Tammy Robinson is a novelist from New Zealand. After the tragic deaths of her mother and a close friend, she sat down in 2011 to write a book and hasn't stopped since. She now has eight novels to her name and is working on the ninth.

She lives with her husband and three young children on a small farm in rural Waikato.

By Tammy Robinson

Differently Normal
Photos of You

Back to You

tammy robinson

PIATKUS

PIATKUS

First published in Great Britain in 2021 by Piatkus

1 3 5 7 9 10 8 6 4 2

A CIP catalogue record for this book
is available from the British Library.

ISBN 978-0-349-42527-6

Typeset in Garamond by M Rules
Printed and bound in Great Britain by
Clays Ltd, Elcograf S.p.A

Papers used by Piatkus are from well-managed forests
and other responsible sources.

Piatkus
An imprint of
Little, Brown Book Group
Carmelite House
50 Victoria Embankment
London EC4Y 0DZ

An Hachette UK Company
www.hachette.co.uk

www.littlebrown.co.uk

For whatever we lose (like a you or a me)
It's always ourselves we find in the sea.

Prologue

The man staring down at me has cheeks the colour of mottled autumn leaves and a chipped tooth. It is greyer than the other incisor, I note. Half as long, with a smooth edge, worn by repetitive use. Unlike my own injury, his is not a new one. I haven't seen mine, that would require effort outside of my current control, but I can feel the blood pulsating out of me, taking my life along with it.

'Keep looking at me,' he says, desperation making his voice tremble. 'Talk. Tell me something about yourself.'

He means well, I know, but if these are my last moments here on earth, I don't want to spend them as if I'm in a job interview. Besides, I don't think I could speak even if I wanted to. I barely seem to have the energy left even to blink. Each time I do, my eyelids get heavier, harder to open again.

I can hear Bonnie nearby; she sounds hysterical. Wailing and crying. I've never heard her sound like that before. I've never heard anyone sound like that before. Things must really be bad.

'Miss? Can you hear me?' He gives my shoulders a little shake. I drag open my eyelids once more.

1

He looks worried, as well he should.

I stare at the buildings over his shoulder, stark against a pale autumn sky, and remember the first time I saw Finn. Will he ever know what became of me? My untimely, horrific end, my life ebbing out into concrete, littered with broken glass and discarded cigarette butts. I hear the echo of his words. 'Throw the coin, make a wish.'

I wish I could have seen him smile one more time.

I wish . . .

Everything starts to fade.

'We're losing her,' a panicked voice calls out.

Four months earlier

New Year's Eve

Chapter one

The kiss was all Bonnie's fault. That's my first instinct immediately afterwards; assign blame. The man stares down at me,
amused, while I try to think of some explanation that will make
sense of what just happened. Well, anything other than 'my
friend told me to do it'. We're not eight and on a playground,
after all.

Bonnie's wide-eyed expression is torn between pride and disbelief as she looks from me to the man and back again.

'I can't believe you did that,' she says.

'You dared me to do something spontaneous.' I remind her.

'Yeah, but I didn't mean kiss a perfect stranger.' She looks him
up and down. 'Although he is pretty perfect, I'll give you that.'
She says the last bit in a voice she thinks only I can hear, but
from the way the man suppresses a smile I'm sure he hears it too.

Drunk on pre-mixed alcoholic drinks and high on the excitement of New Year's Eve, she's been banging on for the last hour
about how we'll never be this young again (obviously), and how
life is 'there for the taking'. She also pointed out that when we're

old and at death's door, we'll only regret the things we didn't do. It's all inspirational clichés she's picked up from the Facebook memes she adores. Usually, I indulge her by smiling and nodding and letting it all wash over me; clichés have never really been my thing. But for some reason, on this night they'd struck a chord. Or maybe it was simply that I wanted to shut her up. Either way, after she'd told me for the twelfth time to 'seize the moment', right as someone bumped into me, I'd instinctively grabbed their arm. My fingers told me it was a bicep, very toned. Most likely male. My eyes travelled up and confirmed this. The owner of the arm had frowned down good-naturedly, with a pair of eyes so dark they seemed almost black.

'Can I have my arm back?' he'd asked.

'Sure. After you kiss me.'

His eyebrows shot up. 'Sorry?'

'I think you heard.'

He'd hesitated for only a moment and then shrugged nonchalantly. 'OK.'

Before I could even flash a grin at Bonnie, he had one arm around my hip, one behind my head and was dipping me backwards, like we were in some sexy, old-time Hollywood movie. It was meant to be a light-hearted moment, a passing whim, a momentary impulse; but when he looked down at me I felt a jolt and the smile stuttered to a halt on my lips. Everything in the background, the laughter and conversation of the crowd, the thump thump beat of the music, it all faded away, and all that was left was me, and him, and this moment. He lowered his head and he kissed me. It might have lasted ten seconds, or maybe it was ten minutes. I honestly have no idea.

Chapter Two

However long it lasted, it wasn't long enough. When he broke free and restored me to my feet, I let go of him reluctantly, utterly confused by the fact that a kiss from a stranger didn't feel in the slightest bit strange at all.

Now he stands, looking at me expectantly, but I can think of nothing at all to say, so I stare back at him. He's taller than me, at about six foot, wearing black jeans and a grey T-shirt that is snug enough to reveal an athletic leanness, but not so snug that it looks like he's trying to show off. His hair is dark, almost black, his eyes the same. They study me curiously, his eyebrows arched, as he waits for me to speak.

'Well that was . . . unexpected,' he says finally, a nanosecond before it starts to get really awkward. 'Not in a bad way,' he adds hurriedly.

I gesture towards Bonnie. 'She dared me.'

'I did not,' she protests. 'Well, not that specifically.'

'I guess I should thank you, then,' he says to her.

She basks in his gratitude and I want to kick her.

'I think I saw Josh, your boyfriend, over by the bar, waving at you,' I say pointedly. 'He might need help carrying the drink order.'

'He's fine, it's three drinks,' she says dismissively. 'How hard can it be?'

The man turns his attention back towards me, and I unconsciously stand up straighter.

'Do you often ask strange men for a kiss?'

'No.' I frown, indignant at the implication. 'Do you kiss any girl who asks?'

He grins. 'You're definitely the first. Can I at least know your name?'

'Zoe.' I hold out a hand, he wraps it up inside his. It seems ridiculously formal to shake hands after what we've just done. 'And yours?'

'Finn.'

'Finn.' I consider it. 'It's a good, solid name. One you don't often hear anymore.'

'Zoe's a schoolteacher,' Bonnie explains to him. 'She has a thing for names. You should hear some of the ones she gets in her class. Weird names, like . . . Andromeda.'

'Andromeda,' Finn muses. 'Isn't that the name of a star?'

'Made-up planet, I think.' Bonnie's nose crinkles. She turns to me. 'Off Star Trek, isn't it?'

'No, it's real, and it's a galaxy,' I tell them. 'On the first day of term, her mother told me that they named her after a galaxy because they want her to go on to do spectacular things in life.'

There's a pause while we all think about this.

'That's a hell of a lot of pressure to put on a kid,' Finn says finally. 'But I suppose it's as good a reason as any.'

'No, it's not,' Bonnie snorts. 'It's stupid. What's wrong with Stephanie? Or Deborah? Helen. Emma. Normal names.'

'I kind of like Zoe, myself,' Finn says.

I suppress a smile. 'Finn isn't so bad either.'

Bonnie looks at us, like she's at a tennis match watching the ball get lobbed backwards and forwards over the net.

'Uh, what's happening here?' she says. 'Are you two . . . ? Is this like a meet cute?' She waves a hand up and down between our faces, but we don't break eye contact.

Finn jerks his head towards the exit. 'I don't suppose you want to get out of here and go for a walk somewhere quieter?'

I open my mouth to reply, but Bonnie interrupts.

'Whoa.' She puts one hand on my arm and plants the other firmly on Finn's chest. 'Wait a second, Zoe. I hate to be a reality check, but are you sure about going off into the night with a guy you literally met for the first time a couple of minutes ago?'

She has a point. From a safety perspective, it would make more sense to stay here, in a public place with my friends around, while I got to know him. But my instincts are telling me that he can be trusted, and I learned to trust those instincts a long time ago.

'I promise she'll be perfectly safe with me,' Finn reassures her.

I bustle Bonnie a short distance away. 'Look, I know that this goes against all the safety protocols we always talk about, but Bonnie, I like him.'

She rolls her eyes. 'How can you like him when you don't know a thing about him?'

'Good point,' I acknowledge. 'But how else am I supposed to get to know him? I mean, look at him, he looks nice, don't you think?'

'He looks like trouble,' she retorts. 'But in a cute, kind of Shawn Mendes way.'

'Bonnie.' I pick up her hands and lean my face closer to hers. 'Have you ever had one of those moments when it feels like the universe is trying to tell you something?'

She screws up her face while she thinks about it. 'No.'

'Yeah, me neither,' I admit. 'But this kind of feels like that.'

'Babe, that's just the alcohol talking.'

'It's not. I've had two drinks. I'm sober. See?' I close my eyes and extend both arms, then bring my right index finger in to touch the tip of my nose.

'Convincing.'

'You know that I'm not actually asking for your permission here, right? Look, I love you, and I appreciate you looking out for me, but you're the one who said that life is there for the taking, remember? If I don't go, I'll always wonder what might have been, and you don't want me having regrets on my death-bed, right?'

She shakes her head sadly. 'I can't believe you're using my own words against me.'

I shrug. 'We always knew it would happen one day.'

Josh fights his way back through the crowd and passes her a drink, then holds one out towards me. Bonnie takes it instead, holding both drinks up in a cheers motion. 'Go. Be careful. And flick me a text every now and then, so I know you're OK. Oh, and have fun.' She winks.

'What's going on?' Josh asks.

'I'll fill you in later,' she tells him.

I turn to Finn. 'Ready?'

He smiles. 'Ready.'

Chapter Three

Away from the crowds, the nerves start to kick in, but so does something else, something I can't put a name to. If forced, I'd say it's akin to anticipation. That feeling like something wonderful is about to happen. It's been thirteen months since my last relationship ended, and in that time, I haven't felt this attracted to, or this excited about, anyone. My mind keeps flashing back to the kiss, and how amazing it felt. 'So,' I say, hoping he can't tell I'm nervous from the flutter in my voice. 'Tell me about yourself.'

We turn left after leaving the bar and walk down a tree-lined street, the oak branches towering overhead like we're inside a leafy tunnel. For the Christmas/New Year period, the council has decorated the thick trunks with fairy lights, hundreds of tiny white pinpricks, guiding us, illuminating our way. It's incredibly beautiful, and romantic.

'What would you like to know?'

'How about we start with your full name.'

'My full name?'

It takes me a few steps to realise he's stopped walking. When I do, I turn to face him, confused. 'Is there a problem with that?'

He sighs and rubs his forehead, his expression pained. 'I was kind of hoping it wouldn't come up.'

'It's a pretty normal thing to ask someone,' I point out.

'I'm afraid that if I tell you, you'll laugh. Or run away.'

'I doubt it. Unless your name is, I don't know, Finn Hannibal Lecter. Oh wait, are you famous?' My eyes widen. 'Or royalty?'

'No, sorry. Not famous, or royal. Merely lumbered with an unusual set of names.'

'More unusual than Andromeda?'

'No, nothing is more unusual than that.'

'Exactly, so tell me.'

'My name is Finlay Archibald Bradford Young. But everyone calls me Finn.'

I try really hard to keep a straight face, and last about five seconds.

'I told you you'd laugh,' he says indignantly.

'I'm sorry.' I cover my mouth with my hands. 'But seriously?'

'Why would I make it up?'

'Good point. Wow. That's . . . wow.'

'I know.' He looks downcast. 'You can understand now why I try and keep it quiet.'

'Did your parents want you to get beaten up at school?'

'Of course not.' He looks thoughtful. 'Then again, apparently I was a bit of a rotten baby. Barely slept. Cried lots. Projectile-vomited all over the furniture. So . . . maybe?'

We start walking again. 'It's like your mum googled a list of the most pretentious baby names that she could find.'

'Actually,' he says stiffly, his face unsmiling. 'They're family names. Handed down through the male generations. There's a lot of history involved.'

'Oh.' My own smile slips. 'I'm sorry for laughing. I didn't mean to offend you.'

His face cracks into a grin. 'Ah, I'm only messing with you. My grandfather's name was Johnny. He was a hunter who brewed his own beer, so more hillbilly than Ivy League. I think my mother, like Andromeda's, thought that if she gave us these illustrious names, we'd go on to great things.'

'Us?'

'I have three brothers. Their names are almost as bad.'

'Three? Wow. That's a lot of testosterone in one house. Your poor mother.'

'We have a sister too, so she wasn't completely on her own.'

'How old are you?'

'Twenty-nine.'

'Star sign?'

'Leo. What is this, thirty questions in thirty seconds?'

'Sorry?'

'You know, like a lightning round on a game show.'

I click my fingers at him. 'Hey, that's not a bad idea.'

'I was only kidding.'

'No really, it'll be like a crash course in getting to know someone, like they do on those speed-dating nights.'

'I've never been to one of those.'

'I have.' I confirm, pulling a face. 'Once. With Bonnie, before she met Josh. It was completely bizarre, but I'll tell you about it another time. First things first. You ready?'

'No.'

'Good. Favourite colour?'

'Uh, blue. No wait, green. No, blue. Definitely blue.'

I stare at him. 'You don't know your favourite colour?'

'There's too many good ones to choose from,' he answers defensively.

I smile, because it's cute. 'OK. I'll allow. Favourite movie?'

He turns and starts walking backwards slowly so we can see each other's faces as we walk. *John Wick.*

'Never heard of it.'

'Lots of fighting.' He does a few half-hearted fight moves. 'What's not to love.'

'Favourite book?'

'Archie.'

'The comic? That's not a book.'

'It has words, so it still counts. I didn't pick you for a bibliophilic snob. For your information, I do read the occasional, actual book as well. In fact, I quite enjoy a good thriller. But you asked for my favourite. And that, my dear, is *Archie.*'

'Well, for your information,' I poke him in the stomach, 'I'm not a snob of any sort. Moving on. Occupation?'

'Barman. Employee currently, but I have grand ambitions to have my own place someday. Big, open fireplace. Dark wooden furniture, tables and chairs, corner booths.' He gestures vigorously while he talks, clearly passionate about the subject. 'Dartboard. Maybe a pool table. Definitely a jukebox.'

'Sounds like you've got it all planned out.'

'I've had a lot of time to think about it.'

We reach an intersection and I put my hand on his arm to stop him from stepping backwards off the kerb.

'Thanks,' he says, smiling at me in a way that makes my pulse quicken. I want him to kiss me again, but this time without me having to ask. For a second, I think he's going to. His face turns serious, his gaze slipping to my mouth. He leans forward, but then a car comes driving past us, going too fast and we both jump, startled. The driver honks the horn loudly, a few heads hang out of the window, wolf-whistling. The moment is broken.

'Where do we go from here?' I ask, not bothering to hide my disappointment.

Chapter four

Over the next few hours we wander the streets of the inner city, getting to know more about each other. He points out the bar where he works, but only from the yellow puddle of a streetlight outside. Neither of us feels like venturing inside and breaking our little bubble of two.

I lead him to my favourite bookshop, then also on to my second and third favourite bookshops. We peruse the titles in the window and compile a list of those we would buy if money were no option. Nearby, I show him the studio where Bonnie and I do yoga on Saturday mornings, then I sheepishly show him the bakery not far from there, where we usually buy coffee and doughnuts afterwards.

Eventually, we stop at a fountain that sits in a courtyard surrounded by retail shops, one of which is owned and run by Bonnie. I work there sometimes in the school holidays when I'm at a loose end, and on the way past I proudly showed Finn the mannequins in the front window that I'd helped dress earlier that day. They were a little out there, fashion wise, but

I'd figured if you couldn't have a little fun on New Year's Eve, when could you?

'I think we should make a wish to mark the occasion,' he announces, looking down into the reflective water of the fountain.

'The occasion?'

'This. Us. Meeting each other.'

I look down into the water, happy he considers our meeting worthy of celebrating. 'I don't have any coins.'

He frowns. 'Damn, me neither.' Then the frown clears. 'I know, we could fish some out of the fountain and use those.' He boosts himself up onto the concrete side.

'Are you serious?'

'What?'

'You can't steal a coin that someone else has already used to make a wish.'

'Can't you?'

I lean my arms onto the cool edge and look up at him sideways. 'No, you can't. I'm pretty sure it goes against every kind of wishing fountain etiquette there is. In fact, do it, and you'll probably get the opposite of what you wish for.'

'You're probably right,' he agrees regretfully. He swings his legs, his hands tucked underneath his thighs. 'Shame. I knew exactly what I was going to wish for, too.'

'Care to share?'

'No way. If I tell you, it won't come true. Duh. I thought you were the expert on wish etiquette.'

'Did you just duh me?'

'I did, but to be fair, I immediately regretted it.'

'What are you, a sixteen-year-old girl? I'm so tempted to push you in right now.'

He leans down so that his face is close to mine. 'If you do,' he says, 'I'll pull you in with me.'

'You wouldn't.'

His eyebrows arch challengingly. 'Try me.'

He's so close. All I'd have to do is lean forward and I could kiss him. The temptation is strong, but all my earlier bravado seems to have disappeared now that I've spent time with him. I have that fluttery feeling you get in your stomach when you meet someone you know you could easily fall for. Swallowing hard, I look back down into the water that glitters beneath the city lights. 'I have an idea.'

'Chicken,' he says smugly. 'I knew you wouldn't do it.'

I ignore the chicken remark. 'Do you have any cash?'

'Yeah, but no coins, remember?'

I hold out my hand, palm facing upwards. 'Give me your wallet.'

He passes it over and watches as I open it and pull out a ten-dollar note.

'Perfect.' I close the wallet and hand it back. 'Wait here.'

'Where are you going?' he calls after me.

'I'll be back soon.' I jog around the art gallery that occupies the corner and find the drink-vending machine exactly where I see it every morning on my way to Bonnie's shop. I feed in the money, choose my option and wait while it spits out the change – a five-dollar note and three coins – and the drink.

'Ta-da,' I announce proudly when I get back and hand Finn his change. 'I got us some coins. You're most welcome.'

He takes the money without looking at it, staring longingly instead at the can in my hand, beads of condensation running down the sides. 'What about the drink?'

'What about it?' I pull back the tab on the top and it makes a satisfactory fizz sound as the gas is released.

'Oh, that looks so good.' He licks his lips.

I take a drink, wipe my mouth and nod. 'It is. Insanely good. Cold. Refreshing.'

After taking another large swig, I hold the can against my neck, my eyes closed with the exquisite pleasure of how cold it is.

'Are you going to drink it all right in front of me?'

'Oh.' I give him a fake look of surprise. 'I'm sorry, did you want some?'

'Well, I did pay for it.'

'I suppose you did. Go on then.' I pass it over and he throws his head back, taking a long drink. Sitting up there, silhouetted with the light from the fountain behind him, he looks like he belongs on an advertising poster.

'You look like you're in one of those sexy Coke ads,' I blurt out without thinking.

He lowers the can and wipes his mouth. 'Does that mean you think I'm sexy?'

Does he seriously have to ask? 'If I say yes, will you give me the rest of the drink back?'

'Let me think about it. Uh ... nope.' He easily downs the rest and then crumples the can up in one hand like it's paper, throwing it towards a nearby rubbish bin. It clunks on the sides and then rattles as it hits the bottom. 'Goal,' he declares triumphantly.

I gape at him, lost for words.

'What?' he asks innocently. 'That was payback, for teasing me so much with it in the first place.'

'I can't believe you did that.'

'Hey, you started it. But I'm not completely heartless. Here you go.' He passes me one of the remaining coins. 'You can wish for another drink.'

'As if I'd waste a wish on that.' Still, I take the coin anyway.

'OK, if not a drink, what will you wish for?'

'Not telling. Duh.'

'I deserve that.' He hops down and puts most of the money back into his wallet, keeping one coin for himself. We stand side by side, staring into the water. I wonder if he is thinking the same thing I am. Closing my eyes, I make a wish, mouthing the words silently, then throw the coin. It rotates in the air a few times, before falling into the water with a tidy little splash.

Finn nudges me with his shoulder 'I really want to know what you wished for.'

'That's against the rules,' I say primly, nudging him back. 'Your turn.'

'You and rules,' he mutters, closing his eyes. He's silent for ten seconds, then flips his coin into the air using his thumb and finger. We watch its trajectory as it arches, reaching its highest point, hovering in the night air for the briefest of moments before plummeting down into the water in front of us.

'Don't suppose . . . ' I trail off, turning to face him.

'No way. Not going to tell you either. But I can say this. You'll know if it comes true.'

'What does that mean?'

He pretends to zip his lips shut and smiles cryptically.

'Tell me.'

'No.'

'A clue?'

He steps forward suddenly, closing the gap between us, and I gasp sharply. His jaw tenses as he reaches out one hand, running his fingers ever-so-lightly down my cheek to rest at my chin. His eyes focus intently on my lips as I feel my body arch towards his. This is nuts. I've never wanted anyone as badly as I want him right now.

'Don't tell anyone,' he says huskily. 'But I wished that before this night is over, I'd get the chance to kiss you again.'

I swallow hard. 'What a coincidence.'

Chapter five

'Whose place is this?' I ask quietly.

The hallway of the old-style apartment building that we're walking down is giving me the creeps. It smells like stale ciga-rette smoke and spilt beer. Only two of the four lights spaced out along the ceiling are working, and one of them flickers ominously like we're in a B-grade horror movie. I snuggle closer to Finn, half expecting some maniac in a mask to emerge from the shadows wielding a chainsaw over his head.

Finn reassuringly pats my white knuckles that are clutching his bicep. 'My brother's, but don't worry, he's not home.'

'How do you know?'

'Because I left him and his mates at the bar. That's who I was out with.'

'Do you live here with him?'

'No, I had my own place until recently, but I do crash here sometimes. It's quite handy having a brother living right in the heart of the city.'

'Had your own place?'

'Long story. Basically, I'm between tenancies right now. Don't judge me, but I'm staying with my folks for a bit, while I save some money.'

'Why would I judge? That's sensible, city living isn't cheap. What's his name?'

'My brother? Connor. Short for Connery. And before you ask, I'm the better-looking one. By far.'

'And what does Connor do?' I cringe as we walk past an old orange stain dripped down a wall. Paint? Tomato sauce? Blood?

He grins. 'Don't worry, I know the hallway doesn't give the best first impression, but the flat's all right. And to answer your question, Connor is a librarian by day, and a drummer in a band by night.'

'So, he's like, a nerdy rocker?'

'Pretty much. But don't let him hear you say that.'

We've reached the end of the hallway and he stretches his hand up towards the upturned lightshade of the flickering light.

'Ouch. Hot, hot.' He curses a few times as he fumbles around inside, then triumphantly pulls out a key which he tosses from hand to hand, blowing on it until it cools down.

'That's the best hiding place they can come up with?'

He grimaces at the red spot on his hand. 'They only have the one key between the three of them. It's either that or under the mat.'

I look down. 'What mat?'

'Exactly.'

He inserts the key into the lock and turns it, then pushes open the door. 'After you.'

Inside, Finn guides me down a short hallway into an open plan lounge-cum-kitchen-cum-diner. I look around while he rummages in kitchen cupboards. As far as bachelor pads go, it's exactly as I would have imagined. Tidy and presentable, yet lacking in the kind of objects that make a house a cosy home. Framed photos, ornaments, cushions and rugs, for example. Everything in the room is here purely for function. There's a couch, a table and four chairs, a deflated-looking beanbag that has seen better days, and a TV, gaming and stereo set-up that looks expensive.

'Aha,' he declares gleefully, pulling from the depths of a cupboard a large bottle of clear liquid and brandishing it towards me.

'What's that?'

'Only the very best vodka that money can buy.' He peers closely at the label on the front of the bottle. 'Actually, that's not true. It's cheap and nasty. But it is strong, and frankly, beggars can't be choosers.'

'OK, so what's the plan here? Get me drunk and then have your wicked way with me on the beanbag?'

We both look at the beanbag that can barely prop itself up.

'That does sound like fun,' he admits. 'But I was thinking instead, we take this up to the roof and ring in the New Year in style.'

I gesture towards the door. 'Sounds good. Lead the way.'

As we step out onto the dark terrace, three rickety flights of stairs later, I gasp audibly.

'I know,' he says smugly.

'This is incredible.' I turn in a lazy circle, taking in the city lights spread out before me.

'Isn't it?' He walks over towards the edge and looks out. 'I like to come up here sometimes and just hang out by myself.

24

Stare out at all the lights. I find it calming. Like I'm on top of the world, away from all the noise, and no one knows where I am.'

'It's beautiful.' Everywhere I look there are lights on buildings, and the streets are aglow with an orange fire. I was already in awe of this city, and now another layer has been revealed to me.

'I told you it would be worth it.'

'I didn't doubt you for a second. Thank you.'

'For what?'

'For sharing this with me.' I walk over to join him by the edge.

'You're welcome. Somehow, I knew you'd appreciate it.'

'Do you bring lots of women up here?' I tease, hoping he won't say yes. It's such a special place, and this is such a special night. I'd be crushed if it was only me feeling it.

'You're the first.' He looks at me intensely. 'Like when you asked me to kiss you. Guess this is a night for firsts.'

'I feel honoured then.'

'I come up with my brother and his mates sometimes,' he says. 'They hang out on those old deckchairs over there' – he points towards a cluster of worn-out plastic lounge chairs, like the kind you'd find around a resort pool – 'to smoke weed and philosophise. It's quite funny to listen to. Load of bullshit, of course.' He takes my hand and guides me closer to the edge of the roof where there is a wide ledge, gesturing for me to sit down. 'Other times I come up by myself, when I need to get away from everything. It's easy to feel lonely in this city, but hard to find anywhere to be completely alone. This is my secret little place. It's perfectly safe,' he assures me when I hesitate.

'That's what they said about the *Titanic*,' I quip, to hide my nerves.

He chuckles, sitting down. Trusting him, I follow suit, relieved to realise that you can't even see the street from where we are because of a ledge that juts out and around the top of the building. Even if I did fall, it'd only be about four feet before I landed on that ledge.

'Do you think that ledge was put there as a safety thing? Like a deterrent to stop people from jumping?' I muse. 'I've always wondered how desperate someone would have to be feeling to do something like that. To honestly believe that their life will never get any better.'

He doesn't answer right away, but I feel his body stiffen. He unscrews the lid on the bottle of vodka and takes a long swig. Then he wipes his mouth with the back of his hand, holding it out to me.

'Did I say something wrong?' I take it and copy him, tipping the bottle up, gulping down a big mouthful. It burns the back of my throat and I cough, my eyes starting to water.

'Careful,' he says. 'That stuff is fifty-three per cent.'

'Tastes like it too. I'm pretty sure my taste buds have all been burned into oblivion.'

'Sorry. I should have warned you.'

'I'll live.' I take another swig and hold it back out to him, but he doesn't notice. He's staring off into space, out over the city, his eyes unfocused. I give him a nudge with my shoulder. 'You OK?'

He snaps out of his reverie and blinks a few times. 'Yeah, sorry, I was . . .'

'A million miles away.'

26

'Something like that.' He takes the bottle and has another drink, staring moodily out over the city. 'Do you ever feel like getting away from it all?'

I frown sharply.

'No, not like that,' he says quickly, realising where my mind went. 'I'd never do that. I meant the city. Don't you ever feel like getting on the open road and heading off into the sunset? Never looking back. Going wherever the wind and the road takes you.'

'I did feel like that once, but not about here. I grew up in a small town. Couldn't wait to get out.'

He looks at me questioningly, sensing a story. Not tonight though. I'm enjoying myself too much to ruin it.

'It's really not that interesting,' I lie.

His expression indicates he doesn't quite believe me, but he drops it. 'God, it's so hot up here!' he exclaims, putting the bottle down and pulling his shirt off. He throws it over his shoulder, then pulls off his shoes and tosses those behind us too. Swallowing hard, I try not to openly stare, but he's like the scene of a car crash, and I can't tear my eyes off him. As suspected, he's nicely toned underneath his shirt, not an ounce of fat around his stomach or waist. Lean living, whether by choice or budget I don't know. There's a light sheen of sweat on his tanned skin, and he smells both earthy and exotic, his sweat mingled with his cologne. It's heady and intoxicating. I fantasise about running my tongue across his chest, nibbling his shoulder, breathing in the scent of him in the curve of his neck.

'You OK?' he asks, and I swear from the glint in his eye he knows exactly what I'm thinking.

'Me?' My voice is squeaky, I clear my throat to fix it. 'Yeah, I'm fine. You're right, it is hot.' I can feel a trickle of sweat making its way down my own back, so following suit, I slide off my heels and fling them. Wriggling my dress up my thighs as far as I can without exposing my underwear, I smile with satisfaction when I hear Finn start to breathe heavier beside me. Two can play at this game.

Chapter six

'Right,' Finn says. 'It's your turn.'

'My turn for what?'

'You've told me what your favourite season is. You've shown me where you like to hang out. But you haven't told me anything about you.'

'What do you want to know?'

'Where you come from. Your family. Why you decided to become a teacher. I want to know the things that make you tick.'

I dislike this part of meeting someone new. Telling them what happened. It changes the way they treat me. It's subtle, but still noticeable. I've found the best way is to get it over with fairly quickly.

'I'm an only child. Grew up near the beach a couple of hours away from here with my dad. My mum, Fiona, died when I was ten years old.'

There it is. Finn's face goes still, his eyes swamped with sympathy.

'She went in for what was supposed to be a routine operation to remove a lump on her ovary, but' – I shrug with enforced casualness – 'she didn't survive the operation.' There's more to it, of course, but a basic summary is all he needs, and all I care to provide. He holds his hand out for the bottle. I take another drink before passing it back.

'Well, that officially kind of killed the mood,' I say drily, when it becomes clear he doesn't know what else to say. He's lost in thought, his brow furrowed. 'Which is why I don't usually tell people. Honestly, I'm OK. I'm fine. It happened a long time ago and is what it is. Can we go back to having a nice night?'

'I know what it's like,' he says. 'To lose someone you love.'

'Oh?'

He shakes his head and exhales briskly. 'But you're right. Tonight, we should focus on the here and now. Forget the past, let's only think and speak happy thoughts.'

'Together we shall fly,' I say quietly.

'What?'

'Sorry,' I smile. 'Peter Pan. Favourite book as a child. If you want to fly, you must think happy thoughts.'

'I like that. Never read it myself.'

'Seriously? Finn, that's tragic. You have to read it, as soon as possible.'

He gives me a little salute. 'I'll get right on it, teacher.'

'Hm. You're easily swayed to do my bidding,' I remark. 'Interesting.'

He looks me up and down deliberately. 'Anything else you'd like to bid me to do?'

I think of a million things, none of which I'm brave – or drunk – enough, to say out loud.

He chuckles, clearly reading my thoughts. 'Tell me.'

'Tell you what?' What I want you to do to me? Not likely.'

'Why teaching?'

I breathe out, relieved to be back on safer ground. His proximity has my whole body on edge, like a jangled mass of nerve endings. 'When I was seven, my teacher wrote in my report card that I would make an excellent teacher because of my personality traits, and the idea kind of stuck.'

'Personality traits like . . . bossy?' He grins.

'Ha-ha. No, not bossy, more . . . commanding.'

'Pretty sure if I looked it up it'd mean the same thing.'

'OK, fine. So I'm authoritative. Do you have a problem with that?'

He holds up his hands, palms facing me. 'No, no problem here. In fact, I quite like being told what to do. In certain situations.' He hooks his bottom lip with one tooth suggestively.

'Anyway, so that's why I became a teacher.'

'You shaped your whole life based on a comment in a report card?'

'I did. And once I made the decision, I never wavered from it. Never once doubted whether I was making the right choice. That's how I knew it was right. Worked hard at school, got the grades I needed to get into teacher training college, and graduated soon after my twenty-first birthday. I applied for and got offered the job at the school I work at now, and I've been there ever since. Sounds boring, I know, but at least I'm lucky enough to be doing a job I love. Not everyone is that lucky.'

'It's not boring at all. I admire your conviction, and your dedication. It must have been liberating, to have something to aim for. I hated my last year at high school. All that pressure to choose a career.'

31

'I agree. For most people, eighteen is too young to be deciding the rest of your life.'

'I couldn't do it. Took me years to figure out what I enjoy doing enough to want to do it for the rest of my life. Had some rather . . . unsavoury, jobs along the way, believe me.'

'Oh yeah?'

'Nothing bad,' he adds hurriedly. 'Or at least, nothing illegal. But I've cleaned toilets and washed dishes and unclogged drains.'

'Hey, someone's got to do it, right.'

'Right.'

'My job is not as pure as one might think,' I admit. 'I've had to clean a few things off chairs and carpets that I'd rather not have seen. Or smelt.'

'Oh gross, you'd have to really like kids to want to be a teacher.'

'You don't like kids?'

'I don't know any.'

'They're pretty amazing little humans. Every single day they blow me away. I always tell people, if you're ever worried about the future of this planet, sit in a classroom for a while. The determination and optimism of the next generation will soon put your mind at ease. Kids are much smarter than some adults give them credit for. I'd like at least four of my own, one day. Maybe five.'

He spits the vodka out. 'Five?'

'Hey, I grew up as an only child, remember? I always thought it would be so much fun to have lots of siblings.'

'Trust me,' he wipes the vodka spray off his lap. 'It's not always.'

'It's got to be more fun than growing up alone.'

'Yeah, you're probably right.'

'Oh, I'm always right.'

'Is that so?' He shuffles across the ledge until our thighs touch. I jolt with the shock of it, wondering if he can hear how laboured my breathing is. It seems deafening to my own ears.

'Zoe?'

'Mm?'

'Look at me.'

My head turns slowly. He's looking at me that way again. The way that makes me feel like I'm sinking deeper and deeper into his eyes until I am a part of him. An unspoken understanding flashes between us; a story has begun, and there's no going back to how things were before. The Zoe and Finn of a few hours ago no longer exist. From this moment, there is only us, there is only this.

He stands up, holding out a hand. I accept it, and he pulls me up to my feet. With him walking backwards, he leads me over to one of the lounge chairs, maintaining eye contact all the way. Sinking down onto it, he looks up at me.

'Are you OK?' he asks.

'Yes.'

'Nervous?'

'Yes. And no.'

'It's OK,' he says. 'We don't have to do anything, I just want to lay with you.'

'I want that too.'

So I do, I lay down beside him, and he puts one arm around me, my head resting on his shoulder. For a while, we say nothing, simply stare up at the stars. They are the one thing I miss from back home. Here, there is too much light pollution. If you'd spent your whole life in the city, you'd be satisfied with the scattering of stars across the sky. You'd think that's all there is. But I know different. I remember a sky so full of stars there was barely any space between them. The hazy Milky Way, a resplendent streak of lights. A solar system, a galaxy. Confirmation we are a tiny part of something vast and immeasurable.

Finn speaks, and I feel his voice rumble through his body. 'Where do you think the Andromeda galaxy is?'

It takes me a second to catch up, that conversation in the bar seems like it happened ages ago now. Has it really only been a few hours?

'I'm not sure.'

'I wonder if her parents can even pick it out in the night sky,' he muses. 'I can find the Southern Cross but that's about it.'

'Another tragedy,' I scold lightly. 'I'll have to educate you.'

'You know about the stars?'

'I spent a lot of nights looking at them when I was younger. Got books out of the library so I could put names to what I was seeing.' I point to a cluster overhead. 'You see that area to the east of the Southern Cross? That's a star nursery, called the Coalsack Nebula. New stars are born there.'

'Seriously?'

'Yes. And that constellation there? The one we call the saucepan ...'

'Oh yeah, I remember my dad showing us that when we were kids. He called it a pot though.'

'We see it upside down to how the ancient Greeks used to see it. Where we see a pot, they saw a giant with a sword, and a belt.'

He tilts his head to one side. 'They had better imaginations, clearly. Or is it just me.'

'No, I can't see it either,' I admit. We lay silently for a while, our eyes on the sky. With my head against his chest, I can hear his heartbeat.

'Do you believe everything happens for a reason?' he asks.

'No. Too many bad things happen to good people. How can there be a reason for that?'

'So you don't think we were always destined to meet?'

'I don't know,' I admit. 'I'd like to think so, but ...'

'I understand. Are you scared?'

'Of what?'

'Maybe it's just me. Or the heat and the vodka. Maybe it's just this night.'

'What are you talking about?'

'I don't know, I have the weirdest feeling. I've never felt it before. You know how people feel déjà vu? It's kind of like that. Like I was always supposed to meet you. Like this night was always going to happen. Like something in my soul saw something in your soul and said, there she is. Does that sound cheesy?'

'Yes. But it also sounds right.'

He pulls his arm out from underneath me a bit so that he can roll onto his side and prop himself up on his elbow, looking down at me. 'You feel it too?'

'I'm not sure what it is, but yes. I do.'

'Welcome to my life, Zoe Calloway,' he says softly.

'Thank you, Finlay Archibald Bradford Young. It's a pleasure to be here.'

His eyebrows shoot up. 'Pleasure?' He grins. 'Oh Zoe, you haven't felt anything yet.'

I roll my eyes. 'Now that's cheesy.'

He laughs, then lowers his head to kiss me. My heart explodes inside my chest, and everything I am feeling is suddenly bigger than the Milky Way and all the galaxies and solar systems and the universe combined.

Chapter seven

When I open my eyes the next morning, it takes me a few moments to figure out where I am, and then the memory of the night before comes rushing in. Finn. In the hazy pink light of a new day, it all seems a bit surreal, like I dreamt it.

We'd kissed and talked for hours, before finally falling asleep spooned together on the sun lounger, but a breeze on my back tells me he's no longer there now. Lifting my head, I feel relief when I see him, standing over by the edge of the roof, his back to me, head bent down. He's still shirtless and barefoot, clad only in his black jeans. In the daylight, I notice for the first time the tattoo that snakes from the nape of his neck across to the edge of his right shoulder. It's handwriting rather than a typed font, and says, 'Love you, kiddo.' There's also the outline of a hand next to it, with the pinkie and index finger raised in a rock-on hand sign.

The city view from the rooftop, spectacular at night, is just as majestic in the dawn, I see when I sit up. Much of the city is still asleep, but noise has begun to seep in as people go about their business. The air is already muggy and stifling; it's going to be another hot day. Standing, I stretch quietly before walking over to his side, suddenly feeling shy. Last night was incredible, but what if daylight has brought with it regrets? What if his feelings have changed?

'Morning,' I say.

He doesn't answer, giving no indication that he's even heard me. Simply stands there, still and silent, looking down at something in his hand. I realise that it's a photograph, a little creased from being folded in his wallet. He makes no attempt to hide it, so I study it. It's a photo of him, three other guys and a young woman, blond hair, huge smile. She's stunning. They're standing in front of a hedge with their arms around each other, and they look happy.

'Nice photo.'

He jumps, and looks at me. 'Zoe. Hey. 'Bout time you woke up.'

'Are you OK?' I ask, as he runs one thumb over the photo that's still in his hand.

'I am.' He smiles at me, and any fears I have melt away.

'Is that your family?'

He looks back at the photo. 'Yeah. That's Connor,' he points at the shorter of the three guys. 'That' – the finger moves along the line – 'is Leighton, Blake. And this . . .' His finger moves to gently trace the face of the blonde woman. I hear him swallow like he has a lump of something stuck in his throat. 'Is . . . was . . . our sister, Paige.'

My heart sinks when I hear the word was. 'She's beautiful.'

'What are you doing this weekend?' he asks abruptly.

'Uh, nothing much.' I'm supposed to work a shift at Bonnie's shop tomorrow afternoon, but the prospect of more time with Finn is infinitely way more attractive than that. 'Nothing I can't change, put it that way. Why?'

'Come away with me?'

'Where?'

'My parents have a holiday home, by a lake. I was planning on going there for a few days anyway, before . . . ' He stops short from finishing the sentence. 'I'd love it if you'd come with me.'

'Um, look, Finn, I'd better get home.'

His face falls. I put him out of his misery quickly.

'To pack, I mean. I can hardly wear this dress all weekend, can I?'

He pulls a face. 'You had me going there for a minute.'

'I know.'

'So, we're really doing this?'

'Looks like it.'

Finn opens up the door that leads to the staircase downstairs. 'You know what?' he says, as I brush past him. 'I'm loving this new year already.'

'It's not too bad,' I agree.

Chapter eight

I wave to Bonnie, who is standing on the pavement outside our apartment building. She has the nervous expression of a parent seeing their child off on their first sleepover.

'Call me if you need me,' she hollers. 'I'll have the phone by the bed.'

'The service isn't great where we're going,' Finn says, as we pull away from the kerb. 'But I can show you the best spots to pick up some bars on your phone.'

I hang out the window and wave as Bonnie recedes into the distance behind us. My stomach feels queasy, a mixture of the vodka from the night before and nerves. When we turn at the end of the block and she disappears from view, I pull my head back into the car and wind the window most of the way back up. Finn reaches over and gives my thigh a gentle squeeze.

'You sure about this?' he asks. 'I can turn around if you want.'

'I'm sure.'

'Last chance to change your mind.'

I look sideways at his profile and feel my nerves start to settle. 'No. Let's do this.'

'I thought you weren't normally an adventurous person, Miss Calloway,' he teases.

'It's about time I started then, isn't it?'

'Cabin, here we come!' Finn whoops exultantly.

I can't help but laugh with him, his excitement is infectious.

After saying goodbye out the front of his brother's building, Finn had headed back to his parents' place to catch a few hours' sleep and pack, while I'd caught a cab home to do the same – after I'd showered and filled Bonnie in on the night before, of course.

On the way out of the city we stop for some much-needed coffee and a late lunch, then head out along the motorway, leaving the city limits behind. I watch the scenery pass by the window, my own smile reflected back at me as I reminisce about the night before.

Chapter nine

Over the next few hours, the road gets slowly narrower and windier. It also gets darker, as the sky is swallowed up by a forest of thick, towering trees. Like dark guardians of the forest, they loom over us, watchful as we weave our way through them. The sun disappears behind the treetops and we're plunged into darkness. Apart from the glow of our headlights, there is no other light around.

'You didn't tell me it takes so long to get to this place,' I comment, yawning.

'Truthfully,' he confesses, 'I'd forgotten. When we were kids, we'd always fall asleep on this last half of the journey. It's been a while since I've been up here. We are close now though, if that's any consolation.'

'Oh good.' I peer out my window into the eerie darkness that makes it feel like we're driving through black treacle. 'It feels weird, like we're miles from civilisation.'

He flicks me a look. 'That's because we are,' he says seriously. 'Out here, this is harsh, remote, wilderness territory. You need your wits about you out here. Here is where you find out what you're really made of.'

We drive around the next corner and I'm almost blinded by a service station, all lit up like a Christmas tree. Opposite, there's a small country school and a few houses, with a takeaway shop tacked onto the side of the service station.

'Gotcha,' Finn grins.

As we leave the small town, he turns off the main road and heads down a long gravel driveway. I sit up straighter on the edge of my seat and try to peer ahead to catch a glimpse of where we're going, but I can see nothing. He rounds one last corner and pulls to a stop, turning the ignition off.

'We have arrived at our destination,' he says in a robotic voice like a satnav then, without waiting for me to reply, jumps out and closes his door behind him. I bend down and lean forward to peer up and out of the windscreen. The cabin is up on a little slope. I can't see much of it in the darkness, but I caught enough of a glimpse in the headlights to know that it's at least twice as big as my flat. I open my door and step out; the only sound the snap of dry pine needles underfoot. Closing the door, I crunch over to stand beside Finn. He's lost in his own world, gazing up at the building.

'Fresh air,' I comment. 'Smells like Christmas.'

'Doesn't it? I've forgotten how relaxing it feels to be here.' He takes a deep breath, closing his eyes, then exhales it slowly.

'Didn't you mention something about a lake?'

'All in good time, my dear.' He bounds up the steps and flicks through his key ring to find the right key while I use the torch on my phone to light it up for him. He slots it into place, smiling at me, and turns it. Nothing happens. He frowns.

'Hang on,' he says. 'This door is always a bit tricky.' He gives it a hard nudge with his hip and smiles triumphantly when it unsticks. 'After you.'

He follows me inside and closes the door behind us. I hear him fumble on the wall and then the lights come on, allowing me to check out the room. There's an open-plan lounge-cum-kitchen-cum-diner, a couple of doors off to the right of the lounge and a ladder that leads up to a loft.

'Over here,' Finn says, striding across the room. He pulls aside floor-length drapes to reveal large glass doors. Outside, he hits a switch and bright floodlights come on, lighting up the area behind the cabin. I squeeze past him. Steps lead down to the ground. There're no manicured lawns, only natural forest floor; bit of dirt, bit of grass, and about thirty metres in front of the deck, there is, indeed, the edge of a lake. There's also an old wooden jetty built out over the water, though it disappears into the darkness and I can't see the end of it. The water is black, calm, and reflective like a mirror.

'This place is insane,' I say, awestruck.

'I know.'

Spying something to the right, about ten metres from the house, I peer at it.

'Is that . . . '

'A wooden hot tub? Why yes, yes it is.'

'No way.'

'Yes way.'

'Can we go for a swim in it now?' I jiggle up and down like an excited child on Christmas morning.

'No can do,' he shakes his head regretfully. 'It's empty at the moment – I'll need to switch the pump on to fill it with water from the brook. Also, it's wood-fired and takes a couple of hours to heat up.'

'Oh.' My face falls.

'Don't worry,' he laughs. 'I'll get it set up today and we can have a swim tomorrow.'

'I guess that'll have to do,' I sigh wistfully. 'You must have some pretty cool memories of being here. How long have your parents owned it?'

'Since I was eight. We used to come here every summer for weeks on and off. Swimming, fishing, hiking. Exploring the forest.'

I picture a younger Finn, carefree and adventurous, scrambling these hills and forests with his siblings. This is probably his first trip here without Paige, I realise.

'I'll unpack the car,' he says. 'I thought we'd do an easy dinner tonight so I bought some cheese and bread and deli meats. We need an early night. Big plans for the morning.'

'What sort of plans?'

'You just' – he waves his hands, ignoring my question – 'explore or something while I get everything sorted.'

'I can help, you know.'

'No way. You're my guest.' He starts walking back inside but stops in the doorframe to turn and smile at me. 'I'm really glad you're here, Zoe.'

I smile back. 'Me too.'

Chapter Ten

I pick up a pebble and throw it into the water, watching the ripples roll across the surface. 'Fishing?'

Finn stretches, releasing tension from his back by sticking his belly back and forward a few times. 'You don't like fishing?'

'I do, it's just not what I imagined we'd be doing when you dragged me out of bed at five a.m. in the morning.'

'What were you imagining?'

'I don't know.' I yawn as I look round at the hills around the lake, a halo of orange beginning to creep over the top as dawn advances. 'A fried breakfast? Dip in the hot tub?'

'I told you, that won't be ready until later. I promised Connor I'd bring him back a feed of fish in return for letting me use his car. We need to strike now at dawn while the fish are most active.'

'Aye aye, captain.' I yawn again as I watch him unpack his tackle box.

He looks up at me, concerned. 'Rough sleep?'

'No, it was fine, thanks,' I lie. In truth, I had lain awake for hours, unsettled, knowing Finn was so close nearby and yet so far away. I could hear him breathe as he slept. Even though we'd spent the previous night practically entwined in our sleep, tonight, Finn was behaving like the perfect gentleman. He insisted I have the bed on the open mezzanine floor upstairs, after first helping me make it with sheets from the airing cupboard. It had a comforter so big and so soft, it was like sleeping underneath a cloud. Finn took one of the sleeping bags and slept on the sofa bed right below. There was also a room off the lounge with two sets of bunks and a single, but he said he preferred the sofa bed. I had a feeling though that he wanted to be close by in case I needed something, which was sweet, but frustrating. I knew he was doing this because he didn't want to rush me into anything, but all I wanted was to recapture our closeness of the night before, when everything had felt so natural and so right. It was impossible to do that with him in another room.

I'd lain there, staring into the dark, craning to try and figure out whether he was awake or asleep by the sound of his breathing. It felt like I'd no sooner drifted off to sleep than I was woken by the smell of freshly brewed coffee rising up to the rafters. He hadn't let me drink it then, pouring it into a large stainless-steel thermos and adding it to a backpack he had packed and ready to go by the door. Refusing to tell me where we were going, he'd led the way through the trees and around the edge of the lake for forty-five minutes, with me following behind, stumbling a little at first in the pre-dawn dark, until we reached the point where a river fed into the lake. From there, we'd followed the riverbank upstream for another twenty minutes or so to reach our current spot, where the river widened and a nice stony beach gave us a place to set our things down.

47

'Is this my fishing rod?' I ask, picking up a dark green one. It's well loved, but still sturdy. I give it an experimental flick.

'Yes, but I haven't baited it yet.'

'I'm sure I can figure it out myself.'

'Oh really?' He pauses from what he's doing to watch, clearly expecting amusement.

'How hard can it be?' I inspect the rod, clicking my tongue disapprovingly. 'This is rigged all wrong. Got any split weights in here?' I rummage inside the tackle box, emerging with one triumphantly. 'Can I borrow your knife?'

Looking less amused, and more impressed, he passes it over without saying a word, and then watches as I set up the line the way I like it, the weight pinched in place two feet above the hook so it will help control how far the bait will drift. Then I flip the lid on his can of worms and push a few aside until I find a big, fat, juicy one.

'You OK?' I ask Finn. 'You look a little pale.'

'It's ... you ... '

'What?' I put a hand on one hip and give him an innocent look. 'You've never seen a woman string a rod before?'

'Not like that, I haven't,' he splutters. 'Bloody hell, that was seriously impressive. Who taught you?'

'My father. We used to fish together all the time before Mum died.'

I wade into the water while Finn sorts out his own rod, bringing the rod tip behind me slowly, pressing and holding the reel with my thumb. Then in one quick move, I bring the top of the rod back directly in front of me and release. It plops into the water upstream. For a while, there's nothing but the sound of mosquitoes hovering above the water, and the gentle babbling of the water downstream as it runs over a rocky patch. After twenty minutes or so, the silence is broken by the soft whirring sound of Finn bringing in his line. He whoops out loud.

'Quick, grab the net, will you?' he calls out excitedly, expertly reeling and releasing the line and letting the fish swim in closer to shore.

I wade back to the bank and pick up the net, then head back into the shallows, watching as he brings the fish in close enough for me to scoop it up.

'She's a beauty,' he crows, splashing through the water to check out his prize. It's a brown trout, long and shiny, magnificent. He clicks something on the handle of the net that converts it into scales. 'Four kilos,' he says. 'Not bad.'

'Not bad,' I agree.

He lowers the net back into the water and unhooks the fish carefully so as not to injure the gills. 'Go on,' he says reverentially to it. 'This is your lucky day.' Then he releases the catch on the net and we watch as the trout swims gracefully out of sight.

'You let it go,' I splutter, pointing out the obvious. 'That was a perfectly decent-sized fish.'

He stands back up and reels in his line. 'My father always said that if you release the first one back into the wild, you'll be blessed by the fishing gods for the rest of the day.'

'Oh really. Does it work?'

'Not usually,' he admits. 'But some habits are hard to break.'

Less than ten minutes later, it's my turn. Finn nets the fish as I bring it in.

'Woohoo,' he crows, 'she's a beauty. And I'm not talking about the fish.' He grins at me and I feel that fluttery feeling in my stomach again. We're starting to get that ease back between us that we had last night.

'Corny.'

He laughs. 'Not even sorry.' He clicks to convert the net to scales and lets out a low whistle.

'Well?'

'A little over five and a half kilos. I'm impressed. Do you want me to clean it?'

I reach out and take the net off him. 'No, it's OK. I like to see it through to the end.'

He watches while I quickly gut, gill and clean the fish. Three quick knife cuts and it all comes away easily.

'Clearly, you've done this before.'

'Once or twice.' I pause from cleaning out the bloodline along the spine. 'Does the fact that you're standing there watching me mean you've given up on trying to catch any more fish yourself?'

'I'm half watching you, and half watching that.' He points to the sky, where the sun has disappeared behind some huge grey clouds, some of them so dark they're almost black. 'I don't like the look of that. We should start heading back. I've seen the weather turn nasty pretty quickly here, and we don't want to be caught out in it.'

We pack up and follow the riverbank back to the lake as the sky continues to darken. I keep my eyes on his feet as he picks out our path home towards the cabin. I've just spied the jetty in the next bay around a small headland, when there's an almighty crack of thunder and the heavens finally open. It's summer rain, but it's still colder than I expected, causing me to gasp out loud and shiver when it hits the back of my neck. The sound of the rain striking the surface of the lake is almost deafening.

'Come on,' Finn calls out over his shoulder. 'We're almost there.'

But instead I stop, dropping my rod gently to the ground and lifting my arms above my head, turning in circles, laughing.

Hearing me, Finn turns and shouts over the incredible orchestra of nature. 'Why are you laughing?'

'Because I can,' I shout back. 'Because this, everything, feels so amazing. Don't you feel it too?'

He runs one hand through his hair, flicking water everywhere. 'I do.'

Tilting my face up to the sky, I let the rain wash my face, plastering my hair to my head and drenching me, feeling years of city life wash off me. It's been so long since I spent any time outdoors, properly outdoors, and it feels unbelievably good.

'You want to know what else is pretty amazing?' he calls, his voice throaty. 'You. I've never met anyone like you.'

I lower my head to stare back at him. God he's gorgeous. I know that I haven't known him very long in the grand scheme of things, but there's something, a connection, and every minute I spend with him it strengthens. This is more than a purely physical attraction. He takes two steps to stand right in front of me. The rain has soaked his hair and I can see droplets in his eyelashes. I reach up to wipe them away and he turns his face into my hand, nuzzling at it with his lips.

'Are you sure?' he asks huskily.

I nod. 'Surer than I've ever been about anything.'

His lips brush mine and I lean into him. But then he pulls away, his face stunned. I see the effort it takes for him to say the next words. 'Wait. No, not here,' he shakes his head. 'This isn't the right place, or the right moment. Come on.'

Chapter eleven

'That smells incredible,' I moan, my stomach rumbling loudly. 'Is it nearly ready?'

'Patience, oh impatient one. It will be ready when it's ready, and not a moment before.'

'You'd better not overcook my fish,' I tease, before taking a sip from the glass of chilled white wine Finn poured for me.

'Stop putting pressure on me, then,' he grins. 'You can't rush perfection.'

By the time we'd made it back to the cabin earlier, the rain had stopped, and the moment between us had passed. Suddenly we were like awkward, love-struck teenagers. All furtive glances, and silly smiles. He'd been painstakingly polite, insisting I have the first shower, and then practically forcing me into an armchair with a book off his mother's shelf, which I'd pretended to read for some of the afternoon, although I didn't take even a single word in. After that, we'd played cards at the table while we drank a couple of beers, laughing and coming up with outrageous ways to cheat. Now he was preparing dinner, and insisting on doing it all himself.

'Are you sure I can't help?' I offer, watching as he bustles in and out of the cabin, fetching plates and utensils to set the outside wooden table on the deck.

'No,' he answers with a smile. 'Enjoy your wine and the view. Everything else is all taken care of.'

'A girl could get used to this,' I say, when he proudly places dinner in front of me. As well as the fish, which he's cooked to perfection in foil with simple salt and lemon slices inside for seasoning, he's prepared a salad with lettuce, tomatoes and cheese, and we have a baked potato each, which he wrapped in foil and cooked on the outside grill. I cut it open and the steam hits my nose with its delicious smell and I moan appreciatively.

'Wait,' he says when I reach for it with my fork. He lifts the lid off a container and cuts a small wedge of butter with a knife, spreading it on top of the hot potato. It immediately starts melting buttery goodness down the sides.

I watch it, my stomach rumbling. 'And there I was thinking you couldn't get any more perfect.'

'I take it you approve,' he says a short time later, watching as I use a finger to scoop up a little melted butter that remains, licking it off with a lip-smacking noise.

'I never want to leave here. Seriously.'

His face clouds, and I immediately feel like I've said the wrong thing, but I don't know what, exactly. 'I was only kidding.'

'Zoe, there's something I should have told you.'

I feel my blood run cold. Jovial, happy Finn is gone. His face is now deadly serious. My head spins from how things changed so quickly. 'Sounds ominous.'

'I'm going overseas for a while. I leave Monday.'

My stomach sinks. 'Oh. Right. Monday as in ...?'

'Two days' time, yeah.'

'Oh.' I force a small smile. 'Going somewhere nice?'

'Africa.'

'Africa?'

He takes a deep breath, exhaling slowly, as if bracing himself. 'Remember I told you I lost someone close to me too?'

I nod, knowing what's coming, remembering his words on the rooftop. 'This is . . . was . . . our sister Paige.'

'Leighton's the oldest. Then Blake, Connor, Paige. I'm the youngest, a surprise addition to the family. There was five years between her and me, and right from the start she doted on me. Carried me around everywhere like I was her baby. I don't remember much of it, but the stories always come out at family gatherings, and there's photos. At school, she looked out for me. And when we were teens, she used to drive me and my mates anywhere we wanted to go. I idolised her. Thought she was the coolest person in the world. She didn't like school, left before her final year and got a job selling make-up. My mother wasn't happy, but Paige made up her own mind about things and that was it. Didn't care what anyone else said. Even when she left home and started flat-sharing with mates, she'd still come back and see me, every weekend, and she said there was always a bed for me at hers if I needed it. I thought her life was perfect. She had so much freedom, did what she wanted, when she wanted. I thought she was happy.'

'What happened?'

'Depression, borderline bipolar. She was officially diagnosed when she was twenty-five, but in hindsight she'd probably been dealing with it since her early teens. Medication helped, for a while, but then she stopped taking it. We didn't know that at the

54

time, only found out after her first suicide attempt. In the hospital, she told us the pills had made her feel like a zombie, like she was sleepwalking through life, incapable of feeling emotion. She stopped taking them because she said she'd rather feel alive, even if that meant living in pain. It didn't make sense to me then and it still doesn't. Why would anyone choose to live like that?'

He looks at me and I see tears in his eyes, but I have no answer for him. I wish I did, I wish I knew what to say to make him feel better, but I'm out of my depth.

'I wanted her to do whatever it took to get well,' he continues. 'I actually got angry with her for not wanting the same thing. How bad is that? I was angry. She was sick, and I was pissed off because I thought she was doing nothing to help herself.'

'You can't help how you feel. None of us can.'

'I can't stop thinking about some of the things I said to her, and ...' He shakes his head. 'It haunts me. I try not to think about it, but it's impossible. Always there. Did she know how much I loved her. Did she know how much she meant to me, or did she die thinking that I was annoyed, angry with her.'

'I'm sure she knew how you felt.'

'When she went missing, we figured she'd gone to ground at a friend's, like she had in the past. Sometimes she got paranoid, thinking people were out to get her. For four days we just went about our lives, waiting for the episode to pass, for her to make contact. We had a plan; we'd admit her back into the psych ward where we knew they'd make her take the medication. It would be against her will, yes, she hated that place. But it would get her back on an even keel, at least for a while, and that was all that mattered. But on the fifth morning some kids found her, washed up on the bank of the river. She'd jumped off a bridge.'

55

'Oh my God.' I cover my mouth with my hands.

'The fall didn't kill her, but it knocked her unconscious and she drowned. They wouldn't let us see her, said it would be too traumatic. That we didn't need to remember her like that.'

'Finn, that's heartbreaking. I'm so sorry.'

'They had to do a post-mortem before we could bury her. Even though she'd left a suicide note beside her bed, they still had to rule out foul play. The coroner told my dad that she broke so many bones in her body that, if she'd lived, she would have had to spend the rest of her life in a wheelchair. You want to hear something really messed up? When my dad told us what the coroner said, I felt relieved that she'd died.'

His face is anguished, awash with guilt.

'Relieved,' he repeats. 'How bad is that? But only because I knew that if Paige had been given a choice between dying that day or living her life completely dependent on others for everything, I reckon she'd have chosen death. She would have hated living the rest of her life in a wheelchair. And as selfish as it sounds, I would have hated seeing her like that too. Her beautiful spirit broken.' He looks at me, his face desperate for me to understand.

'It's not selfish to think about her and how she'd feel living that way. I think it's only natural to think about the what ifs and the might have beens,' I say as I process everything. I don't want to console him with empty meaningless platitudes, I can tell how hard it was for him to be so honest with me. He deserves an honest response. 'But it's obvious how much you loved her. I don't think you're bad or selfish, you're grieving, and everyone grieves differently.'

'Of course, you know what it's like. You know how it feels.'

'I do, but it's a little different. I was only a child when my mother died. I can remember not understanding why she'd gone and wasn't coming back, but when I'd try and talk to my dad, he'd get too upset, so I stopped talking about her. I try not to think about it,' I confess. 'All the things in my life that she's missed out on. It's too hard otherwise.'

His eyes scrutinise my face. 'That's the answer? Pretend they never existed?'

'No, that's not what I meant.'

'I feel like I'm doing a lousy job of grieving for her.'

'There's no right or wrong way, that's one thing I know for sure.'

'Maybe. I still feel like I'm doing everything wrong. Thinking the way I do.'

It's obvious he's being eaten up by guilt and it will take more than me to persuade him he hasn't done anything wrong. 'When did she die?'

'Almost a year ago.' He wipes tears off his cheeks quickly, using the back of one hand.

The reason for his melancholy on the rooftop becomes clear. 'So, the other night was . . . ?'

'My first New Year's without her, yes.'

'No wonder you're feeling so raw about it all. I know that it's a massive cliché, but it does get easier with time, I promise.'

'Yeah, so everyone keeps saying. But I think about her every single day, and every single day it hurts. There are so many reminders of her here.'

'So Africa, that's you running away?'

'No,' he protests. 'Maybe. A little, yeah. I need to get away from here, away from all the memories and reminders and the people who mean well but don't have a clue how I'm feeling. My parents are completely devastated, and it's so hard watching them go through this. I don't know what to say to them. That's why I decided I needed to do something to help others in the same situation as Paige. Mental health has such a stigma attached to it, people fear what they don't understand. I want the world to know that Paige was more than a statistic. She's not merely another suicide victim, she was so much more than that. Then I read an article in a *National Geographic* about a bike ride over in Africa, the Tour d'Afrique – have you heard of it?'

I shake my head. 'No.'

'Eleven thousand kilometres, from Egypt to South Africa.'

'Eleven thou – whoa. That's a long way.'

He gives a small, wry smile at the understatement. 'Yeah, it is. I'm doing it as a charity ride, already have quite a few sponsors, but hoping to pick up more once I'm out there. Any money I raise will go to the mental health foundation, in honour of Paige. It's a small gesture, but one I feel strongly about.'

'I think it's admirable, and if it helps you, then good on you. But eleven thousand kilometres?' I shake my head in wonder. 'I can't even wrap my head around how far that is. How long will you be away for?'

'Five months or so. The ride itself should take around four, but I wanted to allow myself time to enjoy it, not race through without absorbing any of it, you know? Afterwards I'm planning to head to the UK to catch up with an old school friend, Scott. He has a couch I can crash on for a few weeks while I check out a bit of Europe.'

I force a bright smile to hide the sadness I feel at the thought of him leaving, and so soon. 'I hope it goes well for you, I'm sure it will.'

'I'm sorry I didn't tell you about it earlier.'

'Hey, that's fine.'

'No,' he startles me with his loud voice. 'It's not. I feel lousy about it, but when we met, I just figured we'd hang out for a bit. I didn't realise that . . . ' he trails off.

'That what?'

'That we'd be still together. Here, now.'

He stares at me, I can see his chest rising and falling, his emotions right there on the surface. I'm not sure of the exact moment that this crossed over from being a bit of fun to feeling like it could develop into something more, but it did, and it does. Only now he's told me he's leaving, so where does that leave us? Don't get too attached, it'll only lead to heartbreak. Keep it light. Keep it fun.

'You know what,' I change the subject, getting abruptly to my feet. 'This is all getting a bit too heavy for me. I think it's time I finally had a swim in that hot tub.'

He exhales, releasing the tension of our conversation, summoning up a smile. 'Of course, but aren't you going to help me with the dishes first?'

'You said everything was taken care of and you didn't need my help, so . . . ' I move down the steps from the deck, and towards the tub, peeling off my jersey and shorts as I do. I've had my togs on since the shower in preparation for this moment and now I can't wait any longer. There is a whirring sound to my right, and I turn my head in time to see Finn streaking past, naked apart from his boxer shorts. 'Race you,' he calls.

'Hey,' I protest. 'What about the dishes?'

'Ah, I'll just throw them away.' He climbs up onto the little deck beside the pool and dips his toes in the water. 'Mum has enough, she'll never know.'

'You can't do that. It's . . . it's environmentally reckless. Don't you care about the planet?'

He pauses on the edge of the pool to arch his eyebrows at me. 'OK, my apologies, eco-warrior. I'll do them later.' He lowers himself into the water and closes his eyes in ecstasy. 'Oh my God, I'd forgotten how good this feels.'

I reach the side of the tub. He stands up abruptly while I'm hovering at the edge, and before I realise what's happening he grabs me around the waist, lifting me easily off my feet and down into the water.

'Hey!' I squeal indignantly.

'What?' He feigns innocence. 'I thought you wanted to get in.'

'Ohhh,' I say in ecstasy, sinking in until the water is above my shoulders. It's hot but not too hot, and it feels so good on my body. 'I can't stay mad at you, this is incredible.'

'Worth the wait?'

'Oh yes.'

He looks up. 'Hang on a sec, I forgot something.' He pushes over to the side and boosts himself up so his stomach is on the edge. Reaching out to a wooden control box next to the tub and a tree, he opens it and flicks a switch. 'Hopefully this still works.'

I gasp as strings of fairy lights strung through the trees above us light up the dusk, craning my neck to take it all in.

'Like it?' Finn says, from close beside me.

'Love it,' I reply breathily.

'They're solar-powered. My mother is into all things hygge.'

'Hygge?'

'Hard to explain. Not even sure I'm saying it properly. It's some kind of Scandinavian happiness thing.'

'Well, whatever it is, if it means fairy lights hung in trees above a hot tub by a lake in the woods . . . I have to say I like it.'

'You're so beautiful, Zoe. How can it be that I only met you twenty-four hours ago,' he muses softly. 'It feels so much longer, don't you think?'

'It does,' I agree.

'God, our timing sucks,' he moans. 'I almost wish I wasn't going away now.'

'You have to go, it's important. We could always pick this up when you're back.'

'I can't ask you to wait that long.'

Without breaking eye contact, I carefully pull down one bathing suit strap off my shoulder, freeing my left arm, then repeat the action with the right. His nostrils flare and his pupils open as I pull my togs down and fumble under the water to take them off altogether. When I have, I hold them up out of the water between one thumb and finger, then throw them behind me over my shoulder.

'Who said you're asking?' I say. 'I make my own decisions. You go and do what you need to do and I'll be here waiting when you get back. But on one condition . . . I don't want to wait any longer. This is the right moment. And anywhere with you is the right place.'

He rises abruptly, lifting me up again, one arm around my back and one under the knees. I loop my arms around his neck without thinking and yelp, aware of how exposed I am.

'No, don't cover yourself, I want to see you, all of you, when we make love,' he says, his breathing ragged. He kisses me, I

61

kiss him back, hungry and with the knowledge that after this there is no going back, and I will wait for him however long it takes. Out of the pool he stumbles but we don't let go, staggering towards the house, kissing the entire way. Inside, he holds my hand as I follow him upstairs to the mezzanine, where he picks me up again and gently tosses me onto the bed. I stare up at him as he removes his boxer shorts and reaches for a condom out of his bag on the floor nearby.

'You're so beautiful,' he murmurs, kneeling on the bed and lowering himself down on top of me. He kisses me again, tenderly at first and then with more urgency. He nuzzles my neck as I arch my back, desperate to feel him inside me. 'I don't know if I can wait any longer.' Suddenly he stops, pushing himself up so he can look at me properly. 'Are you sure?' he asks softly.

Instead of answering, I summon all my strength and push him upwards and sideways, rolling him onto his back so I am straddling him on top. I lower myself down and move to join us together completely. He moans and his pupils flare like exploding fireworks.

'I'm sure,' I breathe in his ear, as our worlds irrevocably collide.

Chapter twelve

'So that was . . .'

'Yup.'

'I mean . . . the way you . . .'

'Hey, I can't take all the credit. You were pretty sensational yourself.' I trace circles on his chest with my finger.

Our energy depleted, Finn is laying on his back. I'm tucked into his armpit, my head nestled on his shoulder. A steady plop plop plop on the roof indicates that it's started to rain again. I feel myself beginning to grow sleepy, but then he rolls swiftly over onto his side, taking me by surprise, and starts planting butterfly kisses on my forehead. 'You know, I'm feeling a little hot now, aren't you?'

'Well, we did have quite a workout.'

Kiss. 'I know something we can do to cool off.'

'Like what?'

He rolls away from me and gets to his feet. 'Follow me.'

I sit up, reaching for a T-shirt out of my nearby opened bag.

'You don't need clothes,' Finn says. 'Not where we're going.'

He reaches for my hand and I follow him downstairs curiously, outside and down onto the grass. I have a brief hope that maybe he's leading me to the hot tub again, but instead he heads straight for the lake. The rain is sharp on my skin, but I don't feel cold. At the edge of the jetty he stops.

'Are you ready?'

'For what?'

'This.' With a loud whoop, he drops my hand and he's off, running down the jetty, his white bum flashing until he reaches the end where he launches himself into the air, tucking his knees into his chest and wrapping his arms around them. With a large splash, he disappears underneath the water, popping up a few seconds later to shake droplets from his face, laughing loudly and unashamedly.

'Shit that's cold,' he hollers.

I shake my head at him in disbelief. 'You're crazy,' I shout.

'Crazy about you,' he shouts back. 'Come on, join me.'

'I can't believe I'm going to do this,' I mutter to myself, checking the edge of the jetty with one foot tentatively to see if the wood is slippery in the rain. It's fine though. Rough enough to supply grip. 'Here goes nothing, I guess.'

Even though I've braced myself, the water is freezing. It feels like a million tiny needles stabbing at my body. As I rise to the surface all the air is forced out of my lungs and I spend a few seconds gasping, while Finn grins at me and says, 'Doesn't this feel amazing?'

'That's ... not ... quite ... the word ... I would ... use ...' I answer.

'Don't worry, you'll get used to it soon,' he reassures me. 'My siblings and I used to do this all the time when we were kids.'

He bobs close to me in the water, raindrops running down his face. 'Every time there was a big summer storm.' His expression turns wistful, and I realise how hard it must be for him, being back here after Paige's death. Memories of his childhood everywhere. There's one thing I can think of that will distract him from his grief.

'You know what?' I start swimming towards the ladder on the jetty. 'I think I'm going to head back to the hot tub. Much warmer, and far more intimate.'

'Intimate?' He cottons on quickly and starts swimming after me. 'I like the sound of that. Wait for me!'

Chapter Thirteen

'You OK?'

I turn my face away from the car window and face Finn. 'Yeah,' I smile wanly. 'I'm fine. Just a little tired.'

'It was a pretty full-on weekend,' Finn agrees. 'You know, physically.'

'I'm not complaining about that, believe me.'

It's Monday morning, early. When we left the cabin it was still dark, but the sun is starting to peep over the hills to the east now, bathing the trees and paddocks in a soft orange glow that is breathtakingly beautiful. Any other time, on any other journey, I would have stopped to admire it. But not today. Today is the day that Finn leaves.

Originally, Finn had planned on heading back to the city the night before, to catch up with his family for dinner. But when it came to it, he wasn't ready to leave the cabin and neither was I, so he called his mother and told her he'd be home to see them in the morning and they'd have a family breakfast instead. Everything was already packed for his trip so he'd have a few hours to spend with them before he had to leave. It gave us another night together. A night when we slept little, talked plenty, and made love like we would never get enough of each other.

All too soon, we're back in the city and he's pulling up outside my apartment building. It's nothing fancy, a grey, characterless box, no different to all the other ones around it, but it's been my home since I moved in with Bonnie eight years ago, and I'm rather fond of it. He kills the engine and we sit in silence for a minute. I have so much I want to say, but no words with which to say it. In my head, when I practise, it sounds trite and ridiculous. How can I have these feelings towards someone I've only known for a few days? It doesn't make any sense. The thought of saying goodbye to him hurts far more than it should.

'We're back,' he says eventually.

I look out of the window at the city I normally love but which right at that second, I would trade in a heartbeat for a view of a lake and tree-rimmed hills. 'So we are.'

'I had an amazing weekend, Zoe.'

'I did too. Thanks for inviting me.'

'Thanks for accepting.'

I put my hand on the door handle. 'I wish you all the best, Finn, with the trip and everything. I'll be thinking of you.'

'Will you?'

I look at him, surprised he even has to ask. 'Of course.'

He exhales. 'I'll be thinking of you too.'

He develops a sudden interest in his thumbnail. 'Hey, I don't suppose you'd, like to ...' he clears his throat. 'Maybe come with me, to my parents' house? And then the airport?'

I frown, torn. If it was only the airport he was suggesting,

67

I'd consider it. But as strong as my feelings towards him are, it's far too soon to be meeting his family. How would he even introduce me? As the woman he met three nights ago who hasn't been back to her own house since? I don't think so. I can only imagine what they'd think of me after that. Besides, they deserve his undivided attention for his last few hours here, I owe them that after keeping him away an extra night. 'I don't think that would be a good idea.'

'You're probably right.'

I get out and so does he, lifting my bag out of the boot and placing it on the footpath at my feet while I stare at chewing gum stuck to the pavement and think about how it would be really cool right now if I could just not cry.

What follows is, as I tell Bonnie later when she gets home from work around lunchtime, an unsatisfactory goodbye. We hug, once we figure out whose arms go over the top and whose go underneath. I breathe the smell of his chest in deep, as I hear him do the same to the top of my head. There's an exchange of brave smiles, well wishes and a promise to keep in touch as we get out our phones and exchange email addresses. We'll catch up when he's back, we agree, but five months seems so far away and I'm acutely aware how much feelings can change in that time. It's not mine I'm worried about though. It almost feels like a wall has sprung up between us. I wave as he drives away. All in all, it's a disappointing end to our time together.

'So, did you tell him or not?' Bonnie asks with a mouthful of ham salad sandwich, when I finish telling her about the weekend and sum up with the weirdness that was our goodbye.

'Tell him what?'

'How you feel.'

'Of course not.'

'Why not?'

I frown at her. Was she not listening? 'Because that would be crazy.'

'Because?'

'Because I've only just—'

'Met him,' she interrupts. 'Yes, yes. I know that. I was there.'

'Well then you know.'

She runs a finger around her plate to wipe up some errant mayonnaise and licks it off her finger, shrugging. 'All I know is that you're an idiot.'

'Wow, thanks,' I say sarcastically. 'Awesome friend you are.'

She points the finger at me. 'I am an awesome friend, and you know it, because I say it how it is, and not what you want to hear. And I think you're a fool. It sounds like you guys had the kind of connection you hear about, but never truly believe exists.'

I sniff, slightly mollified. 'You honestly think so?'

'I do. And yet you let him go off to wander the desert, without offering him even a scrap of comfort to cling to when he's pining for home.'

'Not all of Africa is a desert, Bonnie, and I think you're being a teensy bit melodramatic now.'

'Whatever. Point is, maybe that's why things were so weird when you guys said goodbye. You were probably trying too hard to act like you didn't care so much, but maybe he thought that meant you didn't care at all.'

'Oh my God, what if he did?' I put my hands to my cheeks in horror. 'What if you're right? What if he thinks it all meant nothing to me?'

She shrugs. 'It's not too late.'

I check my phone and wail. 'It is. He'll be at the airport by now.'

'You can still make it.'

'It would take ages for a cab to get here.'

'It's OK, I'll call Josh, he has a car.' She gets out her phone and starts flicking for his number. 'He's always saying he can get anywhere in the city in thirty minutes, this is his chance to prove it. You go slap a bit of make-up on to hide the fact you've been crying.'

Josh, it turns out, wasn't exaggerating. He screeches to a halt outside the airport drop-off zone twenty-six minutes after he picks us up. Bonnie swivels to look at me.

'OK. We got you here. Now go do your part. Find Finn and tell him how you feel.'

'What if I can't find him?'

'Then at least you'll know you tried.'

I nod. OK. I can do this. I open the door.

'We'll go park in the short-term parking area and make out,' Bonnie says unashamedly. 'Text when you're ready to be picked up. Good luck!' she calls as I head towards the automatic doors.

Inside, there are queues of people at the checkout counters but I jog straight down the concourse to the large screens that display Arrival and Departure details, scanning them as I approach. I don't know his flight number, but I do know which airline he's flying with, roughly what time it's supposed to leave and where it's headed first. It doesn't take me long to find it.

13.15 LH 4235 MELBOURNE
GATE B33 GO TO GATE NOW

I'm too late. He's already somewhere on the other side of the wall that separates the travellers from the people left behind, waiting to board his flight. My body sags dejectedly as my chin sinks to my chest, eyes closed. I've missed him. Exhaling sadly, I turn to head back towards the exit, fumbling in my back jeans pocket for my phone so I can text Bonnie the bad news.

'You came.'

He's standing behind me, only a few steps away. A back-pack slung over one shoulder and a look of disbelief mingled with happiness on his face. It's only been a few hours since we parted, but the joy that surges inside me at the sight of him is unmistakable.

'I thought you'd have already gone through Customs.'

'I should have.' His eyes flash above my head momentarily to look at the board. 'I checked in ages ago but I couldn't make myself go through that final door until I knew there was no chance . . . ' he trails off.

'That I'd come,' I finish.

He nods.

I shrug my shoulders. 'I came.'

'You did. Why?'

'I don't know.'

'Oh.'

'Actually, that's not true.' I step closer until I am only a hand's width from his chest, and look up at him. My heart starts fluttering in my chest at being close to him again. 'I felt funny after we said goodbye earlier, like I'd messed it up. I should have been honest and said how I was feeling.'

His eyes search mine, his expression inscrutable. 'Which is?'

'I think you know.'

'I still want to hear you say it.'

I take a deep breath. Here goes nothing. 'That I'm going to miss you. That I think I'm falling for you, which I know is nuts because, I mean, we barely know each other, right? Although that's not totally true, we have talked, a lot, and I feel like I know more about you than some people who have been in my life for years. Honestly? I can't really explain it, and maybe it's because I've had stuff all sleep over the last few days. Maybe I'm hallucinating and I should stop—'

He moves so quickly I don't realise what's happening until he's kissing me, one of his hands in my hair, the other snaked around me, pulling me in against him as his mouth meets mine. I kiss him back, hard and desperate, feeling like I can't get close enough to him. When he finally pulls away for breath, he grins.

'I was just trying to stop you talking, but whoa, that was . . .'

He kisses me again.

'All passengers on Lufthansa Flight 4235 to Cairo via Melbourne and Dubai, please report to Gate B33 immediately. All passengers on Lufthansa Flight 4235 to Cairo via Melbourne and Dubai, please report to Gate B33. Your flight is preparing to board. Thank you.'

We stop kissing, reluctantly, but don't release each other, standing with our foreheads pressed together. This hurts way more than I thought it would. Way more than it should.

'I have to go,' he says sorrowfully.

I nod. 'I know.'

He pulls his head back so he can look me in the eyes again.

'Don't forget about me, OK?'

'As if I could.'

'I'm sorry,' he says, sounding it, as he lets me go with a

tortured expression on his face like it's the hardest thing he's ever had to do. I hold it together right until he pauses before the big glass doors leading to the Customs area, where he turns and blows me a kiss. I catch it with one hand, then blow him one back with the other, my eyes pooling with tears. Then he is gone.

Outside, trying to text Bonnie but struggling to see the screen through blurred eyes, my phone pings with a message from him.

I love you

Smiling through my tears, I reply.

I love you too. See you in five months xx

Chapter fourteen

From: Finn_the_finster@gmail.com
To: ZoeCalloway@hotmail.com
Subject: I miss you

God, our timing sucks.

I'm on the plane, still on the tarmac, trying to see if I can see you out of one of these ridiculously small windows. I'm not in a window seat, which makes the task somewhat harder. The man who is in the window seat doesn't seem too pleased with me leaning over his lap every ten seconds. Could be a long flight, in more ways than one.

I hated walking away from you back there. It was one of the most difficult things I've ever had to do. You were clearly trying to be brave, but . . . oh Zoe, your face is not one born easily to deceit. Your eyes slick with tears, your bottom lip quivering . . . (Now I can't stop thinking about your lips, about kissing them. How the hell am I supposed to get through the next five months without kissing you??)

I've been counting down to this trip for months now, and not just because the physical challenge of it excites me, or (being honest here) because it feels good to be raising money for a good cause, in Paige's memory. I've also been looking forward to it because it was a way to escape. My grief, my family's grief. Memories of Paige, of her life, grossly overshadowed by the way she died.

This trip, I figured, would buy some time, during which maybe I'd figure out how I'm supposed to live my life now, with the pretty big hole that losing Paige has left in it. She's always been there, and now she's not. And I don't know how I'm supposed to be now.

But then I met you.

And for the first time since she died, I felt ... happy. Then I felt guilty. Am I allowed to be happy? Am I allowed to move on? I have to be completely honest. Our first night together, on the roof, I never expected to fall for you the way I did. I one hundred per cent wasn't looking for anything, but then you asked me to kiss you and ... I can't explain it. I was intrigued, and you took my mind off ... her. I asked you to walk with me because I thought you'd be a good distraction. Help me to get through one more night until I could get on the plane and put some distance between myself and everything that had happened.

But ... by the time the sun came up, I knew it was so much more than that, and it freaked me out a bit, because I've never had a connection like we had, and that quickly, with someone before. Never. I didn't think that sort of stuff even happened in real life.

I was watching you sleep that morning (sounds creepy

75

in hindsight, I promise it was a beautiful moment at the time!) and I thought, maybe my feelings were heightened because I knew I was going away.

But every further minute we spent together, and I'm fully aware this sounds incredibly clichéd, I knew it wasn't a circumstance thing. It was an us thing.

That's why I said I love you. Believe me when I tell you that I've never told someone I love them after only a few days together, and if, pre-meeting you, a friend of mine had done the same thing I would have been scathingly derisive and probably quite mean. Because I wouldn't have believed it was possible.

Now I do.

I love you, Zoe. I know it's nuts, I can barely believe it myself, but I do.

Chapter fifteen

From: ZoeCalloway@hotmail.com
To: Finn_the_finster@gmail.com
Subject: I miss you too

Agreed. Our timing could definitely have been better.

It seems exceptionally unfair that the night I finally weakened and followed Bonnie's special brand of life advice, I met you, fell for you, and then shortly thereafter, lost you.

I know it's for a good cause. I know it was planned long before we met. I know all that.

But it's still unfair.

Yes, I was watching you from the airport departure lounge. I scanned every single window to see if I could see you, but the plane was too big and too far away. Colours, the odd flash of flesh as someone waved a hand. But nothing definitive as belonging to you. I hated watching your plane taxi out onto the runway, hearing its engines kick up a notch, seeing it get faster and faster until the wheels lifted off the tarmac and I had the sinking realisation that we were no longer standing on the same ground, in the same city, or even in the same country. I watched, as it climbed higher into the sky until it was a small dot that gleamed brightly for a moment in the brilliant sun, before disappearing into the clouds.

I cried the whole time. A snotty, blotchy ugly cry, that made everyone else in the lounge keep a wide berth. Attractive, right? It's all your fault. I keep fantasising about being able to rewind time, just enough to give us our days at the lake again. They were hands down the most incredible days of my life.

Hurry up, will you? But be safe. Be safe, but fast. Five months seems like an absolute eternity. I feel like a love-struck teenager in a Shakespearean play. Forced apart by tragedy. Pining, longing, desolate. Sigh.

In reality, I'll act my age. Get up and go to work every day, like always. Eat a beautifully well-balanced diet (in between the post-workout doughnuts, of course), and I'll wait. Maybe the time will go fast. I hope so. I can't wait to see you again and pick up where we left off. It feels like a new chapter my life started the night I met you, and I can't wait to see what happens next.

I love you too.

Chapter sixteen

Finn: Are you awake?

Zoe: I am now

Finn: Sorry

Zoe: Don't be, sleep is overrated. I was dreaming about you anyway.

Finn: Seriously?

Zoe: No, sorry. I don't know why I said that. I was actually dreaming that Bonnie and I got a kitten.

Finn: Kittens are cute. Guess I can't blame you for that.

Zoe: Where are you?

Finn: Malawi.

Zoe: What's it like?

Finn: I should let you get back to sleep . . .

Zoe: Don't you dare! I'll be very grumpy with you if you do . . .

Finn: But you need your beauty sleep . . .

Zoe: Excuse me?

Finn: For work! I meant for work. You're gorgeous, you know I think that.

Zoe: Mm. Nice save. So?

Finn: It's nice. Passed a lot of fishing villages, down by the lake. The road here is paved. First paved section of the ride so far. Hopefully not the last. Much smoother ride.

Zoe: Where are you right now?

Finn: At a bar, in a shopping centre. Drinking a beer while I sponge off their free Wi-Fi.

Zoe: I wish I was there with you

Finn: Because of the beer? Or the free Wi-Fi ...

Zoe: That's a tough one to choose between, but I'd have to go with the beer. I can get as much Wi-Fi at work as I need.

Finn: ...

Zoe: What

Finn: ☺

Zoe: You asked me to choose. Those are the options you gave me. Were you hoping I'd say something else?

Finn: Maybe

Zoe: Maybe like, I wish I was there so I could be with you?

Finn: Keep talking

Zoe: I miss you

Finn: I miss you more

Zoe: Not possible

Finn: Totally is

Zoe: It's really not

Finn: I miss your lips, I miss your eyes, I miss the way your hair won't stay behind your ear no matter how many times you tuck it there. I miss the way your face looks when you laugh, the way your hand feels small in mine. I miss the way your body feels when it's naked, your soft skin touching mine. I miss the tiny gap between your front teeth, and the little freckles across the top of your nose. I miss the way your pupils flare right before I kiss you. I miss being inside you. It's the only place I've ever known I truly belonged.

Zoe: ...

Finn: Say something

Zoe: OK, maybe it is possible.

Finn: I told you

Zoe: God I wish you were here.

Finn: So do I.

Four months later

Chapter seventeen

Stars . . .

Millions and millions of stars, an infinitesimal amount.

All woven together by strands of light . . .

. . . one giant consciousness . . .

Connected . . .

. . . wondrous,

. . . comforting . . .

'I've got a pulse!'

'The IV's in!'

'She's intubated!'

'Someone get hold of the family, they need to get here. Now.'

The stars vanish at the sound of the voices.

Pain rushes back in, worse than anything I could ever imagine.

I'm hot.

I'm cold.

I'm being set on fire, stabbed by a million knives.
I don't want to die
... but I can't bear this pain.
'Everybody clear! Stand back, she's flatlined again ...'

Chapter eighteen

I hear a clang. Metal upon metal, the swish of fabric . . . a curtain? Hushed voices.

'. . . stabilised . . . touch and go . . .'

Sensations

I feel . . . numb

like I am suffocating. Something is in my throat, choking me, unable to move, pinned down

'. . . not out of the woods yet . . .'

A heavy sigh, it sounds familiar. But . . . it can't be?

'. . . we can give you a few minutes with her but then we need to get her back into theatre. The longer we wait, the more her body shuts down. If you've got something to say, you should probably say it now.'

Chapter nineteen

When I open my eyes, the room has a peculiar orange glow, like the world is on fire. It's disorientating and I don't understand why it's that colour, or even where I am. All I know is I feel . . . weird. Fuzzy. There's the recognition of pain too, but clouded, so that even though I'm aware of its presence, it's not unbearable. Just . . . there.

'Zoe?'

A face suddenly looms over me, and I frown up at it, confused. Am I hallucinating? I squeeze my eyes shut, count to five and then open them again. He's still there. I haven't seen my father's face in almost eight years, but it's him, there's no mistaking it.

He looks a lot older than I remember him, much older than he should, but it doesn't surprise me. To buy myself time before I answer, while I attempt to make sense of where I am and why he is here, I study my surroundings. It's too hard to move my head, but I can roll my eyes from side to side. Pale beige walls and a white roof with an old brown water stain in one corner. A small television is mounted on the wall, and on its screen, racehorses are thundering down a field. There's a trolley beside the bed, with nothing on it. Behind me, just out of sight, I can hear a quiet hum, a steady blip. Over my father's shoulder I can see a window, and outside, the city skyline, on fire with a setting sun. Thousands of city windows reflect the colour in all directions, like a glass prism. Finally, I look back at him.

'Dad?' It's hard to speak, my throat feels swollen, sore.

'I'm here.'

I clear my throat and wince when the pain worsens. 'Where ... am I?'

'You're in a hospital, Zoe.' He's clearly uncomfortable. Doesn't know what to do with his hands. Crosses his arms then uncrosses them again, scratches the back of his neck and then lightly slaps one fist into the other palm. 'You had an accident. Somebody called me.'

He looks as confused by this as I am.

'What happened?'

'From what I can piece together, you and Bonnie were heading out to lunch. You were in front and stepped out onto the road between two parked cars where an oncoming van hit you. Whether he was distracted, or simply didn't have enough time to react, I don't know. The police will figure all that out. You're the only important thing right now.'

'Bonnie?'

'She's OK. In a bit of shock, understandably, but she's not injured. Her boyfriend took her home to try and get some rest. I promised I'd let her know when you're awake.'

The sun, brilliant overhead.
The ground, burning underneath.
The sound of my body breaking.
The utter helplessness as I felt my life drain from me.

'I thought I was dying,' I say.

'You almost did,' my father admits. 'You lost a lot of blood.'

'I almost died?'

'Hey now,' he says gruffly. 'Don't dwell on that. You're still here. That's all that matters.'

I try and focus on his face but everything is still a little blurry, like I'm under the influence. And not of anything good. 'You didn't have to come.'

'Course I did.' He grimaces guiltily. 'Zoe, I know things between us aren't in a great place, and I know that's my fault,' he concedes. 'But things are different now.'

'Dad . . .'

'I mean it. I've changed. And I want to make it all up to you. Let me help.'

'They're just words,' I say warily. 'I've heard it all before.'

'I know. I know you have. But I'm still your dad, and I'll always love you. That isn't something that's ever going to change.'

'I'm sure you mean well, but I don't need your help.'

He flushes and looks down at his hands again. 'We can discuss it all later. Right now, you need to rest and recover.'

My blood runs cold. What hasn't he told me?

Chapter twenty

All my life I have been taking decision-making for granted, I realise, rather belatedly and only now that the ability to do so has been taken away from me. OK, that's not completely true. I can still make some decisions for myself. Small ones, like, what to wear, or how many pillows I want to sleep with. I can even decide for myself how long to wait before I need to start the arduous process of going for a wee. And arduous it certainly is. Everything is, when you've lost a leg.

Two weeks. That's how long I've been 'an amputee'. Fourteen days since they decided while I was on the operating table that my lower leg and foot were mangled beyond repair. Twenty thousand one hundred and sixty minutes since they decided the leg needed to come off. One million, two hundred and nine thousand, six hundred seconds since that leg was sliced off and sent to the ... well. I don't know where it ended up. My father said they asked him whether he thought I'd like to keep the foot for some kind of twisted funeral or cremation, but he said no, which was probably the right decision. Still, it was another decision that I didn't get to make.

This one though, I did make. And it's the reason Dr Finch looks frustrated, even as he tries hard to pretend he's not.

'I hear we had a little wobble yesterday,' he says carefully.

'Something like that.'

'Can you talk me through it?'

I shrug. 'Not much to say. I decided I couldn't go through with it.'

'But you were all prepped and good to go,' he points out. 'The surgical team were scrubbed in and standing by. You were right there.'

'I know,' I reply through gritted teeth. 'But at the last minute I realised I couldn't do it. I'm sorry for wasting everyone's time.'

The doctor looks across the bed to where my father is sitting in a blue faux leather armchair that, frankly, has seen better days. It squeaks every time it moves even a fraction, and the reclining mechanism is broken so when my father tries to recline it to sleep at night, his feet end up higher than his head.

'Don't look at me,' my father shrugs. 'It's her decision.'

Dr Finch laces his fingers together and clasps them in front of them. 'Perhaps things weren't explained clearly enough,' he says carefully. 'If I could go over it all with you one more—'

'No, I understand perfectly,' I cut him off. 'The infection is finally under control. However, it's affected the way the . . . ' I close my eyes and shudder, 'stump, has healed. That, and the way the first amputation was carried out—'

He opens his mouth to interrupt but I beat him to it.

'Yes, I know, it was a life-and-death situation and the doctor did what he had to do. But it means I'm not a viable candidate for a prosthesis.'

'Unless—'

'Unless I agree to another operation to let you cut off another chunk of my leg.'

He winces. 'We would surgically remove another eight to ten centimetres, yes. Clean out the affected tissue and shape and repair the bone and skin that cover the stump.'

'I can't.'

'But, Miss Calloway, Zoe. This is the only way you'll be able to walk again. If you have this operation, we can have you back on your feet in a couple of months.'

'I understand that, and I want that too, believe me. But I need more time.'

He tries a different tack. 'OK. Maybe if you can talk me through the reasoning behind your decision, Zoe, your fears about the operation, I could help to allay some of those.'

'You know what happened to my mother, right?' I sense Dad stiffen beside me. 'You've read her file?'

'I have, yes. But what happened to your mother was very rare and, as far as we know, not hereditary.'

'But you don't know that for sure.'

'No. Like I said, her condition is very rare, so there's a lot of unknowns about it. However, the fact that you've already been through one operation successfully—'

'Doesn't mean it won't happen the second time,' I cut in.

'The chances of that happening are very slim.'

'Dr Finch, if you can look me in the eye right now and guarantee that nothing will go wrong, I'll consent to the operation.'

He wants to, I can tell. His face twitches as he's torn between his confidence and his training, but it's drummed into them at medical school to never set yourself up for culpability. In the end, he's not prepared to risk his career.

'I can't,' he says. 'No one can. But as I say, the risks are very low.'

'Then the answer is no. Or at least, not now. I'm sorry.'

He looks again to my father, this time for help. His expression clearly says, you're her parent, you should want what's best for her! But what he doesn't realise, and what I'm counting on, is that my father is just as scared as I am.

'Does it have to be done right now?' Dad asks. 'Can't she take a bit of time to get used to the idea, and then we'll get back to you when she's ready.'

'Yes. I suppose so.' Dr Finch looks at his watch. He doesn't understand my decision, but he's wasted enough time on me already. 'If that's what you want. In that case, I'm happy to discharge you at the end of the week. We need to make sure that infection won't reoccur, and then you can go. You'll need to start making plans.'

'Plans?' I frown at him, not understanding.

'Yes. Where you'll live. You will need either a wheelchair or crutches, probably both. The hospital will loan you some, but your house will need to accommodate those access requirements. We need to be satisfied that you're going to be able to look after yourself. We recommend you have someone full time to help you, at least for the initial period until you start to get a grasp on things. Speak to the nurses about the services available to you – they can get the ball rolling.'

His voice starts to fade into the background, and all I hear is the loud thump of my own heart beating. How could I have been so stupid? I haven't given any thought to what life would be like after the hospital. I was so focused on getting out of here, I didn't think about what would come next. I naively thought that I could leave and go back to my flat and my job. Any minor, technical details could all be worked out later. A few wheelchair ramps and support bars and I'd be fine, or so I figured. But now it's becoming apparent that it's not going to be as easy as that.

I turn to look at Dad, panicked. 'What am I going to do?'

'It's OK,' he says quickly. 'Don't worry. I've got a plan.'

Chapter twenty-one

'Did you check under the bed?'

I close my eyes and take a deep breath. 'No. How would you suggest I do that without falling over?'

'Right,' Dad replies guiltily. 'Sorry. I'll do it.'

He crouches down and has a look, then straightens up. 'All clear.' He zips up my blue duffel bag and casts one last, long look around the room. As soon as I leave, it will be stripped and cleaned and disinfected, ready for the next patient. Like I was never here. Like my life didn't just change irrevocably inside these walls.

'That's everything,' he says. 'Including your phone charger. I've made arrangements with Bonnie to box up your things at the flat and I'll sort out a truck to pick them up ...' he trails off, aware he's repeating things he's already told me. Things I have no wish to hear.

'Thanks.' It comes out less grateful than I intend, but it's either that or scream. None of this is fair, and I'm angry.

'I know this isn't what you want, Zoe.'

'I don't think what I want comes into it anymore, do you?'

A nurse pushes open the door, saving my father from trying to reason with his unreasonable daughter, yet again. I've got to hand it to him, with everything I've thrown at him over the last few days since it became clear I wouldn't be returning to my 'normal' life here in the city any time soon, he's still here. Still standing. Still coming up with solutions that are practical, though unwanted.

'Ready to go?' the nurse asks chirpily. 'You must be excited to get out of this place finally.'

'Excited isn't quite the word I'd use,' I mutter, but still, the thought of breathing air that hasn't been pumped through a filtration system does seem inviting.

She pushes the wheelchair over to the side of the bed and I awkwardly manoeuvre myself down into it, the way the physio and occupational therapist have been teaching me for the last couple of weeks. Dad passes over my bag and I rest it on my knees.

'I can take it from here,' he says, and the nurse stands back to let him get behind the handles of the chair. 'I'm so grateful for everything that you and the other nurses have done for my daughter. If you could pass on my thanks at the next staff meeting, I'd appreciate it.'

'All part of the job,' she smiles. 'But of course, I will.' She rests a hand on my shoulder. 'Take care of yourself, Zoe. I know at this moment it feels like things will never be normal again, but trust me. You'll find a new normal. You'll be OK.'

'Thanks,' I say, thinking how easy it is to say something like that when it's not your life that's had a grenade lobbed at it. But she means well. 'For everything.'

'You're most welcome.'

It's a weird feeling, leaving the room and the ward that's been 'home' for just over two weeks, and suddenly I'm struck by the painful thought that I'm not ready for this. Maybe if I was going home, back to Bonnie and the flat and the job that I love, I'd feel ready. But that's all gone now. I can't walk because I can't get a prosthetic without another operation, and I can't bring myself to consent to that. Not yet. Maybe not ever.

I can barely push myself around corners in the chair, and as for crutches, well, they're OK for short distances, but to use in a classroom? Around a school? Leading the children in our morning physical exercise around the playing courts? No. Impractical, not to mention dangerous.

Without a job, I can't afford to pay rent, and even though Bonnie broached the idea of her covering the rent and utilities until I'd had time to adjust and figure things out, there's no way I could let her do that. Which left me with only one option.

Downstairs, Dad parks my chair to one side of the hospital outside the ER drop-off zone, while he goes to the nearby multi-storey car park to retrieve his car. There are far too many people around and I'm conscious of curious eyes as people pass through the automatic doors. I should have worn jeans, tried to hide the bandaged stump, but it's still swollen and getting anything over it is too much of an effort. Plus, when I knock the newly healed wound – which I inevitably, clumsily, do – it hurts. I'm wearing shorts, even though it's early winter and there is a definite chill in the air, along with a heavy smell of woodsmoke.

Dad pulls into a parking space in front of me and leaves the engine running while he jumps out and comes around to help. I let him wheel me to the car and stand as a support while I attempt to manoeuvre myself into the back seat. Have cars always been this small? The entrance through the doorway seems ridiculously narrow and even when, with a great deal of effort and a few swear words, I get my bum onto the seat, I can't turn to swing in either the stump or my remaining leg.

'Why don't you try shuffling backwards,' Dad suggests, sensing how close to tears I am. 'Sit long ways across the seat instead of facing forward. Here, I'll help.'

Somehow, with his help, I manage to do as he says. He shuts the door and I sink against the seat and close my eyes, hearing him put the bag in the boot and slamming it closed, then getting back into the front. He takes a deep breath.

'You ready?'

'No.'

'Should I help you with your seat belt?'

Even though I wouldn't normally dream of being in a moving vehicle without wearing one, I say, 'Fuck the seat belt. I'm sitting sideways, it's not exactly going to work anyway, is it. Plus, it'll be too uncomfortable. I'll take my chances.'

I hear him suck air in sharply then blow it out with a little squeak. He wants to argue but resists, for which I'm grateful.

'All right then, let's get on the road.' The car starts to move. 'I was hoping to beat the three o'clock school traffic on the motorway, but I think we're going to hit it. I don't know how it took so long for them to track down a doctor to sign the discharge form, but it is what it is. Can't be helped. I thought we'd stop and grab some dinner somewhere along the way. Takeaway,' he adds hurriedly. 'You don't have to get out of the car. But if you need to go toilet or stop for any reason, let me know. I'm sure we can figure something out.'

The thought of my father having to help me get from the wheelchair into a toilet stall in a public bathroom is enough of an incentive to hold my bladder. 'I'll wait till we get ...' I trail off, unable to bring myself to say home. It doesn't feel like home anymore, where we're going. Truthfully, it didn't feel like a home for a long time before that either.

I open my eyes and watch as we leave the city behind, with all its beautiful and broken idiosyncrasies that I love so much. I do cry, now. Silently, tears roll down my cheeks and drip off onto my chest and I do nothing to stop them. I am in mourning. How can it all have changed, gone wrong, so quickly?

Just a few weeks ago, I spent an hour on a video call with Finn. We were excited, crazily so, because it was only another month until he'd be home. The countdown was on. I was still so excited after we'd talked, buzzing from seeing his face for the first time in weeks, so when Bonnie suggested we head out to lunch, I jumped at it.

I didn't see the van coming as I stepped out between the cars. I've tried to remember whether I even looked, but it's all a blur. I remember Bonnie screaming behind me, and then nothing but bits and pieces after that until I woke up in the hospital.

My life changed, in a second. Forever.

Chapter twenty-two

I fall asleep as we leave the city, closing my eyes to avoid remembering the last time I drove this road, with Finn, on our way to the lake, then sleep fitfully on and off during the journey home. I don't know what it is that wakes me, maybe the reduction of speed, or the twists and turns of the car as it hugs the coastal road that makes up the last half an hour of the trip.

'You awake?' Dad asks quietly.

'Yeah.'

'We're almost home.'

I stretch and adjust my position a bit higher so I can see out the window. An ocean made up of shadows greets me, dark and brooding to match my mood. I haven't seen it since I drove out of town nine years ago, but strangely, I feel no nostalgia at the sight of it. This isn't a trip down memory lane I ever wanted to take.

The road veers sharply inland away from an impenetrable cliff, we crest a hill and there on the other side is the town of my childhood. I barely have to turn my head to see from one side of it to the other. Nestled in a little bay, the town consists of one main road with a few blocks of houses either side that bleed gently out into farmland. School on the eastern limits, rugby grounds over the single-lane bridge to the north. I know all the streets, all the alleyways, all the shortcuts.

I've often wondered how I'd feel seeing this place again, and now I know. Indifferent towards the town itself, but a gut-heavy dread towards the idea of living here again. It's temporary, I keep telling myself. I can leave at any time. Spirals of smoke circle upwards from chimneys, silhouetted against a darkening dusky sky along with trees and the large cross that sits high on a hill above the graveyard. As we drive closer, white, yellow and orange dots of light blink on: streetlights and kitchens, chasing away the night and the cold.

Main street is deserted, the shops all locked up tight for the night. Nothing stays open past five o'clock here, or on a Sunday at all. A few are different to what I remember, though most are the same. There are more empty ones than I recall.

'Place brings back some memories for you, I'm sure,' Dad chuckles. You can tell he's chuffed to have me back.

'Especially Charlie's,' I answer pointedly as we drive past the only business still open.

He sighs heavily. 'Oh, Zoe. I'm sorry about . . . all that,' he says sadly. 'Sorrier than you'll ever know.'

'Yeah, you said.'

'And I mean it.'

'You can't blame me for having doubts.'

'I know,' he says, determined. 'But you'll see.'

He takes a right turn on Main South, then a left on Cherrywood. The road gets narrower and bumpier the further along we go, as the houses get smaller and older. My phone pings as Dad pulls into our driveway and just like that, I'm home.

Chapter twenty-three

From: Finn_the_finster@gmail.com
To: ZoeCalloway@hotmail.com
Subject: One week!!!!

One more week! I'm so packed and ready, counting down the days until I get to board that plane and fly my way back home and to you. I've been looking forward to this day for so long, and now it's almost here.

I tried to video-call you a couple of times last week but you were offline. Probably working? Sleeping? I've lost track of the time difference thing now that I'm in the UK. Is it twelve hours? Day before or after? If you get a chance, call me, whatever time it is. I want to hear your voice and see your face, even though I'll see it for real very soon.

I have a confession to make. Brace yourself. I've thought long and hard about admitting this, because it makes me look like a bit of an ungrateful bastard. But here goes.

(Deep breath.)

Europe SUCKS.

OK it doesn't. But it sucks to be here without you. Scott's doing his best to show me the sights and last week's trek in Spain was pretty cool, but I keep thinking about how amazing it would be to be exploring all these countries with YOU rather than a six-foot, bearded banker. I have so much to tell you about, not only the ins and outs of the bike trip (prepare yourself for the mother of all slide shows, by the way, consider yourself warned). But mentally, and (don't think I'd admit this to anyone else) spiritually. That's right. I don't want to go into it over email, I wouldn't even know where to start. But all those months on the road, I had time to think about life, and what it is I want from it, and I can't wait to talk about it all with you.

The last time we spoke, just before I left Africa to fly to the UK, you asked me how I was feeling about Paige's death now, and you probably noticed that I changed the subject. I'm sorry. The truth is, it's not something I can explain easily. I've tried to put it in an email to you, but I can't find the right words. All you need to know at this point is that I'm doing OK, I am. I thrashed out a lot of my anger on the roads in Africa.

I also met up with a group of riders at a campground in Namibia. There was a woman from Switzerland who was biking the trail in memory of her husband. He'd always wanted to do it, but got a brain tumour in his early thirties and died twelve months later. He'd talked about doing the ride since their first date, but like everybody else, he figured there would always be time later in life. She told

107

me that as part of her grief therapy, she would write him letters, or emails or even texts, to say the things that she still wanted to say but never got the chance to.

So, I wrote Paige a letter. On my last day in Cape Town. The words came out easier than I expected. It hurt though, not going to lie. Felt like a final goodbye, which I guess it was, as I never got to give her one face to face. I didn't want to keep the letter, once I'd got all those feelings out, so I borrowed a lighter from a guy smoking dope on the hostel's balcony, and I burned it. It felt like a weight was lifted.

Anyway. I know this all probably sounds weird, but I'll explain it better when I'm home. X

Chapter twenty-four

Dear Paige,

I'll start with the question that's bothered me ever since you died . . . Why?

Why did you do it?

Do you have any idea how seriously mind fucking it is to have a question that you know you'll never, ever get an answer to?

I could have helped you. If not me, our parents. Our brothers. Aunts, uncles, friends, cousins, the fucking mailman. Any one of us would have done anything for you, in a heartbeat. All you had to do was say something. If you had told us how you were feeling, that you were in so much pain that you could seriously see death as the only way out, we could have helped you to realise that it wasn't. We could have got you the help that you needed. Somewhere, someone could have helped you. I am one hundred per cent sure of that.

All you had to do was say something.

But instead, you kept your feelings/fears/anxieties locked up inside. Slapped on a brave face. Pretended everything was OK, when clearly that was far from the case. Tell you what, you were a far better actress than I gave you credit for.

I'm sorry.

I'm sorry that at times I've almost felt close to hating you. Hating you for what you've put this family through. And then, I hate myself for feeling that way. I shouldn't feel hatred. I shouldn't feel anger. See, that's the thing about feelings, we have no control over them.

Why didn't you trust us, your family, to help you through it? Why couldn't you see that we'd never have judged you? Never have abandoned you? You should have given us the chance to help you. But no, you gave up instead. I know I'm not supposed to see it that way. I know that when you made the decision to jump, you weren't thinking straight. Something was broken in your mind. I know all that. But what torments me is . . . when you made that decision to die, could anything have stopped you? Anyone?

I don't think you wanted to die, I think you wanted peace. I only wish you'd realised that you could have had one without the other. It didn't have to come to this.

You were larger than life, Paige. The life of every party. You know the 'rock-on' hand sign you used to pull in almost every photo (not to mention the poked tongue Mum used to get so mad about)? I got that sign tattooed on my back, in your memory. Probably not my best decision, and one made while I was overwhelmed by grief and to be honest, drunk. But I haven't regretted it yet. I don't think I will. It's like you're looking over my shoulder in life. I also got the words you used to say to me when we were little. Love you, kiddo. Do you remember? I do. You were always there for me, Sis. Why couldn't you let me repay the favour?

You should have heard the clichés people kept telling us at your funeral.

110

Life goes on.

Time heals all wounds.

It gets easier.

She's in a better place.

She's at peace now. (OK, this one might be true. Still hate it.)

But the worse fucking one of all?

Everything happens for a reason.

Nah. I call bullshit on that. There is no possible reason for your death that could ever make sense. And I've tried to come up with one, believe me. I've tried to find a reason even if only to make myself feel better, but there isn't one. It doesn't exist.

Out here on the road, I've had a lot of time to think and reflect. Somehow, I have to accept things the way they are now. That your death will never make any sense. That I will never know why. But if I let the grief and the regrets take over my life, then I'm not doing you any justice. Your death shouldn't mean I stop living. And as guilty as it feels, moving on doesn't mean I've forgotten you, or that I don't care. Because I'll never stop caring.

I don't want to look back and realise I wasted this all too fragile life. So, here's my promise to you. I'll grab every opportunity that comes my way, for you, Paige. I won't settle, and I'll live the hell out of this life I have. That's the best damn tribute I could ever give you.

You'll be in my mind and my heart forever.

Love you always kiddo,

Finn

Chapter twenty-five

There's a line of light around the closed curtains when we pull into the drive but I don't think anything of it at first. In the glow of the headlights and the security lights over the house that have just clicked on when they sensed us, I take in my surroundings, surprised. The place is looking great, better than I ever remember it looking, even when my mother was still alive. She didn't live long in this house, dying less than six months after we moved in, before she had time to see any of her plans for the place come to fruition. And although she was good at a lot of things, gardening wasn't one of them. Dad used to keep the lawns trimmed, and we had a few small trees and plants that survived more through their own efforts than anything my parents ever did.

After she died, my father mowed the lawns more sporadically, at least until I was old enough to figure out how to fill the tank of the mower with fuel and turn it on myself. I worked hard at keeping them the same length as everyone else along the road, because I hated being the unkempt house, the one with the knee-high weeds in the garden, the overgrown hedges and the cardboard taped over the small window by the front door, a permanent reminder of my father's shame. One of them, anyway.

That window has been replaced, I see now. The house given a new lick of paint. A kind of powdery baby blue, or is it grey? Hard to tell in the yellow glow of the outside lights. It's not a colour I would have chosen, but it looks OK. The lawns are trimmed and the edges sharp. Where there was once an overgrown area along the fence inside which snuffling wildlife lurked unbothered, a pretty flower garden now stretches, pops of winter colour to brighten up the space. A sapphire blue birdbath in the middle, and a pole with a birdhouse on the top.

Dad gets my crutches out of the boot and then opens my door. 'Welcome home.'

I edge across the seat until my remaining foot is on the concrete of the driveway. 'Are you sure we have the right address?'

'What? Oh.' Dad looks around proudly. 'You noticed, then.'

'Hard not to. It looks nothing like the house I left.'

'Do you like it?'

I shrug. 'It looks fine.'

His face falls, he'd clearly hoped for more.

'I mean it looks good. Pretty.'

'Thanks.'

'Did you do it all yourself?'

Instantly he's cagey. 'Mostly. I had a little help with the design and some of the grunt work. Let's get you inside, out of the cold.'

We come to a stop at the bottom of the steps that lead up to the deck at the front door. Three small steps. When I was younger, and had two legs, I took them easily and naturally without a thought. Sometimes, with enough speed, I leapt up

them with one quick stride. Now, even though I've been practising how to do this, they look insurmountable, like my own
personal Everest, and the thought of climbing them is exhaust-
ing. I swallow hard, determined not to cry in front of him.

'I've called Harry Taylor about installing a couple of ramps
and he says he'll get on it this week,' Dad says. 'For now, though,
do you think you could kind of hop up? If I help you?'

I give his question the disdainful look it deserves. 'How about
you try hopping up the steps first, and let me know how well
that works out for you.'

'Sorry. Maybe if you sat, we could—'

The door opens, yellow light spilling out onto the deck and
steps, a beacon, inviting us in. I see only a silhouette, gender
unknown, at least until she speaks.

'Hi, Greg,' she says warmly. 'Welcome home, Zoe. I was
starting to get worried.'

'Yeah, the drive took a hell of a lot longer than I remembered,'
Dad says ruefully. 'Plus, I went slower than normal, to keep it
more comfortable.' He gestures with his head at me.

'For the cripple,' I say.

'That's not what I meant.'

'It's true though.' I try briefly to think of a tactful way to ask
what I need to ask, but I'm tired, sore, and a little unnerved
by this woman standing in the doorway of my family house,
looking for all the world as if she belongs there, so I just blurt
it out. 'Who are you?'

She steps forward, and now I can see that she's vaguely familiar. Late fifties, her hair the kind of colour that in some lights
looks blond, but in others, grey. She's tall, a bit taller than me,
and I'm 5' 9". Broad shouldered. Not a feminine figure, but an

athletic one. 'Sorry, of course. It's been a long time, you might not remember me. I'm Linda, a friend of your father's.'

I frown, trying to place the name and face, but draw a blank. 'What do you mean, "remember"? Do I know you? And what kind of friend are we talking about, exactly. The kind who lives here?'

'No, I don't live here.' She laughs loudly, her eyes flickering sideways at my father for a second. 'I live down the road, in the cottage. You don't know me, know me. But I used to wave when you'd walk past on the beach.'

I search my memory. 'The pink cottage? The one with the big climbing rose?'

'That's the one. Although it's not pink anymore, that was the old owner's taste. Mine runs a little more traditional, so I had it repainted off-white.'

Another memory jogs into place. 'You were that mad ... person, always swimming, even in winter.'

She holds up her hands. 'Guilty.'

'I think you moved in during my last year of high school.'

'I'm not sure.'

'That sounds about right,' Dad says. 'Let's figure out how to get you inside and worry about proper introductions later. If you're OK with Linda helping on one side, and me on the other, I think we'll be able to manage it.'

'No, it's fine, I can do it myself. This is the kind of stuff they've been teaching me in the hospital.' Although Dad had stayed at the hospital on and off over the last few weeks, also coming back here a few times to check on his business, he hadn't been required to attend any of my occupational therapy sessions, so he has no idea what I've been practising. Now, seeing Linda, I wonder if he was coming back for another reason too.

Using the railing and my crutches for support, I make it up the three steps by myself, conscious of them both watching and the fact that my dad is hovering, ready to catch me should I fall. It takes far longer than it would have if I'd let them help, but screw that. I have my pride, and I'm determined not to be a burden on anyone. It's a matter of principle.

'I'll get the bags,' Dad says, and they exchange a look I'm not meant to see.

'Good idea,' Linda smiles at him. 'I'll wait with Zoe until you're back, and then I should probably get going. Let you guys settle in. I've lit the fire, and there's a casserole and some garlic bread in the oven. It's all cooked, just keeping warm now, so dish it up when you're ready. I didn't want you both coming home to a cold, dark house and then have to worry about pre-paring something.'

'We already ate on the road,' I tell her.

'That was hours ago,' Dad says quickly. 'And I don't know about you, but I could eat again. Hot casserole sounds perfect.' He rubs his hands together theatrically. 'I think we might even see a frost tonight.'

'I hope not,' Linda frowns. 'We'll lose those cyclamens we planted if there is.'

Dad looks at the garden. 'I thought you said they liked the cold?'

'No, I said they prefer it. But cold is one thing, freezing is another.'

'I am a little hungry, but I don't like casserole,' I say, for no real reason.

Linda's face falls. 'Sorry, Zoe, I should have checked with your father first.'

I shrug my shoulders. 'He probably wouldn't have a clue what I like anyway.'

Another look flashes between them, and I'm left feeling like an outsider in my own home. I don't like it at all.

'You know what?' I fake a yawn. 'I'm going to hit the sack. It's been a long' – day? Week? Year? All of the above – 'and I'm tired. Why don't you two enjoy the casserole together.'

'Oh, well, I mean . . . if you're sure? I don't want to intrude on your first night back.'

'You're not intruding at all,' Dad reassures her. He goes to put a hand on her arm and then, as if remembering my presence, lets it drop awkwardly instead. 'I'll get those bags.'

'Is there anything I can get for you, or help you with?' Linda offers, while we wait for him to finish carting my bags into my room. 'I don't know how it all works with . . . ' she trails off.

'My leg?'

'Yes. Do you need help now? With . . . ' she trails off again, this time gesturing towards the closed door of the bathroom.

'No, you're all right.' I hold up my hands and waggle my fingers. 'I still have these, so I'm quite capable of wiping my own arse. But thanks.'

She flushes. 'That's not what I meant. I thought you might need some help getting in there, or sitting down.'

I hold her gaze steadily. 'Even if I did, which I don't, I'd hardly want a complete stranger helping me during a pretty personal moment, don't you think?' I hobble on the crutches over to where a picture of my mother hangs on the wall above a china cabinet, and make a great show of straightening it, even though it was perfectly straight to begin with.

I hear her swallow. Message received. 'Of course.'

117

Dad reappears in the hallway and claps his hands together. 'Right, your stuff is all in your room Zoe. I wasn't sure if you have any warm pyjamas, so I bought you some. They've been washed and are on the bed, as well as a few toiletries that Linda picked up for you. Sleep well, and if there's anything you need in the night, just yell out. I'll hear you.' He pauses in the door-frame leading into the kitchen. 'Welcome home, Zoe.' Then he disappears.

'Thanks,' I say stiffly to Linda. 'For the toiletries.'

She lifts her chin. 'I'm a nice person, Zoe. And I hope we can get to know each other better. I know it'd mean a lot to your father.'

I hold her gaze steadily. 'What makes you think I care about making my father happy?'

She flinches, then I turn and crutch into my room, closing the door firmly behind me while she still stands there, her expression sad.

Chapter twenty-six

My father is in the kitchen, rinsing his coffee mug in the sink when I slowly make my way out the next morning. He's always been an early riser, even when he was at his worst. I haven't, unless I've had somewhere I'm paid to be, but my sleep patterns are all over the place since the accident and I don't want to spend all my time lying in bed because, when I do, I keep thinking about Finn.

Last night I laid there for hours going over everything in my head before I finally drifted off, only to wake again in the early hours of the morning, chasing the tail of a bad dream, the details of which I can't quite remember. Heart racing, rapid shallow breathing, tears on my cheeks. I assume it's a symptom of the trauma and that it'll ease in time. At least that's what I keep telling myself.

'Morning,' he says. 'Another beautiful dawn. How was your night?'

I crutch over to the table and awkwardly pull out a seat, dropping my weight down on to it, pulling out another chair to rest the stump on. It throbs if I don't elevate it enough. 'Fine.'

'Get any sleep?'

'Some.'

'Pain OK?'

'It's fine.'

He pours me a coffee and brings it over to the table, placing it on a coaster in front of me. Peering at my face, he cringes at what he sees. 'You don't look so good.'

I pick it up and take a sip. It's like the nectar of life and I feel it flood to warm up my insides. 'Thanks. That's just what every woman wants to hear. Do you compliment Lydia like that?'

His eyes flicker nervously. 'Linda. Yeah, about that. I know I probably should have told you about her before you got home, Zoe. I didn't know how to bring it up though.'

'Pretty simple if you ask me. "Hey Zoe, I've replaced your mother with a lady from up the road."'

'That's neither true, nor fair,' he says levelly.

'So, what's the deal there anyway?'

He rinses out the dishcloth and starts wiping the bench. 'There's not much to tell. I mean, she's a friend. A good friend. We enjoy each other's company.'

'When you say friend, do you mean the sort you meet for a cup of tea, or the kind you fall into bed with?'

'Bloody hell, Zoe. Do you have to be so blunt?'

'It's a simple question.'

'Fine.' He stops wiping. 'You want the truth? Yes, we're . . . more than just friends.'

'If you think I'm going to start calling her mum, you're in for a rude shock.'

He shakes his head sadly. 'Of course not. You're an adult, for one thing. No one could expect you to do anything you don't want to, and no one could ever replace your mother. But it's been almost eighteen years, I don't think you can begrudge me for finding a bit of happiness.'

'Maybe if you'd told me about it first, instead of me arriving here to discover that she's already made herself well at home. I mean, the gardens are clearly her work, am I right?'

'She helped, yes. Linda's very creative.' He smiles proudly and I feel sick. 'She helped me with the colour choices and the design. You said yourself it looks miles better.'

'Mm.' I drink more of my coffee.

'Anyway, maybe if you'd actually answered the occasional call, I'd have been able to tell you about her,' he adds pointedly. 'I've had more of a relationship with your voicemail than I have with you, these past years.'

'And that's my fault, is it?'

'I didn't say that.'

He's right though. Whenever I saw it was his name lit up on the screen, I'd reject the call, or let it go to voicemail. Our phone conversations were never easy, often awkward. Trivial and stilted discussions about the weather in the city compared to back home. Crime statistics. He'd say he could never live there. I'd tell him I loved it, couldn't live anywhere else. Hear his sadness and regret that would echo through the phone. I'd end up in a black mood afterwards, so it became easier to avoid him. I'd flick a text every couple of months, to show I hadn't completely forgotten him. It was enough for me.

'Can you give her a chance?' he asks. 'Please? I know you'll like her if you get to know her.'

'How long's it been going on?'

'Almost two years.'

121

I spit coffee across the table. 'Two years? Are you serious? And the first I know about it is her greeting me in the doorway of my own family home? The home you bought with my mother?'

He picks up the dishcloth again and walks around the bench to mop up the spilt coffee. 'We haven't done anything wrong, Zoe. Stop making it sound worse than it is. Anyway, we were just friends for the first year. It only turned romantic last year, on my birthday.' He flushes.

Realising what he means, I pull a face. 'Stop talking. Seriously. I don't want to hear about that.'

'Hey, you started this conversation by complaining that I hadn't told you about her. So now I'm telling you. I don't want you to think it was easy for me. I didn't jump into this lightly. You know I haven't been with anyone since your mother.'

'Why would I know that?'

'OK, maybe you didn't know. But that's why I'm telling you. This isn't some casual fling.'

'I can't even believe we're having this conversation.'

'I like Linda. I really do. In fact, I love her. She's made me the happiest I've been since your mother died.'

The words stab at my heart like tiny knives, and he has no idea. 'Yeah, well. We both know your own daughter didn't make you happy.'

He flinches like I've slapped him. 'That's not true. You don't honestly believe that, do you?'

I push my chair back from the table and fumble for my crutches, sensing tears are on the way and having no wish to shed them in front of him. 'I'm tired. I need to lie down.'

'You're the most important person in the world to me. I love you, I always have and I always will. I might not have always shown it, and believe me, I'll never forgive myself for that. If I could make up for it, I would. I want to, that's why I brought you home, to show you that I've changed, to try and fix things—'

I pause at the doorway, cutting him off. 'Does she know?'

I don't even have to elaborate. He knows exactly what I'm referring to, and nods. 'Yeah. She knows everything. We have no secrets.'

'And she still wants something to do with you.' I snort bitterly. 'She's more of a fool than I thought.'

Chapter twenty-seven

My room overlooks the beach, but that's not anywhere near as romantic or beautiful as it sounds. Nugget Bay, where I grew up, is a desolate place. Named because of the old gold mines in the hills, the landscape is harsh, the beach more rocks than sand. The waves make a hell of a noise washing ashore on them, and while I was used to it once, I'm not anymore, so I can't sleep again, no matter how much I lay there willing it to happen.

Eventually, I give up, but not wanting to leave the room in case he decides to continue our earlier conversation, I manoeuvre myself into the wheelchair the hospital has given us on loan, and wheel myself over to the big window in my room that looks out over the beach. It's not an easy thing to do by myself, I'm still weakened and my muscle mass is not what it was before the accident.

The least hours of sunshine in the country, that's the dubious honour our little town holds. For so much of the year, the sea and the sky are so grey that if you were looking only at them, no land, you'd be forgiven for thinking the world existed only in black and white. Or greyscale. It's depressing as hell, and part of the reason I couldn't wait to get out of here. A small part. To get away from my father was a much larger incentive.

I spent hours in this room, sitting on my bed and staring at a grey world, wondering why my mother had died. Why my mother? She brought light, laughter and joy to a place that badly needed it, so why her? It didn't make sense, it still doesn't, but I don't ask so much, anymore. I know now that these things happen. People die every single die, in a variety of ways. It's horrible and cruel and incredibly unfair. The death of a loved one brings the ultimate pain and confusion.

I was only a child. Nothing made sense.

Finn is an adult, but still, nothing made sense for him either, when Paige died.

Perhaps it never does.

My laptop emits a chirrup noise, signalling an incoming video call. My first instinct is to ignore it, he'll know something is wrong. But my heart won't let me. I feel so alone here, I need this, I need him. To see him, to hear him. To know that some-one out there hasn't forgotten I exist. That by coming back here, I haven't disappeared.

Maybe the physio in the hospital was right, maybe I'm my own worst enemy, because I certainly get back on the bed a hell of a lot quicker than I got off, proving that I can 'do it if I want to'.

Pillows propped behind me, I open the screen and accept the call. Since Finn left, visual contact has been sporadic and for the most part, the quality has been unsatisfactory. We've messaged more than spoken, both due to time difference and dodgy connections.

His face fills the screen and the emotions that I feel are almost overwhelming. His expression tells me he feels exactly the same.

'Oh Zoe, you're a sight for sore eyes,' he moans, touching the screen with two fingers.

I'm struck by a desperate desire to see and touch him in the flesh. He's so real, he's right there! His curls have gone, replaced by a buzz cut that emphasises the shadows on his face from where he's lost weight. His skin is deeply tanned, his eyes startlingly clear and bright against it. His smile hasn't changed at all though, nor has the way he looks at me, like he wants to devour me. I reach out and touch my screen too, it's not enough.

Then he frowns. 'Are you OK?'

'Yeah, I'm fine,' I lie. 'Much better now that I've seen your face.'

'You've lost weight.'

Nine kilos since the accident, but I don't tell him that. 'Maybe a couple of kilos. A nasty stomach bug went around the school. One of the many hazards of working with kids, unfortunately.'

'That'll explain why you're so pale too, then.'

'It's winter here, remember? We're not all lucky enough to be off sunning ourselves on the other side of the world. Anyway, enough about me. What happened to your hair?'

He runs a hand over the top of his head. 'It was too hot when I was biking, so I paid a barber in a small town to shave it all off. Then I got a sunburned head,' he chuckles ruefully. 'That was fucking painful, I'll tell you. But it's all healed up now and grown back a bit.'

'Finn,' I say, exasperated.

'What?'

'You're supposed to be looking after yourself. You promised.'

'I am,' he protests. 'I have. I still have all my bits and pieces.' He grins wickedly. 'Especially the piece you like.'

'Happy to hear it.'

'So, tell me how everything's been with you? It feels ages since we've spoken.' He pouts, looking miserable. 'Not through lack of trying on my part, either. I was beginning to get worried.'

'I'm sorry. I have to go to this annoying place called work, sometimes, and do this irritating thing called sleep. It's very selfish of me, I know.'

He rolls his eyes. 'Nice to know where your priorities lie.'

'Hey, if you were here, my priorities would be very different.'

'Oh yeah?' He leans towards the screen. 'Tell me more.'

'Finn. Why torture ourselves?'

'Can't help it. Can't stop thinking about being with you again. I've spent so many nights in my tent,' he says huskily, 'lying awake, remembering the lake house and how insane that weekend was.'

It physically hurts in my chest, remembering the same thing. How strong and sexy I felt, how much I delighted in knowing how badly he wanted me, and how adventurous our lovemaking was. And now, out of his sight, the bandaged stump on the bed that I'm trying not to look at. The one that means I'll never feel that way again. 'I can't stop thinking about that too.'

'We should head back there, first chance we get. Have some time for the two of us to reconnect. What do you think?'

'I think there's probably nothing I've ever wanted more in my life,' I say truthfully.

'This is so hard. I want to be there right now.' His expression turns cheeky. 'Maybe you could help me get through the next

127

few days by telling me exactly what it is you plan on doing to me when you see me again?'

I open my mouth to answer, then hear a noise out in the hallway. A muted thud, quickly silenced. Is someone out there? 'Sorry, but you'll have to wait and see,' I tell Finn, rattled.

'Ugh,' he groans. 'No fair. Though probably sensible.' He looks over one shoulder. 'I'm in a flat with three guys. Not exactly an appropriate place to indulge in sex chatting.'

'Yeah, that could get awkward.' We laugh.

His face turns serious. 'I can't wait to see you again. Not long now. Two days until I get on a plane and start that epically long, but totally worth it, journey home. Are you going to meet me at the airport or . . . ?'

I swallow hard. 'Um, you know what, I lost the email with your flight details, must have accidentally deleted it. Can you send it to me again?'

'Yeah, sure. I get in Monday, but you'll probably still be at work now that I think about it. Might be for the best, I can head to Connor's and freshen up, then meet up with you later? I'm being polite here, but do you want to do the whole dinner thing or do we skip straight to the—'

'Hey,' I interrupt him loudly, still nervous about that sound in the hallway. 'Buy a girl dinner first, then we'll see what happens.'

'Fine,' he says, in a pained voice, with a smile though to show that he's joking. He leans even closer to the screen. 'I know I'm not even home yet, but I'm already planning to save up and do some more travelling. I've seen so many cool places I want to show you.' Then he looks unsure. 'That is, if it's something you might be interested in. I mean, I know this isn't the time to be discussing this, and we'll have plenty of time for that later. But do you think you might want to do some travelling with me? Not right away, but at some point?'

This is it. The moment for me to tell him about the accident and the amputation. I even open my mouth to do so, but when it comes to actually saying the words, I can't do it. They won't come. Instead I nod, my heart breaking. I'd love to travel with him more than anything. How can I tell him that everything's changed? That I can't even walk from one room to the next unaided. For the past two weeks, his words from that morning on the rooftop when he told me about Paige have been going over and over in my mind like a song I can't get rid of.

She would have hated living the rest of her life in a chair, dependent on others ... As selfish as it sounds, I would have hated seeing her like that.

What if he feels the same way about me? I'm too scared to find out. I'm filled with the sense of an ending, and I have a powerful urge to reach into the computer and pull him out, wrap myself tightly inside his arms and never let go. My face must betray my emotions, because suddenly he looks concerned.

'Are you OK?'

'Yeah, I'm fine. It's just so good to see your face again.'

'Soon you'll see it for real,' he grins.

I swallow hard and summon a smile. 'Can't wait.'

He blows me a kiss as the screen goes blank and I squeeze my eyes shut, trying to imprint the sight of his face into my memory forever.

An hour later:

Finn: I love you.

Chapter twenty-eight

Dad's pushed the boat out for dinner, cooking his speciality, lamb chops. They're his favourite. He thinks that they're mine too, because growing up we ate them more often than anything else, but they're not. Not even close. He's even laid the table with a neatly laundered tablecloth that I suspect is Linda's doing, because I don't remember ever using one when I lived here before.

He buys the bulk packet of chops, the ones marinated in a thick rosemary and mint sauce. It's merely a disguise to hide all the gristly and fatty bits so that some poor sucker will still buy them. My father obliges. Some of the chops you'd be lucky to get a tablespoon of meat off, but if you're like my father, who eats the whole lot, that's not a problem. He eats everything except the bone, and even that gets a good going over, his tongue poking the marrow out of the little hole. Nothing is wasted. Mashed potatoes, boiled carrots and beans and a floret of broccoli complete the meal.

I stare at the plate, not quite able to believe this is my reality again. I thought I'd left all this behind, but here I am, under this roof, feeling as trapped as before. If anything, it's worse this time. At least when I was a teenager, I had a plan to escape. I knew what I needed to do, where I was going to go. Study hard, get good grades, qualify for the country's best teacher training college in the city. When I left, I never looked back. Being fresh out of high school and on my own in a strange, large city could have been terrifying. But it wasn't, not for me. I loved the freedom, the energy, the people. The fact I could buy a milkshake at three in the morning if I wanted one.

I spent the first two years in student accommodation, studying hard and working night shifts at a laundromat. Then I met Bonnie through a friend of a friend, we hit it off immediately and I moved into her spare room. Even after I graduated and got my first teaching job, we lived together. We have no secrets. We know all each other's habits, weird quirks and trigger points. She's my best friend. And the thought of never living with her again, or even near her, is incomprehensible, so I'm trying not to think about it. Denial is probably not a strategy recommended by the therapist I saw at the hospital, but it's about all I can cope with. Because if I part the curtain for even a second to take a glimpse at what my future looks like, the shock starts to set in pretty quick.

'Something wrong with the lamb?'

'Sorry?' I blink, looking up at my father. He's elbow deep in his meal, bones piled up on one side of his plate, lips and chin greasy from the juices.

'The lamb. You haven't touched it.'

'Not hungry, I guess.'

'Not even for your favourite?'

'It's not my favourite, Dad. It's yours.'

His face suggests he doesn't believe me, that he thinks I'm saying it to be difficult. I don't correct him. What's the point?

'You need to eat. Put some weight back on, you're all skin and bone now. You know how cold the winters get here.'

I do. They're not something you forget in a hurry. It's like a chill that gets into your bones and never leaves.

'House is a lot warmer now though,' he carries on. 'I got most of the windows double-glazed and the old wood changed to aluminium joinery as I could afford to. Only the laundry and spare room still to go. I also installed a panel heater in your bedroom, and there's spare blankets on the top of your wardrobe. Sing out if you need them and I'll make the bed up warmer.'

'I don't know if I'll be here all winter,' I say. 'But thanks.'

His face freezes and he slowly puts his last chop down, wiping his fingers on a paper towel. I watch him, waiting. He clears his throat and rustles up a half-hearted smile.

'Oh?' he says, then coughs to clear his throat. 'So, where were you thinking you might go instead?'

'I don't know.' I shrug, poking my broccoli around the plate. 'I'm considering my options.'

'Zoe . . .'

'Yeah?'

'I doubt you'll be going anywhere in a hurry.'

'Like I said, I haven't decided.'

'I think the accident kind of made that decision for you, don't you?'

'I'm not the only amputee in the world,' I say tersely. 'Other people manage.'

It's true. I've been obsessively searching blogs and Instagram, and have been comforted by the discovery that there are other young women out there like me. So many, all over the world. Some missing one leg, and some with both legs gone, or even legs and arms. I look at them and try to tell myself I'm lucky, but I don't feel lucky.

'Have you thought any more about having the other operation?'

'No.' A lie. I've thought about it plenty. But I still reach the same decision every time. I visualise having the op, getting a new leg. What that would mean for me, how it would change my quality of life. But then the fear kicks in, and I think about my mother. As far as I'm concerned, the medical profession can tell me that what happened was rare until they're blue in the face, but until they can tell me with one hundred per cent certainty that the same thing won't happen to me, I can't do it.

'Maybe we need to consider it?'

'Not your leg, so not your decision.'

'No, of course not. Only you can decide. But I'm here to help you, if you'll let me. We can talk it through, try and overcome some of your worries.'

'Worries?' I pull a face. 'I'm not worried, I'm terrified.'

He exhales. 'I'm only saying that maybe we shouldn't rule it out completely.'

'I haven't.'

'Good. I'm not trying to pressure you into anything. It's just, it's hard. Seeing you like this.'

Finn's words flash through my mind again.

'If it's too hard for you, I can find alternative accommodation,' I say coldly. 'Or is it because I'm in the way of you and – what was her name again?'

'It's not hard. You and I both know that I owe you for everything I put you through. And I care about Linda, yes. But you're my daughter. I'm always going to be here for you.'

Like it or not, I need him. No matter what I might say, I have nowhere else to go. No one I can call on. Even if I could figure out a way to move back in with Bonnie, modify the flat to suit my needs, swallow my pride and hope that a disability benefit might cover the bills while I'm not working, that ship has well and truly sailed. Bonnie couldn't afford the place without me, but she didn't like the idea of a strange room-mate either. She and Josh decided maybe it was the push they needed, after two years of dating, and now they've moved into his place together. She's messaged me almost every day to complain about something trivial he's done, and to tell me how much she misses me.

'I meant what I said about talking,' he continues. 'I know it's never been an easy thing for us, but I want that to change.'

I study his face for the familiar signs of guilt and deceit. He has no idea how many nights I cried myself to sleep, wishing things were different. How many times he told me he was better, things were going to be good from now on. How many times I believed him, let myself get my hopes up, only for it to all crash down around me like it always did. He looks different now, though. Older, obviously. But also, healthier, less like an extra from the *Walking Dead*. His eyes have a sparkle to them that I haven't seen since, well, since before my mother died. Somewhere, deep down inside, I feel the tiniest bud of hope blossom. Then I squash it. 'We'll see.'

'I know I need to work at it. And I will ... ' He hesitates. 'I want us to have an open and honest relationship. I want you to be able to talk to me about anything, Zoe. So, on that subject, I have to ask. Who's Finn?'

I drop my fork with a clatter. 'I knew it. You were listening.'

He holds up his hands in a conciliatory gesture. 'I didn't mean to, I was making a cuppa and I was coming to ask if you wanted one too, and I inadvertently overheard you talking. Yes, I'm sorry. Who is he?'

'A friend. None of your business.' I remember some of my conversation with Finn and cringe. Just when I thought life couldn't get any worse.

'Why does he think you're going to go travelling with him?'

'I don't want to talk about this with you. For God's sake!' I push my chair back from the table roughly, hanging on to the edge, teetering. I look around for my crutches; one is leaning against the table where I left it, the other is gone. Bending sideways, I can see it has fallen to the floor, out of reach. If I let go of the table to try and retrieve it, I'll probably fall. 'My crutch is on the floor; can you pass it to me?' I ask through gritted teeth, feeling embarrassed and useless that I can't even storm out of a room if I want to.

'Of course, but I think we should talk about this first.'

'I'm not a kid anymore, I'm a grown woman. I have my own life, a professional career.' Or at least, had. 'You can't eavesdrop on my private conversations. That's wrong on so many levels.'

'I know it was, and I'm sorry. I'm worried about you, that's all. I think you're in denial about what's happened, and from the sounds of it, this Finn is encouraging you by talking about things that are now outside your capabilities. At least for now. He's just putting pressure on you and getting your hopes up to be disappointed, and I'm sorry, but it's wrong, and I don't like it.'

'Thanks for stating the obvious.' I give up and plonk back

down on my chair before I fall, feeling frustrated and angry. 'I'm well aware that my life is fucked beyond recognition. OK? I don't need you to remind me.'

'No, but maybe this Finn needs to be reminded. If he's filling your head with all these plans, when right now we should be concentrating on—'

'He doesn't know!' I snap.

'What?' He stares at me, confused.

'He doesn't know, OK?' I repeat, quieter.

'I don't understand.'

'He's someone I met a few months ago, before he was heading off overseas. We've kept in touch and he's coming back soon.'

'Just . . . someone?'

I stare at the table, blinking away hot tears. 'No. Not just someone. Someone I thought I might have had a future with.'

His eyes widen. 'Wow. OK, that's . . . but if you feel so strongly about him, why haven't you told him about the accident?'

'Because I don't think he'll be able to handle it.'

'You don't know that. I mean, I don't know the guy, but I doubt you'd have feelings for someone so flaky.'

'He's not flaky, he's amazing.'

'Then tell him. Let him be a support for you. God knows you could never have too many people willing to support you through this.'

'I can't.'

'You can.'

'No, I can't. I really can't.' Because it's the only way to shut him up, I tell him about Paige, and how much it broke Finn, losing her like that. I also tell him about Finn's feelings around her death being preferable to being paralysed.

137

'That's pretty messed up,' he says when I finish.

'He's not a bad person,' I add quickly.

'No, I know, that's not what I meant. All I know is that these things are never black and white. He might think she'd have hated living her life paralysed, but that doesn't mean that's how she would have felt. You've been through a trauma, yes, but you survived. And you're not paralysed . . .'

'As good as. I'll never walk again.'

'Not without the operation, no,' he says cautiously, 'but—'

'Anyway,' I cut him off before he starts talking about that again. 'Now you know. That's why I can't tell him. I don't want him to pity me, or feel like he's stuck with me. I'd be holding him back from doing the things he wants to do, and he's so nice he'd put up with it. I don't want that.'

'What's the alternative?'

'I don't know. It was wrong, I know, but easier to pretend that nothing has changed when he was out of the country. Now he's going to be home in a couple of days and wants to see me, but this' – I rub my thigh – 'is not going to be so easy to hide then.'

'I think you know what you need to do.'

'Yeah, run away. Disappear.'

'Zoe.' He cocks his head. 'I didn't raise you to be a coward.'

'You didn't raise me at all,' I snap, and he flinches. 'Sorry. That wasn't fair.'

'It's OK. I deserved that. The way I see it, you need to tell him. Give him a chance to decide how he feels about things. You might be surprised.'

'Maybe.'

He gets up and walks over, scooping up my crutch and passing it to me. 'You just got to be brave, kid.'

Chapter twenty-nine

Finn: Are you there?

Finn: ...?

Finn: Guess not. Well, I can tell you that we definitely made the right decision. I haven't showered in three days, have barely slept on either of the flights (too excited) and have indulged in too many complimentary drinks (always been my downfall).

Finn: So I'll head to Connor's to freshen up before I see you.

Finn: You're probably sleeping. I have no idea what time it is there. But I will soon! Currently sitting in Hong Kong airport, awaiting the last leg of the trip. Should be called to board soon. Got that whole, uncontrollable leg-jiggling thing going on because I'm so wound up and just want to get this flight over and done with. It's been an epic five months, but I'm well and truly ready to get home and SEE YOU AGAIN. Sorry, shouty letters. Excited, see?

There's the call! Time to board, see you soon x

Chapter thirty

On Thursday, Harry Taylor and another guy I've never seen before turn up and spend the better part of the day installing two ramps, one outside the front door and one off the back deck. They leave the steps, but knock down part of the veranda railing on one side and install the ramp there, so that the overall angle isn't too steep. The next day he comes back and fits safety rails in the toilet and shower and by the bathroom vanity. Dad's also bought one of those plastic chairs like the hospital have, for me to sit in while showering. They're awkward and uncomfortable, and I decide to avoid the task as much as possible. Who have I got to smell good for anyway?

On Saturday, Dad drives me into town for my first rehabilitation appointment post hospital. The medical centre is located in an old, three-bedroom weatherboard house on a residential street. There are three GPs working in rotation, although one is seventy-four and on the verge of retirement. According to my father, he's been sitting on that verge for the past eight years, so nobody's holding their breath it'll happen any time soon.

Dad wheels me up the ramp in the hospital loaner wheelchair, and straight away I recognise the woman sitting behind the reception desk. If I'd been in control of the chair I'd have probably hit reverse and rolled right back down the ramp, but I'm not, so I can only sink lower and brace myself as Dad wheels me over. She looks at me with a well-rehearsed smile, which turns into a look of surprise, then morphs into an actual, genuine smile, not one reserved for the punters.

'Zoe!' she exclaims. 'How are you?' Then she freezes at the connection between the question and the sight of me sitting in a wheelchair. 'Oh, fuck. Sorry. That was a stupid question.' She gets up and walks around the desk, bending down to give me a hug. 'I heard about what happened. Awful.'

'Thanks.'

'I can't even imagine how hard it must be.'

'It hasn't been easy, not going to lie. But I'm getting there. How are you, Olivia? It's been a while. You're looking good.'

'Liar.' She grabs hold of the spare flesh around her stomach and gives it a jiggle. 'Three kids in the last five years have ruined me. But I'm working on it. Zumba classes two nights a week in the church hall. You should totally come ...' she freezes again. 'Shit. Still haven't learned to engage my brain before speaking. Sorry. I blame pregnancy. Haven't been the same since.'

'It's fine.'

'Are you home for the reunion?'

I give her a blank look. 'Reunion?'

'Next Saturday. Our senior class. Ten years, can you believe it? People are coming from all over, even Brian's flying back from the UK, last I heard.'

'Brian?'

'Jenkins. He plays rugby now for a pretty big club over there. Doing well for himself.'

'Oh right.' I vaguely recall him. Tall guy, muddy blond.

'Kylie and I have organised everything. The RSA is booked, DJ's locked in, decorating committee's all set.' She frowns. 'Aren't you in the group on Facebook? I can't believe someone didn't add you. Wait, I'll do it now.' She whips out her phone.

'I do remember seeing something,' I say vaguely. A notification, a few months ago. An invite to join. I deleted it.

She taps at her screen. 'There. Done. Come on, you have to come.'

'I'm not sure if I'm up to it.'

'Oh, don't worry, the RSA is disability friendly,' she bulldozes on, misunderstanding me. 'Ramps, the paraplegic toilet. You'll be fine.'

She means well. 'We'll see.'

'Let me know if you need a ride. I'll be there early to make sure everything is set up, but I can organise someone to pick you up, and drop you home.'

A door opens to our left and an elderly man pops his head out. 'Olivia, is my next patient here yet?'

She rolls her eyes at me, out of his eyeline. 'Not yet, Dad. You don't have anyone booked in until the afternoon. Why don't you take a long lunch?'

'Long lunch?' he snorts. 'We don't all share your half-baked work ethic, sweetheart.' He notices Dad and me, and immediately you can see his interest is piqued. He steps forward and holds out his hand.

'Greg, good to see you. You keeping well?'

'No complaints here,' Dad answers, shaking his hand. 'You remember Zoe?'

'Of course,' Dr Gillard mutters, his eyes on my leg. I start to feel a prickle along my spine. He waves his hand, and the gesture encompasses both Olivia and me. 'You girls all used to hang out together once upon a time. I heard about the accident. Terrible thing to happen, Zoe. You have my condolences.'

'I'm not dead.'

He doesn't seem to hear me, instead he rucks up his trousers at the side and crouches, gesturing towards my stump. 'Do you mind if I take a look?'

'Are you my doctor?'

'Sorry?'

'Are you the doctor I'm seeing today?' I feel calm on the surface, but all hot fury and seething indignation underneath.

'No, you're seeing Dr Ashton,' Olivia answers. 'She won't be long.'

'I'll wait for her then.'

'Still, I'd like a look, for interest's sake,' Dr Gillard says. 'It's a while since we've had an amputated limb through here, I wouldn't mind seeing how they're doing it these days.' He reaches out towards my rolled-up trouser leg, but stops short when I lift up my remaining foot and place it in front of his chest, preventing him from reaching.

'I would mind.'

'Zoe, he's a doctor.' Dad frowns, embarrassed.

'Yes, but he's not my doctor. And I'm not a freak show.'

Dr Gillard gets back to his feet, looking at me like I'm being ridiculously sensitive. 'I apologise if my request upset you,' he says stiffly, not sounding sorry at all.

'Put it this way, if a breast cancer survivor walked in here right now, would you ask her to lift her top in the waiting room and show you the scar from her mastectomy? You know, purely for interest's sake?'

'Of course not.'

'Same thing,' I say, before anyone can say it's not. 'My body. My choice.'

'Absolutely right.' I turn at the voice. A woman in her forties is standing in an open doorway, smiling and nodding. 'Zoe? I'm Dr Ashton. Please' – she steps to one side and gestures with her hand – 'come in.'

Still upset, I consider asking Dad to wheel me out for a second, but Dr Ashton looks friendly enough, so I push myself forward and into her exam room, only banging on the doorframe once, an improvement on how I've been going at home.

Dad hovers. 'Do you want me to come in with you?'

I shake my head. 'I'll be fine.'

'OK. I'll just wait out here then.'

'I'll let you know when she's ready,' Dr Ashton smiles, closing the door. 'I'm sorry about my colleague,' she says, crossing to sit on the chair in front of her desk.

'It's not your place to apologise for him.'

'I know, but still, he was out of line. He's from a different generation.'

I snort. 'That's not an excuse.'

'I agree completely, and I will discuss it with him later, I promise.'

'Isn't he your boss?'

She pulls a face. 'Sort of. Technically. But that's no reason

145

not to call someone out on bad behaviour, however innocent his intentions. Otherwise, how is anyone supposed to learn?'

It may be a simple thing, to have her understand why it irked me so much, but to me, it's huge. 'Thank you.'

'You're welcome. Now' – she turns to her computer and clicks to bring up my file – 'I have to be honest, Zoe. I'm not a specialist in the kind of rehabilitation your injury requires, but I have spent the past two days discussing your case with the doctors and specialists at the hospital where your operation took place, so I'm well versed in what we need to be working on. Some of it we'll cover here at your weekly appointments, and I also have some literature for you to take home to read over and have a go with as well. How does that sound?'

I shrug my shoulders. 'OK.'

'The doctor I've been speaking with has also asked me to refer you for counselling,' she adds tactfully. 'That's if you would like me to. We do have a very good counsellor here in town, however, if that feels a little too close to home, we can organise for you to have online counselling sessions. It's up to you.'

'There's no need.' I say curtly. 'I'm fine.'

She nods. 'Absolutely your decision, of course. But please know that you can change your mind at any time if you find that you're struggling. Make an appointment with me, or if I'm not here, leave a message with Olivia and I'll get back to you. There's plenty of support available. We all want to help.'

She looks at me kindly, clearly expecting a response. She doesn't get one. I'm still fuming from my run-in with Dr Gillard. If that's the kind of help on offer, they can keep it.

'All right, I'll lower the bed, and we'll get started on these exercises, shall we?'

She has a caring, almost motherly smile. It's making me feel a little shaky, so I look at my phone to distract myself. Shit, it's still on silent from during the night and I have an email notification from Finn. My heart starts beating quicker when I see the subject line: See you soon.

'Sorry, but I have to go.' I slap the phone down on my lap and reverse the chair. It bangs into her desk, knocking a pile of papers to the floor.

'Zoe?' She turns, concerned.

'I'm sorry, I've just remembered I have somewhere else I need to be. But I'll come back next week, I promise.'

I wheel straight past Dad in the waiting room, but am forced to stop at the automatic doors when they fail to open. Even when I lean back and wave at the black sensor above the door, nothing happens.

'Finished already?' Dad asks, surprised. He puts down the magazine he was reading. 'You've only been in there five minutes.'

'I'm not feeling well.' I wave as high as my arm can reach. 'Can you take me home? What the hell is wrong with these doors?'

'Sorry,' Olivia calls out. 'They're programmed to only register people of a certain minimum height. We got annoyed with kids making them open and shut for the hell of it.'

'Are you kidding me?' My waves get wilder, angrier, determined to prove I'm still capable of doing something as basic as opening a door. 'Open the damn doors. I want to go home.'

'OK,' Dad soothes. 'Then that's what we'll do.' He puts his hands on the handles of the chair and immediately, the doors open. I feel completely humiliated.

'Let me know about the reunion,' Olivia calls out as we leave.

I don't answer. There's no way in hell I'll be going.

147

Chapter thirty-one

According to the results of my online search, the flight home from Hong Kong takes around ten hours and fifty minutes, or ten hours forty-five, depending which site you believe. Either way, Finn sent that email at 3.20 a.m., which means he's now only about an hour away from landing back in the same country that I'm in. On the same soil. Breathing the same air. Awake in the same time zone.

The thought has me hiding away in my bedroom, staring at the little clock on the top right-hand side of the screen on my laptop, watching the minutes tick over, feeling an ever-growing sense of dread creep over me. My father is right. I can't keep up the pretence much longer – not that it was ever a deliberate, conscious move on my part. In the initial aftermath of the accident, I wasn't capable of processing what had happened to me, let alone trying to explain it to Finn, all the way on the other side of the world. And I knew he'd feel helpless, being so far away. I suspected he'd fly back to be with me, and I didn't want that. Not only because I didn't want him to see my new physical self when I couldn't bear to look at it, but also because I didn't want him to cut short his trip. It was important to him, and that made it important to me. He needed to finish the bike ride, to accomplish the goal he'd set for himself.

As the days went by, it became both easier and harder, because how do you suddenly drop something so big into a conversation? Oh, I keep forgetting to tell you, I wasn't looking where I was going and kind of collided with a van. They had to cut off my leg, but never mind that, how's the weather in Africa today? In my head, I convinced myself I was doing the right thing by Finn. Right or wrong, that's how I sold it to myself: I'd tell him in person on his return.

Now that moment is almost here, I have no choice but to be honest with myself. I'm absolutely terrified. Terrified of rejection, mostly. I know that I'm supposed to love my own body, flaws and all, and maybe one day I'll get there. But right now, the stump has to be one of the ugliest things I've ever seen, and I hate that it's attached to me. I'm scared that he'll think I'm a coward for not having the second operation. The doctors aren't buying my fears, will Finn? I somehow doubt it. He's brave, courageous, adventurous. He might not like this side of me, the frightened and anxious woman I've become. But most of all, I'm scared that he'll feel pity towards me. That he'll stick with me out of a sense of obligation.

I stare out at the moody grey scenery and wonder, is this it now? Is this my life? Stuck here in this hellhole, feeling like I'm trapped in some horrible time warp. One minute, a grown woman, with a professional job that I loved, a life in the city that thrilled me, and friends I adored. The next, back under my childhood roof in a town I couldn't wait to get out of. Jobless, friendless, lifeless.

149

Tears roll down my cheeks as I open up my social media accounts one by one, and delete them. Not deactivate, but completely delete. I don't trust myself not to change my mind. In a moment of weakness, it would be all too easy to reinstate them. A warning flashes up, asking me if I'm sure. I hesitate for only a second, then choose yes. These websites are not doing me any favours, merely emphasising the fact that for everyone else I know, normal life goes on.

After that, I try and get the SIM card out of my phone but it's damn near impossible. I'm crying too much to see properly, so after a few fruitless attempts, I give up and throw it down hard onto the floor. The screen cracks, a tiny sliver, but the phone stays in one piece, so I get down on my hands and knees and bash at it with a heavy stone doorstop painted like a cheerful whale. It bears all my frustration and anger and I smash it over and over until it's in a million tiny pieces. When I'm sure it's completely destroyed, I sink back against the side of the bed with my head on my knees.

There's a knock on the door. 'Zoe?'

'Go away.'

'Normally I would do that, but I'm a bit worried about the noises I've been hearing. Are you OK?'

'No.'

'Can I come in?'

He takes my silence as acquiescence, and the door gently opens. 'Zoe?'

'Down here.'

He walks around the bed and clocks the phone smashed to smithereens and his daughter's tear-stained face. His eyebrows arch, but to his credit, he says nothing. He sinks down onto the bed and puts a hand on my shoulder. We both survey the carnage.

'I had a little accident.'

'I can see that. It's fine, I'll get you a new phone.'

That makes me look up quickly. 'With a new number? It has to have a new number.'

'Sure, if that's what you want.'

'I do.'

'Do you want to talk about . . . anything?'

I chuckle bitterly, wiping my nose onto my jersey. It's too little, too late. 'What's the point? I've done what you wanted. Finn is now officially out of my life.'

His hand tightens. 'You told him? What did he say?'

'It doesn't matter. He's gone. I'll never see him again.'

'Oh Zoe, I'm so sorry.' His voice wobbles. 'But honestly? He's not worth it, not if he ups and abandons you at the first sign of something difficult.'

'You'd know all about that, wouldn't you?'

He exhales sharply as if I've sucker-punched him. 'Zoe.'

'It's fine,' I sniff, shrugging his hand off my shoulder. 'I'm used to it. Can you go? I want to be alone now.'

Chapter thirty-two

Exhausted from crying, I sleep away the afternoon, waking when the sky outside has darkened and the temperature has dropped. I'm about to crawl underneath the blankets when I hear the unfamiliar murmur of voices through the wall. Lifting my head off the pillow, I crane to listen. Not just voices but, unless I'm mistaken, music.

My mother loved music. When she wasn't singing, she was humming, and when she wasn't humming, she was whistling. Badly off-key, but happily. We had a big old stereo in the kitchen and whenever we were home she'd have it blasting out some old-time station that I used to hate with a passion. I wanted to listen to the latest pop music, but instead we'd have Karen Carpenter or Fleetwood Mac filling the house, telling me how on top of the world they were, or that I should go my own way.

Then she died.

I don't remember the stereo ever being on after that. My father couldn't bear to listen to any song that reminded him of her. The soundtrack of my teenage years was uncomfortable silence. The house echoed with it. We barely spoke unless necessary, so to hear the sound of voices through the wall now is both unfamiliar and disconcerting. Then I hear laughter and realise who it is.

Linda.

I'm tempted to stay in my room and avoid dinner and them altogether, but there's a part of me that seems to have regressed into a petulant teenager. How dare this woman listen to music on my mother's stereo? In my mother's kitchen? With my mother's husband? Is this a regular thing? Does she . . . sleep over? In my mother's bed? Angry, I focus all my rage on her. Shuffling to the edge of the bed, I pick up my crutches. There's a knock on my door.

'Zoe?'

It's her. I hobble over to the door and throw it open. 'What?'

'I hope I didn't wake you.'

'You did.'

'Sorry. I didn't mean to be so loud, it's your father – he always makes me laugh.'

'He does?'

'Yes, he was telling me about one of the tricky customers he had to deal with this week, but I'll let him tell you all about it. You know how good he is at storytelling, I wouldn't do it the same justice.'

I stare at her.

'Anyway, I was coming to see if you felt like joining us for dinner? Your dad has cooked his famous fish pie, and I brought over some cheesy garlic bread. Perfect meal for a cold night like this.' Her eyes focus over my shoulder. 'Oh, your curtains are still open, no wonder your room felt like an icebox when you opened the door.'

She bustles past me and starts closing the curtains.

'You're inviting me to dinner?' I ask.

'Yes.'

'In my own house?'

'Yes.' She's less certain now.

'With my father.'

'And me, if that's OK.'

I don't answer.

She smiles, a little nervously. 'I know this must be weird for you.'

'Weird? Why would it be weird?'

Without waiting for an answer, I leave the room. She follows me down the hallway, silently. Stepping into the kitchen, for a second it's almost like I've stepped back in time. The lights and the lamps are all on, the room is cheerful and bright and warm. The stereo is playing – something by the Seekers, if I'm right. The table is lit, amazing smells emanate from the oven, and my father is humming, humming as he wipes down a chopping board and places it on a dish rack to dry. I could close my eyes and imagine my mother in the other room, folding the washing, singing along. A family. My family, before it was ripped apart. I'm seized by such a sense of nostalgic longing for that simple time that it takes my breath away.

But then I see it, and the bottom drops out of my world all over again as a horrible sense of déjà vu hits me.

My father turns and sees me, his face brightening. 'Oh, there you are, feeling any better? I called Tim at the appliance store and he's going to sort out a new phone for you ASAP. Perks of having a mate who owes you a favour. He reckons I should be able to pick it up Monday afternoon.'

'You lied,' I say, my voice shaking with my sense of betrayal and anger.

He frowns. 'What?'

'You lied,' I repeat, shaking my head in disbelief. 'And stupid me, I almost believed you this time.'

'What are you talking about?'

'You'd think I'd have learned by now, right?' I snap bitterly, angry at myself, angry at him. 'But no. It's always the same old shit.'

'Zoe,' Linda places a hand on my arm, but I rip it away savagely.

'Don't touch me.'

'I'm sorry—'

'You could never replace my mother. No matter how much you replant the gardens, or what colour you paint the house.'

'Zoe!' Dad says. 'That's not fair, Linda has done nothing wrong.'

'You told me that she knew all about your history.'

'She does.'

'OK, so what – she's enabling you anyway?' I point at three champagne glasses on the bench, an open bottle of sparkling wine beside them. Dad follows the direction of my finger, and his shoulders subside with understanding.

'You've got it all wrong,' he says. 'But I don't blame you. It looks incriminating.'

Linda finally clocks on to what we're talking about and walks to the bench, spinning the bottle so that the label is facing me.

'Sparkling grape juice,' she says. 'No alcohol, I promise.'

I give her a distrustful glare and walk to pick up the bottle myself, reading the label. She's telling the truth.

'Your father has been very honest and open about his struggles,' she continues. 'I know that after your mother died, he turned to alcohol to numb the pain.'

I snort. 'Don't make it sound so glamorous. He was a down-and-out, filthy alcoholic. Fell asleep in his own piss and vomit some nights, did he tell you that? That his thirteen-year-old daughter would have to try and roll him into the recovery position, to make sure he wouldn't choke to death on his own sick while he was passed out. Not asleep, unconscious.'

Dad winces. Linda puts a comforting hand on his back.

'Or that sometimes,' I say through gritted teeth, 'I'd have to sit awake all night, on a school night, watching him, making sure that he was still breathing. Hoping I'd be able to work out what the tipping point was. When should I be calling the ambulance? When he coughed up blood? Because he did that, sometimes. Or maybe when he'd fall over and crack his head on the floor and lay there. Not moving. Breathing, but not moving. Should I call then? Knowing that the whole town would be talking about it by sunrise?'

My father stands with his head down, eyes squeezed tightly closed. He doesn't even try to defend himself, knowing there is no defence. 'I'm sorry, Zoe.'

'Or how about all the times I had to drive to Charlie's Bar to pick him up. Before I even had a licence to drive. I'd get a call: "Your father has passed out drunk. Again. Please come and get him. Again."'

My father looks up suddenly, his eyes desperately pleading. 'Zoe, please, don't—'

'Don't what? Tell your new girlfriend about that night?' Tears start pouring out of my eyes, but I don't stop. I couldn't stop even if I wanted to. 'Sorry, Dad, but I thought you two were all about honesty?'

'I think we should all take a minute to calm down,' Linda says. I ignore her.

'Tell her, Dad. Tell her how you tried to kill us.'

He makes a shuddering, sobbing noise. 'I . . . '

'Tell her how I was driving you home, and you were passed out in the passenger seat but then you woke up and grabbed the wheel, trying to steer us off the road into a tree. You never said a word, but I knew what you wanted. Us, dead. Reunited with Mum. The family back together. I was seventeen, Dad, and I had to struggle with you for my life. Struggle to stop my own father from killing us both. But you were too strong.' I blink away hot, angry tears. 'I thought we were goners for sure, but then for some reason . . . you let go. Keeled over and fell asleep, as if nothing had happened.'

'I thought I dreamt it,' he sobs. 'You never said anything, and I knew it couldn't be true. I'd never hurt you, not knowingly.' He takes a step towards me. 'Oh God, I'm sorry, I'm so, so sorry.'

'Don't.' I step back, my tone a warning. 'Don't come near me. I don't want to be part of whatever this is.' I look angrily between them both. 'OK? This is not a family, so leave me out of it. As soon as I can figure out a way to get away from here, you won't have to worry about me anymore. Enjoy your fish pie.'

I hobble back to my bedroom, listening to the sound of my grown father crying behind me. My heart and my mind feel like they're going to explode. Everything in my life has fallen apart. I have nowhere to go, no one I can ask for help. I'm on my own.

Chapter thirty-three

From: Finn_the_finster@gmail.com
To: ZoeCalloway@hotmail.com
Subject: Where are you?

Hey Zoe, sitting in a bar. Bit confused, but trying not to leap to any conclusions and freak the hell out. I'm home! I've been to Connor's, where I'm temporarily storing my stuff until I find my own place again. Showered, smelling A LOT better. Managed to put off the rest of the family until tomorrow (not easy) but I know that once I'm in their clutches it'll be a while before I can escape again and all I want to do is see you. I've planned/dreamed about little else for the past five months.

But here's where I've hit a wall. Where are you??

I've tried calling your phone but all I get is some automated out-of-service message. Texts don't go through. I can't find you on Facebook, Instagram, Snapchat or WhatsApp. It's like you've clean disappeared off the face of the earth.

Aha! Brainwave! I'll come around to your flat. I can't remember exactly how to get there from that time I picked you up to go to the lake, but I'm sure I can figure it out. I do remember what the front of your building looks like. Pretty sure, anyway. Then we can figure out what's going on. OK, I'll just finish this beer and then I'm on my way.

Chapter thirty-four

After the argument in the kitchen, I can't stop shaking. I've never had a panic attack, but I imagine that what I'm feeling is approaching something similar. Caged, trapped. This spiteful, nasty woman is not me. I am not her. I am Zoe, I teach children how to fill the world with kindness, not hate. I choose compassion and empathy, always, even when someone is truly horrible to me. I don't take it personally because I know we all have our inner battles. We all have our struggles.

But all these years of repressed hurt, combined with the accident and losing my sense of self and the life I thought I had ahead of me, has unleashed itself like a perfect storm, and my father and Linda are the only ones here to bear the brunt of it. I knew I still harboured anger and pain towards him, that I have so many questions that have tormented me over the years.

Why?

Why wasn't I enough of a reason for him to stay strong so we could find a way through it together?

It was all about him. What he'd lost. His wife, the only woman he'd ever loved. It never seemed to occur to him that losing your mother is a pretty big deal too, that I was grieving just as much. That I was in as much pain as he was, only I didn't fall to pieces as spectacularly as he did. I thought I'd managed to put it behind me, move past it, accept that some things simply are, and we don't always get the answers we seek in life. But now I know that there's a difference between recovering and repressing. Not talking about it didn't make it go away. It's been festering away inside of me instead.

I need distraction, something to take my mind off the never-ending stream of conscious running through my head that my life is effectively over. I know that I should go back out to the kitchen and apologise to Dad and Linda. But I can't, and a part of me doesn't want to.

There's nowhere I can go. Even pacing the room is a non-starter, with only one leg. The TV proves to be more noise than I can handle, so I turn it off. I've never felt like this in my life, not even when I was younger and my father was at his worst. I had an end goal in sight, then. Something to aim for, look forward to. Getting out of town, getting my dream job, building a life for myself where I didn't need to rely on anyone.

But this time, I can't see a way forward. There's the operation, of course. But every time I think about that, I picture that terrifying moment when they'll medicate and send me off to sleep. Being unable to fight it, feeling myself sliding under. What if that's my last moment? Things go wrong. You read about it every single day. There are no guarantees except that nothing can be guaranteed.

I don't even have the escape of social media anymore. It's a weird feeling. I've had some of those pages for years, since high school. Even though their demise was self-inflicted, it wasn't thought through, and it's only now that I realise I've lost all the photos I've ever posted. All the messages I've ever sent. It's all gone.

My laptop chimes an email notification. I figure it's probably a loyalty card discount offer, or something equally uninteresting, but it's a distraction, so I reach for the laptop and open up my emails, freezing when I see his name.

Finn.

I forgot about emails. I sit bolt upright, my breathing shallow and quick, as if he's in the room, as if he can see me. How could I have forgotten about emails? It's OK, I remind myself. Emails are not like any of the other message mediums, where you can tell instantly when someone has seen your message. He has no way of knowing if I've even received the email, let alone read it. It was a stupid mistake on my part, but a fixable one. Clicking on the little icon at the top-right side of his email, a list of options comes up and I move the cursor until it hovers over the 'Block Contact' option.

But I can't do it.

It's like the universe offered me a lifeline when I thought I was adrift with no chance of rescue. A light in the dark. A chance to keep him in my life. But it's not going to be easy. Sooner or later, he's going realise that I've ghosted him with no explanation, and then he'll be hurt, angry, and confused. I'm pretty sure I'm not going to like what he has to say then.

Deciding I'll make that call when it comes to it, I click the cursor somewhere else on the screen. The option list disappears. I read his email, my heart breaking as I picture him sitting in a bar, hopeful and excited at the prospect of us reuniting.

What have I done?

Chapter thirty-five

From: Finn_the_finster@gmail.com
To: ZoeCalloway@hotmail.com
Subject: confused

Guess where I am?

The rooftop. Our rooftop. Without the vodka this time, although I tell you what, I could sure do with it. Confused doesn't even begin to cover how I'm feeling. Did you ever see that old show called the Twilight Zone? That's what I feel like I'm in right now.

This roof is the place where I first started to fall in love with you. Did I ever tell you that? That night was the most incredible night of my life. Sitting up here with you, a stranger but someone I felt completely at ease with. I can close my eyes and remember it all vividly. The lights of the city on your face. The way you looked at me that made me want to kiss you and never stop.

Where are you?

I don't understand what's going on, I really don't. In the last hour, I've come up with a million possible explanations, but none of them make any sense.

I found your apartment, after a few wrong turns. I wish I could tell you how I was feeling, standing outside your door, my hand up ready to knock, knowing I was seconds away from seeing you again. I don't know how to describe it though, only that it was like every Christmas morning all rolled into one. Then I knocked, and some woman I've never seen before answered. When I asked where you were, she said she'd never heard of you. I apologised, thought OK, maybe I had the wrong apartment, but then I mentioned Bonnie and she knew her name. Said she was the previous tenant, that they were still receiving the odd piece of mail for her in the weeks that they'd been living in the apartment. No forwarding address (I asked, of course).

So, what? How does this work? You move, but somehow forget to mention it? How can someone forget to mention something like that? If not forgotten, then it was a deliberate omission, and here's where I start to get a horrible feeling. I don't know why you'd move and not mention it, or why you've completely disappeared from all social media, or why your phone is disconnected. Why you aren't answering these emails. It's not like we've been out of contact for years. We spoke a week ago for fuck's sake. Sorry. I'm . . .

Maybe I'm too jet-lagged to figure this out. It's messing with my head. I know you exist. I know you feel the same way I do, you told me you did. What the hell is going on?

If you're reading this, please, let me know you're OK.

Whatever's going on, we can figure it out.

Please.

Chapter thirty-six

The following week is the longest week of my life. The weather is gloomy and depressing, perfectly matching my mood. A storm off the coast settles in and lashes the shore with giant waves that roar like angry wild animals, keeping me awake. Relentless rain floods the lawn and driveway until it's one large, murky pond that I half expect to see fish swimming in. Dad is forced to park his car out on the road and wade through the water to get to the front door. If I didn't feel isolated before, I feel completely cut off from the world now.

Every morning, I wait until I hear the front door close behind him and his car rumble into life before I leave my room in search of breakfast. We've barely spoken two words since the night I went off at him and Linda. I try not to live with regrets – what's the point? – but I'm well aware that I acted like a child, not the grown woman I'm supposed to be. And I know that we can't carry on like this, that difficult conversations must be had, but I don't know how, or when, to start them. Neither of us have ever been particularly good at communicating with each other. Clearly, or we wouldn't be in the mess we're in now.

Alone in the house, I eat at the kitchen breakfast bar, surveying the battered bay outside. I'd forgotten how miserable winter can be in this place. It's a misery that seeps into everything, everyone. The local paper has a crime column, and in winter, it blossoms to cover half a page, sometimes more. People get edgy from all the rain, sick of being stuck inside their houses. Domestic abuse increases, as do pointless acts of vandalism. When I was fifteen, some friends and I painted a bright pink bra on the bronze statue of a mermaid that sits on rocks at the far end of the bay. Some kind of misguided attempt at feminism, outraged that her perfectly perky breasts were on display for all to see. It made the front page of the paper, perpetrators never caught. I still have a clipping of it somewhere.

As selfish as it sounds, the rift between my father and me is not what occupies my thoughts ninety per cent of the time. After all, it's nothing new, so I don't expect anything to change overnight.

It's Finn I can't stop thinking about, and I make the firm decision several times a day to block his email address so he can't send me any more messages that, quite simply, break my heart. But then I think about never hearing from him again, and I can't go through with it. It's torture, reading how confused and upset he is, but I know it's nothing compared to what I'm putting him through and so I deserve every ounce of punishment coming my way. I read them over and over, and sometimes, my resolve crumbles and I start to reply, try to explain, but then I remember Paige, and I imagine a look of horror and pity on his face at the sight of me, and I hit delete.

Chapter thirty-seven

From: Finn_the_finster@gmail.com
To: ZoeCalloway@hotmail.com
Subject: Not giving up

I have no idea if you're getting these emails, but I'm hoping, based on the fact that they're not bouncing back to me, that you are. Whether you're reading them or not is another matter. But it's outside my control. All I can do is keep trying, and that's what I wanted to tell you. I'm not giving up. Don't get me wrong, I've thought about it. Connor thinks I'm an idiot to carry on looking for someone who clearly doesn't want to be found, but he doesn't know you. He doesn't know us.

We might not have had long together, but I know that whatever happened between us wasn't fake, or all in my head. You had the same feelings I did. And that's what I need you to remember. Think, Zoe. Think about the time we spent together. That weekend at the lake, the night here on the roof. All our messages while I was away. It was real, and it was special. For whatever reason you've done this, whatever you've got going on, remember that. What we had was, is, special. Not many people are lucky enough to find that.

Don't give up on me, and I won't give up on you.

Chapter thirty-eight

Linda hasn't been back since that night. Dad says she's 'giving us some space' to try and sort things out. Things between us are at an all-time, unhealthy low. He's even tried, several times, to initiate a conversation about that night, but although I give him props for doing so, I shut it down quickly, retreating to the sanctuary of my room. Pleading tiredness/pain/I-can't-do-this-right-now. He stood outside my door and cried and told me how sorry he was, for everything. How much he hated himself for not being there for me, and for what he had put me through. I sat on my bed and I cried too, but I didn't answer him. I couldn't. I didn't know what to say.

It's my fault, I know that. I'm the one who vomited the ugly truths out. But now that Things Are Out In The Open (that's how he said it, with stiffly enunciated capital letters) things that must be addressed if either of us is ever to move on from the past, I'm legitimately worried that those things might be beyond repair. That if we pull that thread, the whole jersey will unravel and all we'll be left with is a tangled pile of wool that could never be shaped into anything even remotely recognisable ever again.

He tries the guilt card. It's part of his recovery, he says, to make amends. Face up to his wrongs, do right by the people he's hurt. I, perhaps cruelly, point out that he couldn't even remember half of what those wrongs were until I reminded him.

'Doesn't matter,' he says. 'We can lump them together into one big pile and go from there. The important thing is that we start. We can't fix our problems if we don't even bother to address them.'

'If only it was that easy.'

'It could be.'

'No, it can't.'

'Zoe, you're my kid. I haven't done much to be proud of in life, but I'm proud of you. I want to fix things. I want us to get through this.'

I'm torn. All I ever wanted was to hear words like these from him. But now that he's saying them, I don't trust it. I want to, but something inside of me is holding me back. Like an inbuilt self-defence mechanism, designed to protect me from hurt. I can't seem to override it.

'Look, give me some space,' I tell him. 'The timing is lousy, I'm dealing with too much, all at once. I can't promise anything, but maybe if you stop trying to push a relationship on me, we can see what happens. Organically.'

'OK, sure. I can do that.'

Chapter thirty-nine

'How did you get this number?' I stare at the landline receiver, disconcerted.

'Easy, I looked up your dad's file at work,' Olivia replies cheerfully.

'Is that even legal?'

'Probably not.' She doesn't sound in the least bit bothered. 'But the number on your file wasn't working, so what choice did I have?'

'I ... broke my phone,' I mutter. I knew I shouldn't have answered, but when the phone lit up as I was passing it in the hallway I stupidly thought about how many days it had been since I had heard the sound of another human's – apart from Dad, of course – voice. And how even if it was just another tele-marketer, it was still someone. Proof that the rest of the world hadn't washed away in all the rain and there was only us left alive. So, I picked it up.

'Ugh, they're so flimsy, aren't they,' she commiserates. 'My screen is always getting cracked. Bloody kids keep dropping it. I know I shouldn't let them use it, but honestly, it's easier sometimes to let them play a game instead of listening to them whining. You're not one of those anti-screentime people, are you?'

'No. As a teacher, I know there are some merits to it.'

'Oh my God, I keep forgetting you were a teacher,' she chortles. 'Do you remember Mr Lincoln from high school? Fuck, he was such a prick. Angry all the time, and such a power-tripper. Now that I think about it, all of our teachers were pretty shit.'

'Are.'

'Sorry?'

'Are . . . am, a teacher. I'm still registered, just not currently practising.'

There's a few seconds of silence. 'Right. Anyway, I called to see if you needed a lift tonight?'

'Tonight?'

'The reunion, remember?'

'Completely forgot,' I say truthfully. 'Don't even know which day of the week it is.'

'Well, it's Saturday, and the reunion is tonight. So, lift? I can swing by and pick you up, but it will be an hour earlier than it starts because I have last-minute things to do and check. Or I can organise someone else to collect you on their way. You'd be amazed how many people are coming, it's going to be so cool to see everyone again.'

'Yeah, cool.' Not the word I would have chosen. 'I appreciate you thinking of me, but I'm going to have to give it a miss. Sorry.'

'No,' she wails. 'You can't. This is huge, our ten-year reunion. It's a once-in-a-lifetime thing.'

'I know, believe me, I'm devastated,' I lie. 'But the pain has been incredibly bad this week, really, really bad. That's why I had to cancel my rehab appointment.' Well, I made Dad call to do the actual cancelling for me.

'Can't you pop a few painkillers?'

'It's a bit more than a couple of paracetamol can handle.'

'This sucks, I can't believe that you're going to miss out. What if I call my father, ask him to prescribe something stronger?'

'Unless he can mainline morphine into my veins, it's not going to help.'

'Are you sure you can't come?'

'Positive.'

'All right.' She sounds miffed, though, as if I've rejected her personally. 'I'll tell everyone you said hi. And if you want, I can send you some photos, so you can see how much every-one's changed.'

'Sure. Thanks. That'd be nice.'

I hang up the phone, pick up the crutch I'd leant against the hall side cupboard, and swivel on my foot, coming face to face with my father standing in the afternoon shadows of the hallway behind me.

'Jesus, you nearly gave me a heart attack,' I scold him.

'Sorry. Who was that on the phone?'

'No one.'

'Didn't sound like no one.'

'OK, I'll rephrase. No one you need to worry about.'

'Was it Olivia calling about the reunion?'

I glare at him. 'How did you know that? Were you listening in on another phone somewhere? Are you monitoring my calls now? Because if you are, that's seriously overstepping.'

'No, there's no other phones. She reminded me about it this morning when I called to cancel your appointment.'

'So why the third degree if you already know?'

He blinks. 'Is that what this feels like? I'm only trying to show interest.' He waves his hands around vaguely. 'In your life. It's what dads do.'

'That might have been somewhat appropriate when I was a teenager, but it sure as hell isn't now.'

His looks dejected. 'Can't seem to get it right, can I.'

'Stop trying so hard. I told you, this isn't easy for me. I need time. Boundaries. You have to remember that I'm an adult now. I make my own decisions and choices.'

He holds his hands up, palms towards me. 'OK. Backing off as we speak.'

'Good. Thank you.'

He flattens himself against the wall as I hobble past him. 'I'm glad you're not going, anyway,' he says.

'Why?' I pause, my back to him.

'Because I've asked Linda to come for dinner.'

I'm thankful he can't see my face as I squeeze my eyes shut and mouth the word fuck.

'Zoe, she's nice, I promise,' he says, almost pleadingly. 'I'd love it if you two could get to know each other. You're both so important to me.'

I imagine the scenario of dinner and know that I can't do it. I'm sure he's right, and she's a perfectly nice, normal, completely lacking-in-ulterior-motives kind of person. She's obviously been a good influence on him, so I should be thankful to her for that. And in the past, I've always prided myself on never judging someone until I've gotten to know them. But it's weird. I know it's irrational; after all, my mother has been dead for a long time. It's not like Linda and my father are betraying her. And I do want him to be happy. It's just … weird. Plus, I'm ashamed of the way I acted the last time I saw her. I saw the bottle of what looked like wine, immediately assumed the worst, and said a whole lot of things that would have been better delivered in a different time and place, and in a calmer tone.

I look over my shoulder at Dad. 'Who says I'm not going?'

He looks understandably confused. 'You did. Didn't you?'

'You must have misheard.'

He frowns at the phone as if for answers. 'You told her your pain was too much.'

'I'm feeling better now.'

'So … you want to go?'

'Of course. It's my high school reunion.'

He looks at me doubtfully. 'What about …' he gestures towards my leg.

'Got to start facing the world at some point, don't I.' I take a deep breath to quell my nerves at the thought. 'At least these people kind of know me. That might make it easier.'

'I'm not sure this is a good idea.'

'It's lucky that I'm not asking for your permission then. Boundaries, remember?'

He smiles weakly. 'Understood. Have you got something to wear?'

'I'll find something. It's not like anything would be open in this town on a Saturday afternoon anyway.'

'No, you're probably right. You want me to drop you off?'

'Yeah. If you don't mind,' I mumble, feeling about ten years old.

'Of course not.'

'Thanks. Suppose I better go and sort out an outfit.'

'Want me to make you a sandwich?'

'No, I'm OK.' The thought of eating makes my stomach feel queasy.

He gives me a look.

'What?'

'Keeping the whole boundaries thing in mind, with me not telling you what to do ... can I just say that you should eat something. You need to rebuild your strength. Plus, I don't know if you're planning on drinking at this reunion – and I know it's absolutely none of my business if you do – but keep in mind that painkillers and booze don't mix.'

I start to say something snarky, but stop myself. He's trying. 'Fine. I guess a sandwich couldn't hurt.'

Chapter forty

'You sure about this?'

'No.'

'Because I can take you home again, if that's what you want.'

We're parked across the street from the RSA hall. It's just gone six o'clock, but it's been dark for almost two hours already. Night sets in early in winter, as does the cold. At least it's stopped raining for a while, though the fact the stars are all blotted out by clouds suggests this won't last.

'I'm here now,' I say, with false bravado. 'I may as well go in.'

'And you're sure about not taking the chair?'

I cringe at the thought of being wheeled into the hall in front of all those people. 'I think the crutches will be enough. Don't you think the crutches will be enough?'

He shrugs. 'Only you can decide, it's not me who will have to use them all night. If you think you can manage, that's your call. But I'm happy to push you inside in the chair.'

Neither option seems appealing. I'm still weak, and the crutches do tire me out easily. But at least with them, I'm upright, and I figure I can find a seat and camp out until I'm ready to leave. Or need the bathroom, but I'll cross that bridge when it comes to it. In the wheelchair, I feel like a complete invalid. 'The crutches will be fine.'

'At least let me help you get inside.'

'No way.' I shake my head. Being chaperoned inside by my father will just draw attention to me. 'Out of the question.'

'OK, well you have your phone, right? Call me anytime you've had enough and I'll come and get you. Even if it's in ten minutes' time. No judgment here.'

'Relax. I should know most of these people, it'll be fine.' I'm not sure whether it's him I'm trying to convince, or myself. Probably both.

'When was the last time you had anything to do with any of them?'

'Probably when I walked out of the school gates for the last time.'

'That's what I figured.' He fidgets with his watch, clearly nervous on my behalf. 'Well, good luck. You look nice.'

My hands flutter at my dress. 'Thanks.'

Picking an outfit had been an easy task in the end, due to the majority of my wardrobe being ruled out from the offset. First, I thought I'd go nice casual, but all of my skinny jeans have had one leg cut off at the knee to make them easier to get on over the stump. Short dresses were, for obvious reasons, completely out of the question. The majority of my dresses were of the mid-thigh variety, including the one I wore the night I met Finn. I'd fingered the hem of it wistfully and then shoved it into the shadows at the back of the wardrobe. No emails for a few days now, and it's driving me crazy, not knowing how he is.

In the end, I settled on the only long dress I own. A black stylish number that I wore to my teacher graduation ceremony. When I wear it with heels it falls to ankle length, but tonight, I wear a flat ballet shoe on my right foot, so the dress skims the floor. With a cute round neck and elbow-length sleeves, it's fitted at the top with a wide, billowing skirt. As a bonus, it even has pockets on the sides. It's far too big on me now that I've lost so much weight since the accident, but it hides the stump, so it's perfect. Over the top, for warmth, I wear a faded denim jacket, my favourite.

'OK.' I put my hand on the door handle and take a deep breath. 'Here goes nothing.'

It's obvious my father wants to say something, but he manages to rein it in. 'Try to enjoy yourself.'

I get out, carefully, and wait on the kerb until he drives away. Watching his tail lights disappear around a corner, I immediately start regretting my decision to come. Light from inside the hall streams out of the windows and the open door. On the footpath at the bottom of the steps is a blackboard announcing the event and the fact that it's private. I can hear music and laughter from inside, but now that it's come to it, I'm frozen to the spot. This was a dumb idea. Planting the crutches firmly in the gravel for balance, I fumble inside my pocket for my phone. Dad won't have got far, he can circle around and come back for me. I'll just have to face the music with Linda and apologise.

Before I even enter the passcode to unlock the screen, a black car pulls into the car park beside the RSA, crunching on the gravel and screeching to a halt, distracting my attention momentarily. The car park lights aren't great, but I see a man's figure get out, slamming the door closed behind him. He leans

181

against the car, lifting his hands to his mouth, and I see a brief flare of orange light as he sucks on a cigarette, which he then throws down and extinguishes by grinding it into the gravel with his shoe.

He fixes his jacket lapels, then strides towards the entrance, but as he gets to the bottom of the steps he glances around and notices me standing on the other side of the road. Doing a double-take, he stops.

'Are you OK?' he calls out. 'Do you need help?'

'No, I'm fine, thank you.' I pull out my phone and try to flip open the case, but my hands are cold and I clumsily drop it. 'Damn it.'

He crosses the road and stoops to pick it up. 'Let me get that for you.'

'Thanks.' My cheeks burn with a mixture of embarrassment and regret. I was so stupid for thinking I could do this.

'I know what it's like,' he says, passing the phone over.

I eye him warily. 'What what's like?'

'Getting around on crutches. Pain in the ass.'

I look him up and down. He's very clearly able-bodied. He reads my mind.

'Not now, obviously. But last season I pulled a hammy.'

I continue to stare at him.

'Hamstring,' he clarifies, pointing to the back of his thigh.

'I know what a hammy is.'

He grins. 'Four weeks I had to use those stupid sticks.' He gestures towards my crutches. 'Longest four weeks of my life.'

'I can imagine.'

'What did you do?'

'It's a long story.'

'You're here for the school reunion, right?' He looks around. 'Of course you are. Nothing else is open in this town. Why don't we head inside, grab a drink? You can tell me about it.'

'I was actually going to head home.'

'Already?' He pushes a button on the side of the very expensive Apple watch on his wrist, and it lights up. 'I'm not that late, am I? Nope. Party's just getting started.' He drops his arm again. 'So, why are you leaving?'

'I can feel a migraine coming on.'

'Nothing a drink won't fix.' He grins again, clearly used to it winning women over. 'Come on. It's Zoe, right?'

'Yeah,' I answer, surprised. 'How do you know that?'

'We were in a few of the same classes. Don't ask me to name them though, cause as soon as I left high school I forgot everything I'd ever learnt and never looked back. School wasn't exactly my favourite place in the world. Being on a field, however . . .'

The penny drops. 'You must be Brian Jenkins.'

'Guilty as charged.'

'I remember you now. You and that friend of yours, Matthew. You used to throw spitballs into the hair of that girl who sat in front of you. Bridget, wasn't it?'

He sucks air in between his teeth and looks guilty. 'Yeah, not my finest moment. If she's here tonight, I should probably apologise for being such a jerk.'

'Careful, she might be here solely to exact her revenge.'

'You think?'

'You've seen the movie *Carrie*, right?'

'If she gets pig blood on this suit, she'll be paying the dry-cleaning bill,' he retorts. 'Italian. Very expensive. Come on. Let's go inside. One drink, then if you still think a migraine's coming on, I'll drive you safely home myself.'

I study his friendly face, feeling a little more at ease now. 'OK. Just one.'

'Deal.' He looks at my crutches. 'Do you need help?'

'No, I'm OK.'

It quickly becomes apparent though that I'm not. The crutches have rubber tips, but still struggle to find purchase in the gravel. One slips forward and for a brief, horrifying moment I think I'm about to fall at his feet, but he gently grabs my arm and steadies me.

'You sure you don't want any help?'

'OK. Maybe some help would be good. Thank you.'

He takes one of my crutches and slides an arm around my waist, pulling me in so I'm leaning into him. With his support, I hop and he walks towards the steps.

'Can't put any weight at all on that other leg, eh?' he remarks.

'Nope, none at all,' I reply truthfully.

When we walk into the hall, there's an immediate hush in the volume level, as people turn to check out who's walked in. I hear excited voices when they see that it's us, or at least, Brian, who is, as it turns out, a minor celebrity in the sports world. A few men cheer out his name and flock forward to pretend tackle him. Luckily, I manage to grab my other crutch back in the nick of time, and balance myself out of harm's way.

'You came!' Olivia appears in front of me, her cheeks flushed and eyes shiny, clearly a few glasses of wine down already. Her breath confirms this when she leans in for a cheek kiss. 'And with Brian Jenkins! You must tell me everything, leave nothing out.'

184

'Tell you what?'

'The details,' she hisses. 'Of you and him. I want to know everything.'

'There is no me and him, and there's nothing to tell.'

She pouts. 'Oh, don't be like that. I'm married, remember? Romance is practically non-existent, and as for sex?' She pulls a face. 'If I have to live vicariously through you to get my kicks, I will. So, spill.'

'OK, first of all, that's all kinds of weird,' I tell her. 'And secondly, there really is nothing to tell. I met him outside in the car park about forty seconds ago. He helped me up the stairs. End of story.'

She looks disappointed, but also relieved. 'Are you sure? The way he had his arm around you when you guys came in, I thought . . . '

'He was being kind. That's all.'

She brightens. 'Oh well, your loss is my gain. He's free and available then.' She bites her lower lip and cranes to look around the room.

'Is your husband here?' I ask deliberately. 'I'd love to meet him.'

Her good mood temporarily evaporates. 'No, he's not. He stayed home to look after the kids. Sophie has a bit of a cold. Between you and me, I think he was glad. This way he can stay home and watch the rugby. He's not what you'd call a people person, in that he doesn't like people all that much.'

'Really? But you were always such a sociable person,' I muse. 'I guess it's true what they say, opposites attract.'

'Something attracted, initially,' she mutters darkly. 'Didn't last though.'

Sensing trouble in paradise, I try to make my excuses so I can search out a dark corner from where I can sit and people-watch while hopefully avoiding too much interaction. Olivia is having none of it.

'I'm here to help you, whatever you need,' she announces, like I'm her latest charity cause.

'I don't need anything, but thanks.'

She looks me up and down. 'You can carry a drink while using those things?'

I tilt my head, conceding she has a point. 'No, I cannot.'

'That's what I thought. Now, you take a seat over at that table,' she points to one in the middle of the hall, nearest to the stage. 'And I'll get you something from the bar. Wine? It's so cheap here.'

'In that case, you'd better make it two.' I reach for my phone to get out my money card, but she brushes me off.

'I'll get them. Honestly, they're like seventy cents or something stupid. Got to love the RSA – cheap booze.' She suddenly looks thoughtful. 'I should come here more often.'

Chapter forty-one

I have only hazy recollections of my parents' marriage, and a few gleanings picked up from married colleagues in the school staffroom to go by, but I'm pretty sure Olivia's marriage is doomed. She's been hanging off Brian's every word during our meal of steak and roast vegetables, and occasionally even his arm. In fact, if her cleavage was any closer, it would be in his lap. Not that Brian's complaining. He's been happily regaling our table with stories of his time in the UK. The places he's played, even blow-by-blow accounts of some of his best matches. I tune out after a while.

There are a lot of familiar faces here. I never had a best friend, growing up. Kids found it hard to know what to say to me after my mother died. And when Dad started to drink, I distanced myself rather than risk getting too close to anyone. Couldn't exactly bring a friend home after school for fear we'd find him passed out on the couch surrounded by empties. It wasn't something I knew how to explain to someone else, when I couldn't understand it myself. The weird thing was, he didn't even seem to enjoy it. When sober, he looked like death warmed up, and he'd swear black and blue that he'd never touch a drop again. Sometimes he'd even pour whatever was left in the house down the sink. But it never lasted. That itch would steal over him, the uncontrollable desire to quench a thirst he couldn't control, and he'd leave the house to buy more.

Bonnie was my first real friend, and thinking about her brings a lump to my throat. I miss her so much. Being here, surrounded by happy people who all seem to know each other, I feel so lonely. I pick up my phone and fire off a quick text message to her. It doesn't take long; my new phone has only two contacts: Bonnie, and my father. I know that she doesn't agree with the way I've cut Finn out of my life, but she respects that it's my decision. Or at least she's trying to.

'You OK?' I hadn't heard Brian sidle into the seat beside me until he leans in and speaks, a little too close to my left ear.

'Hmm?' I pocket my phone and draw away. 'I'm fine. You?'

'Bored.'

'Really? You haven't stopped talking for the last hour. Looked like you were having a great time.'

'Hey, I'm simply giving the fans what they want.'

'Are you serious?'

He bursts into laughter. 'No. But you should see your face. Relax. I'm not that up myself.'

I laugh along with him, grateful for a bit of company. 'I don't know. Olivia has you pretty high up on a pedestal.'

'That's only because I'm the most – and these are her words by the way, before you look at me like that again – famous person here.'

I snort. 'She said that?'

He nods. 'She did.'

'She must be pretty disappointed with what the rest of us have achieved.'

'I don't know. The world wouldn't get by without' – he starts pointing at random people around the room – 'doctors, lawyers, hairdressers, construction workers, accountants, mechanics, farmers, mothers, and of course' – the finger points at me – 'teachers.'

I smile. 'What about everyone else? What do they do now?'

'Haven't a clue.'

'Isn't Bridget a renowned scientist?'

'She is. She has also, as of five minutes ago, graciously accepted my apology.'

'Wasn't that nice of her.'

'I thought so.' He looks around. 'I forgot Ted.' He leans close again. 'Local drug supplier.'

'Bullshit.' I look at where Ted is shovelling a strawberry cheesecake into his mouth. Ruddy cheeked, he's wearing jeans and a shirt that's too small. It gapes across his belly where the buttons do up. He looks completely harmless. 'Isn't he a travel agent? I'm sure that's what Olivia said.'

'By day, yes. By night?' He waggles his eyebrows.

'You make him sound like Batman.'

'No, he's the guy Batman's after.'

I watch Ted. He uses his thumb to wipe something out of his ear, inspects it quickly and then wipes it on his shirt. 'Are you sure?'

'Hundred per cent.'

'Huh.' I drain the last of the wine out of my glass. 'Guess you never can tell with some people.'

189

Brian gives me an unreadable look. 'What about you, Zoe. What's your secret?'

The tablecloth suddenly looks incredibly interesting. I brush a few breadcrumbs onto the floor. 'Me? No secrets here.'

Olivia, who has been giving us funny looks from across the table, springs to her feet. 'Awards time,' she announces loudly.

I feel a sudden dread. She wouldn't, would she?

'What awards?' someone asks.

'Nothing serious.' She picks up a folder. 'Kylie and I thought it would be fun to present a few certificates.' She turns to Kylie. 'Have you got the trophies?'

Kylie holds up a plastic bag. 'Right here.'

'Good. Let's do this.'

'I'm going to need more drinks,' Brian mutters to me. 'You want another one?'

'Only one?'

He grins. 'Understood.'

Olivia does the old one-two-testing thing into the micro-phone and the room quietens down. Someone dims all the lights except the ones over the small stage by the dance floor, where she's standing. She makes a speech, thanking everyone for coming. Brian returns with a beer for him and a couple of wines for me. The first goes down far too quickly. It's been a long time since I had a drink, the last being probably a week or two before the accident. I'd forgotten how relaxed it can make you. In fact, I feel the calmest I've felt since I got back here.

Then the 'awards' start. Brian, naturally, wins the award for Most Famous, which he graciously accepts, modestly refusing to make a speech.

'Christ, that was embarrassing,' he mumbles, when he gets

190

back to the table and slaps the trophy down in the middle. It's a little gold cup, about ten centimetres high, with his name engraved on the front.

'I don't know. You looked thrilled if you ask me,' I say, and he pulls a face.

They proceed to give out more awards, calling the recipients up to the stage while the room gives scattered applause.

First to register

Hardest person to find

Person who travelled the furthest to be here

High school sweethearts who are still together

Person whose hairstyle hasn't changed since high school

Most tattoos

Weirdest job

And then, Olivia announces, the next recipient has the honour of receiving two awards. She looks straight at me when she says it, and I feel my body start to tremble. I shake my head at her, warningly, but she ignores me and carries on talking. Blood rushes to my ears, so I hear only every third or fifth word, something about an award for never leaving school (teacher) and then she places a hand over her heart and her expression gets serious, and I instantly realise what's coming. Somehow, I've managed to get through an entire evening without anyone mentioning my leg, mainly because I don't think many people know. It's not like I ever broadcasted it on social media, but now she's about to broadcast it to the world. I can feel Brian's eyes on me, curious.

'Are you OK?' he asks.

'No.' I shake my head. 'No, I'm not.'

'Zoe,' Olivia says into the microphone. It echoes off every

corner of the hall. 'I'm so proud to present to you the award for overcoming the worst odds,' she says tearfully. 'I can't even imagine how hard it's been for you, but you're so brave. I honestly think you're amazing.'

Everyone turns to look at me. 'Um,' I stammer. 'What about Rachel? I heard that she survived breast cancer?' I look around the sea of faces until I find the one I'm looking for. 'Is that right?'

Rachel looks annoyed at the attention, as well she should because I'm effectively throwing her under the bus to save myself, but she gives a small nod.

'Well, there you go,' I tell Olivia. 'She's more deserving of that award than I am.'

'Zoe, you lost your leg.' Olivia grimaces. 'That's way more brutal.'

I hear gasps and murmurs around the room, and I want to slink down off my chair and hide under the table.

Kylie, determined to participate in this freak show, pushes in front of the microphone. 'Don't worry about trying to get up here on the stage, Zoe. I'll bring the trophy down to you.'

'Can you just move on to the next person? Please?' I keep my eyes on the table in front of me, hating the attention. Why did she have to do this? I was out of the house, feeling a little bit normal for the first time since before the accident, and now everyone is staring at me with a mixture of curiosity and pity. I feel like the biggest freak on the planet, so, when Brian scrapes back his chair and asks quietly, 'Want to get out of here?' I don't even hesitate.

Chapter forty-two

If Brian realises that I'm crying as he drives back through town and towards the beach, he's gentleman enough not to comment. It's not an out-of-control, sobbing kind of cry. More of a gentle trail of tears as I rest my head against the glass of the passenger window and stare at the dark façade of the old buildings passing by. I never thought I'd be back here, and certainly not under circumstances like these. What happened to my life? How could everything have gone so wrong? A split second that altered my life irrevocably. A minute of fun that ended in disaster, and my life as I knew it was over.

'I don't think she meant any harm,' Brian says eventually. 'Olivia. She didn't think things through.'

She'd been upset when we left, but the fact that she had no idea why I was upset, pissed me off to the point that I knew if we didn't get out of there, I'd end up saying something I shouldn't.

'I know that her heart was in the right place,' I agree through gritted teeth. 'But I wish she'd spoken about it to me first, so I could have told her I didn't want the attention. Would you? If you were me?'

He has the decency to think about it. 'No. I wouldn't. But like I said, she doesn't think. She likes the attention, and grand gestures. In fact, I think she jumped at the first marriage proposal that came her way purely because she wanted a big wedding. No thought at all about the commitment that comes after it.'

I sniff and wipe my cheeks, turning towards him. 'How do you know?'

He chuckles wryly. 'Because she spent the better part of the night moaning about her boring husband, chaotic kids, and unsatisfactory sex life.'

'Are you serious? She actually told you about that?'

'Sure did. Oh, and she propositioned me. Hard. Seriously, there was no innuendo whatsoever. She practically offered herself to me on a platter.'

'Her poor husband.'

'Yeah. Wonder if he has any idea.'

'Have you ever been married?'

He flicks me a quick sideways glance. 'Hell no. Marriage, kids, the whole shebang, it's not for me. Not to say never, but we're still too young. Don't you think?'

'We're only a couple of years away from thirty,' I point out. 'Not exactly spring chickens.'

'Yeah well, I still feel eighteen. Speaking of which ...' He reaches over towards the glovebox in front of me, opening it and fumbling inside. The car starts to drift towards the left shoulder of the road, so I grab the steering wheel and lightly correct it. 'Thanks,' he grins, straightening up to put both hands back on the wheel, only this time one of his hands is holding a flask-sized bottle of brown liquid. He unscrews the cap and takes a swig, shaking his head roughly afterwards and grunting. 'That's the stuff.' He holds it out towards me.

'What is it?'

'Whisky. And not cheap stuff either. The best Scottish whisky you can buy.'

If I'm supposed to be impressed, I'm not. And I don't like the fact that he's drinking while driving. I try and remember how many beers I saw him drink at the RSA, but I wasn't taking any notice. Why would I have? I didn't know he was going to be my ride home. He seems OK, though. Not slurring his words, eyes seem clear. Not obviously drunk. I take the bottle from him gingerly and inspect the label.

'It won't poison you,' he says. 'But it might put hairs on your chest.'

'Just what I've always wanted,' I answer drily, and he laughs. I take a mouthful and it almost blows my cheeks out, like in one of those cartoon mouthwash ads. When I swallow it, my throat burns like I've swallowed pure fire. 'Bloody hell,' I splutter, inspecting the front of the bottle again. 'Is it a hundred per cent proof?'

'Told you it was good.'

The car turns into Cherrywood, the road on which I live, but instead of heading down it, Brian drives the car up onto a grassy reserve overlooking the beach and kills the ignition, leaving the stereo on low. There's little light, once the car's headlights fade out, apart from a few stars overhead. The clouds have blown to the east, revealing a crescent moon. Its light reflects along the top of the ocean like a pathway.

'What are you doing?'

He takes the bottle out of my hands and takes a long swig, wiping his lips dry afterwards. 'Thought we could hang out for a while. Night's still young, nothing else to do in this hellhole.'

'I'm lousy company at the moment. Plus, I'm kind of tired. So, if you don't mind, I'd rather—'

'How did it happen?' he blurts out, interrupting me, like the question has been burning a hole in his tongue.

I don't need to ask what he's referring to. 'It's not something I find easy to talk about.'

'Oh, no, yeah. Absolutely. I get that,' he says, but it's obvious he's not getting it at all. 'Super traumatic, I'm sure. But like, was it in a vehicle accident? Or while you were doing something cool, maybe a rock-climbing fall.'

He takes another mouthful of whisky, then offers it to me. I shake my head.

'Nothing as exciting as that,' I say stiffly. 'Sorry to disappoint.'

'So?'

It's obvious he's not going to give up. My instincts are starting to wave little red flags at me.

'Maybe you should take it easy on the whisky,' I say cautiously. 'You still have to drive home and while there might be only two cops in this town, they'll probably be out in force knowing the reunion is happening.'

He snorts. 'You mean that old fucker, Jerry? That guy has had it in for me since I learned how to drive, man. Don't worry, I can, and have, outraced him any day. Anyway, stop changing the subject.' He reaches over and puts a hand on my thigh, and the red flags start waving madly. I push his hand off.

'I got hit by a van, OK? Sorry, it's probably not dramatic

enough for you. Now can you take me home? I sent my father a text when we were leaving the RSA,' I lie. 'He'll be worrying if I don't turn up soon.'

He smirks. 'No, you didn't. I was watching.'

'Do you have any idea how fucking creepy that sounds? Brian, I'm not sure why the sudden personality change, although I have my suspicions.' I eye the bottle of whisky in his hand. 'But I'd appreciate it if you'd keep your morbid curiosity to yourself and take me home. Now.'

'Speaking of morbid curiosity, can I have a look?' He grins at me, like this is a completely normal thing for someone to ask. Like we're co-conspirators up to fun and mischief.

'No, you can't have a look.' I glare at him. 'I can't believe you'd even ask me that.'

I don't like the way he's looking at me, like in his head we're already half undressed.

'Sorry,' he mumbles, and now his words are starting to sound slurred. 'Didn't mean to offend you.' He says it snippety, like I'm being unreasonable. 'I've never seen one up close before.'

'You mean a leg? You know you have two of your own, right?'

'You know what I mean.'

'No, you cannot see my leg. But what you can do is drive me home. It's like, five hundred metres that way.' I point into the darkness. 'Not far at all, would take this big fancy car of yours all of twenty seconds.'

'Come on,' he wheedles, pouting his lip like it's cute and not completely ridiculous on a grown man. 'Why have you suddenly gone all shy on me? You've been flirting all night. I thought you were up for a bit of fun.' He reaches for my leg again and I slap his hand harder this time.

'The back seats recline almost flat,' he says, not caring. 'Plenty of space back there.'

'You need your head read if you think anything's going to happen between us.'

He fakes a wince. 'Harsh.'

'Seriously. If you can't tell the difference between someone being friendly, and flirting, you've got big issues. Huge.'

'Bullshit. I know when someone wants me.' He rests his arm on the headrest of my seat. 'Why else would you get in the car with me?'

'Because you offered to drive me home,' I point out. 'Because I was upset, and because I thought you were being nice. If I'd known you were thinking like this I would never have got in, believe me.'

He takes another swig of whisky and his hand drops to rub my hair. I smack it away again, feeling my panic rise. I've never been in this kind of situation before, where someone won't take a hint. Not that I'm hinting, I've told him straight up that I'm not interested, but he's so full of himself and so unused to women saying no, that he seems to think I'm joking, or playing hard to get.

I start thinking quickly. Home is so close, but along a rough, gravel road. There are a few houses between here and there. Maybe one of the occupants can help me, if I can get to one of them. I pick up my crutches and reach for the door handle. He touches a button on his door and I hear a click as my door locks.

'Open it,' I instruct him, as calmly as I can.

He grins at me as if he's not behaving like a massive creep. I have the horrible thought that maybe he genuinely doesn't see anything wrong with his behaviour.

'Come on,' he wheedles. 'Why are you being so prissy all of a sudden?'

'Brian.' I look him dead in the eyes, to make sure he's listening to what I say next. 'I'm not being prissy. I'm saying no. And I'm not going to change my mind. You're scaring me .'

His eyebrows furrow. 'That's a bit of an overreaction, don't you think?'

'Not at all. I mean, did you seriously think that because I let you drive me home, I'd have sex with you?'

'Yeah, I thought you were as keen as I was. I mean, you were happy to laugh and flirt with me back at the reunion.'

'Smiling and laughing and general conversation does not constitute flirting. And back at the reunion, you were acting like a normal, decent kind of human being. Not like this.'

A thought occurs to him. 'Is this about your leg?'

'Is what about my leg?'

'It's OK, I understand if you're feeling nervous, but I promise I won't freak out at the sight of it. And I'll do all the heavy lifting. I mean, I have no idea how it all works when you're . . .' he gestures at my legs.

'You're unbelievable. You really are. It's like talking to a brick wall. Stop being a fucking creep, and let me of this goddamn car!'

He reels back from the vitriol in my voice, finally getting the message. 'I knew I should have gone with Olivia,' he says angrily. 'She was a sure thing, none of this bullshit.' He takes another pull on the bottle. The whisky is now half gone. 'You know, I'd have thought you'd be grateful for the attention. I'm guessing you don't get many offers these days.'

I do a double-take, unable to believe he thinks it's OK to say these words to another human being. 'So, what, you thought I'd jump at your offer of a pity-fuck?'

'Why not? I'm sure you're gagging for it. Has anyone even looked twice at you since the accident? I was doing you a favour.'

I stare at him, realising that, no matter what I say, he's still going to believe he's the wounded party here. 'Open the door.' I remember my phone and fumble for it, cursing myself for not thinking of it sooner. 'Or I'll call the cops, and my dad, who could be here in less than a minute with his shotgun. And I'll tell everyone, Olivia and all your fans, exactly what kind of person you are.'

He clicks the button. 'Fine. I wouldn't touch you with a bargepole now. In fact, I probably would have thrown up if I'd seen it anyway.'

My hands are shaking as they find the door handle. Pushing the door open, I swing myself around on the seat so I can plant my right foot on the ground, along with my crutches.

His personality suddenly takes another flip, and he calls after me with a wheedling tone. 'Aw come on, Zoe, don't leave like this. Look, I'm sorry, OK? My life is a bit messed up at the moment. There was some trouble, back in the UK, that's why I came home. Needed to lay low for a while until it blows over and the club can sign me again. Which I know they will, I'm sure they will.' He sounds bitter and angry.

I can guess exactly what sort of trouble he's in, if his behaviour tonight is anything to go by. Pushing myself up off the seat, I say stiffly, 'Maybe they're waiting for you to take ownership of your actions instead of believing that everything is someone else's fault.'

'Whatever,' he says scornfully. 'You know nothing. You're just a small-town handicapped nobody. Look at you. What the hell was I even thinking? You're disgusting.'

'Well, that makes two of us,' I retort, snatching the bottle of whisky off him before he realises what I'm doing.

'What the hell?' he grabs at it, but I slam the door in his face.

'I'll take that,' I shout. 'You're drunk, you shouldn't be driving.'

He winds the window down and starts the car, revving the engine loudly. 'Boring as well as frigid. Aren't you the whole package,' he snarls.

'You need help. Seriously.'

He takes off, his tyres squealing when they hit the asphalt of the road again, making a hell of a racket. A light comes on in the nearest house, and a curtain is pulled to one side. I stand there, holding my breath, staring at the dark silhouetted figure. Can they see me? I should wave, try and get their attention. Ask for help. But inexplicably, I'm frozen instead. The curtain drops, the light switches off. I'm on my own.

Chapter forty-three

Somehow, I manage to hold on to the neck of the bottle as I make my way across the grassy reserve and towards the beach, like the ocean is luring me in with its promise of anonymity. There is no one, nothing around, to witness my shame. Because that's how I feel. Ashamed. I know I shouldn't. Whatever Brian thought, I was not flirting with him. Not even close. Even if Finn had never existed and I wasn't completely, totally and hopelessly in love with him, I still wouldn't have flirted with Brian. Not my type.

His comments though, about being disgusting and not exactly inundated with offers, touched a nerve. I can barely stand the sight of the stump myself, how could anyone else ever find me attractive? What if that part of my life, love, romance, sex, is done? Over for good? I think of my weekend with Finn and the way my body felt, being with his, and it's like a punch to the stomach. I might never feel that kind of connection again. But without Finn, I don't want to. Now I know how incredible it can be, when you're with the right person. If I can't be with him, I don't want to be with anyone else.

I should tip the whisky out, then be a responsible person and put the bottle in the rubbish bin over by the fence.

I should call my father, ask him to come and get me. Then again, I should have the operation. Call Finn. Forgive my father. Stop treating Linda like she's done something wrong when she hasn't.

Instead, I do the opposite of all that.

But it's like I'm outside of my body, floating somewhere above in the chilly night air, watching the unbearably sad woman below. The one with the tears and the regrets and the total disregard for her own safety. She's reckless, this woman. Someone in her condition shouldn't be teetering on the edge of a bank, not with one leg to stand on. Not only because of her leg but because she's had a few drinks tonight. Alcohol courses through her blood. She drank far more than she should have, more than she's had in a while. Pre-accident, it wouldn't have had much of an effect on her, but she's so skinny now. Her body can't process it like it used to.

She seems to quite like it anyway, the feeling it gives her. See, she's lifting the bottle to her lips, drinking it like it's water, smiling with her eyes closed and the moon on her face, as the fire floods through her body, numbing everything it touches, burning the nerve endings, dulling her pain. So much pain. She doesn't think it will ever go away.

She hears her phone go off in her pocket, pulls it out, closes her eyes to summon the strength to look at it. What she reads makes her howl, like a wounded animal. Then she's falling, rolling, bouncing to the bottom of the bank, onto the sand.

And there she lays, on her back. Weirdly, she's laughing. It's the laugh of someone who thinks they have nothing left to lose. She lifts her head and stares, mesmerised, at the waves breaking on the shore.

Chapter forty-four

From: Finn_the_finster@gmail.com
To: ZoeCalloway@hotmail.com
Subject: Why?

Do you know what I've realised tonight, Zoe? That the only thing worse than someone breaking up with you is someone thinking that you're not even worth breaking up with. That you're not worth an explanation, an apology, or even a goodbye.

It's 3 a.m. I think. Maybe that's a 2. It's hard to tell because the numbers on my phone, and these words, are a little bit blurry and they keep going in and out of focus, which is really annoying. I've just been around almost every bar in the city. All the ones near your old apartment, anyway. You never said whether you had a local, so I cast the net wide, starting at the bar where we met.

Do you ever think about that night? YOU asked me to kiss YOU, remember? I didn't even question it. It's something I thought I'd always be proud of; that I seized the moment. A story for the grandkids. We would have had cute kids, Zoe. I know it's not cool for a guy to say something like that. To admit he's thought about what his babies would look like with someone. But I had a lot of time to think, in Africa when I was biking. Not much else to do but think.

Now, I have this awful feeling that the moment I was so proud of is going to end up being one of my biggest regrets. Definitely the source of my biggest hurt. That's for fucking sure.

More than once tonight I saw someone with the same colour hair as you, or a similar hairstyle, and I thought, there you are. And each time I'd freeze to the spot, my heart in my mouth, convinced that I was about to come face to face with you. But then the woman would turn around, and it wasn't you, and my heart got ripped into a million pieces all over again.

Now I'm at the fountain, our fountain. It's a cold night, but I don't feel cold. I don't feel anything, except lost. I know that sounds dramatic, but that's what you've driven me to. Melodrama and drinking. Feel guilty? Good. Because you're the only one who can fix what you've broken. I need you to fix me, Zoe.

There's hardly any stars. In Africa, there were more stars than I've ever seen. More than I even knew existed, scattered across the sky from horizon to horizon. Some nights, I would sleep outside underneath them. When the weather was OK and I was too tired to put the tent up. I'd stare up at them and think about you. About how crazy everything was. Because it was crazy. If anyone else told me the story of us? I wouldn't believe them. Hell no. Meeting and falling that hard for someone, so quickly?

Nah. That stuff doesn't happen. Only in movies and books. But that night, it did happen. For me anyway. And I thought it did for you too, but I was obviously wrong about that. Because you're not here. And I don't know where you are.

You know how people say they see their whole life flash before their eyes when they're near death? When you asked me to kiss you and I looked into your eyes for the first time, I saw my future flash before me. Not snapshots or specific moments, but a sense. That this was it. You were it.

I know I'm probably not making any sense. I've had too much to drink, but also not enough. If I fall asleep here, maybe I'll get hypothermia. Maybe I'll die. Would you care then, Zoe? I don't care about anything, except finding you.

I want to know, I need to know. What did I do wrong? If you've changed your mind, I can handle it. It will hurt, sure. Horribly so. But eventually, I'd be OK.

But this? This is fucking torture.

I'm not giving up on you.

On us.

Chapter forty-five

'You're the weirdest-looking mermaid I've ever seen,' a voice remarks drily, dragging me out of the deep, alcohol-induced sleep I've been languishing in. I open my eyelids and then immediately shut them again.

'Oh fuck. Too bright,' I mutter. My tongue feels swollen and thick, and dry as a desert, and there's someone in my head bashing a hammer against my skull. It's been a while since I've had a hangover, and it takes me a moment to recognise it for what it is. 'Where am I?'

'On the beach.'

I frown, still without opening my eyes, trying to recall the events of the night before. It comes to me in a rush. The reunion. As soon as that piece of the puzzle falls into place, the rest follows quickly. Brian. The whisky. An email from Finn. A series of bad choices.

'Did you wash up out of the sea during the night?' the voice, a female, asks. She speaks slowly, sounding out every word carefully. 'I read a thriller like that once. This woman washed ashore on a foreign beach, with no idea who she was or how she got there. She'd been shot three times, but they had to figure out by who, and why.' She pauses. 'You do know you're missing a leg, right?'

Despite myself, I chuckle at the absurdity of the question. 'Yes. I'm well aware of that fact, thank you.'

'Oh good. I'd hate to be the one to have to break it to you that you were the victim of some international, leg-thieving organisation.'

'Does such a thing exist?'

'Dunno. Would make a cool book though.'

I groan a reply, feeling like if I move even an inch, I'll throw up. My body is one giant ache and, now that I'm awake, I'm acutely aware of how bloody freezing it is. My denim jacket even has dew on it. I need my bed, and medication. Stat.

'How'd you lose it?'

'Are you always so blunt with people you don't know?'

'How am I being blunt? I'm only asking a question.'

'Shark attack.'

'Seriously?' She sounds impressed. 'That is an epically cool injury story.'

With effort, I prise open one eyelid to look up at her. It takes my eyes a few moments to adjust to the light. The sun, as wintery pale as it is, hangs in the sky directly behind her, so at first all I can make out is a vague silhouette. I blink a few times to bring it into focus.

'Hi,' the girl smiles, giving a little wave. 'I'm Katie. You don't look so healthy, by the way.'

I can't help it, bubbles of disbelieving laughter boil up out of me, even though it hurts. 'Thanks.'

My phone vibrates, and I pull it out of my pocket, remembering that after Finn's email I'd turned the sound off. 'Sorry, hang on a sec.'

It's Dad. No doubt he's discovered that I didn't come home last night and is concerned as to my whereabouts. It's natural, of course, but I can't help feeling annoyed. I'm twenty-eight years old. Other twenty-eight-year-olds go out and stay out all night, do they have to deal with questioning phone calls from their parents the next morning? Not likely. Why should I? Swiping left to reject the call, I slide the phone back into my pocket and turn my attention to Katie.

'Where were we?'

She gives me a knowing look. 'You were about to tell me the real version of how you lost your leg.'

'Didn't believe the shark story, huh?'

'Nope, not for a second.'

'I lost it in an accident. Not looking where I was going. Walked out in front of a van.'

'Ouch.' She studies the stump curiously. 'Does it hurt?'

'Sometimes,' I admit. 'But the phantom pain from the part of my leg that's no longer there is worse.'

She nods. 'I've heard of that. It's actually real? You can feel your foot, even though it's not there anymore?'

'Oh, it's real all right,' I answer resentfully. 'I can even feel myself wriggling my toes. I wish it wasn't. It's like someone peeled all the skin off and stuck my leg into a naked flame. Some nights it hurts so much that I even wish I'd ...' I was going to say 'died instead'. But it feels wrong to say it in front of someone so young.

'Died?' she guesses anyway.

One of my crutches is nearby, within reach. Once I have it, I roll onto my hands and knees and push up carefully, the way the occupational therapist in the hospital showed me how to do. It was one of the most important moves to learn, she'd told me, because you'll probably fall a lot and need to get yourself back up. At the time, I thought she was exaggerating, but I've fallen at least once a day since getting home to my father's.

'What does whisky taste like?'

I follow the line of her eyesight to the bottle in the sand beside me. It's empty. No wonder I feel so rough. Bending down, I pick up the bottle. 'Disgusting stuff. You should never touch it.'

'Oh, hey, Linda.' I hear her say, and I squeeze my eyes shut and say a silent prayer that there might be two Lindas living in the vicinity. Opening my eyes again, I take a deep breath and turn, my heart sinking. No such luck. It's Dad's Linda, standing at the top of the bank and looking down at us, my other crutch in her hand.

'Hello, Zoe,' she says.

Chapter forty-six

I summon up a weak smile. 'Linda. Hi. What a weird coincidence, running into you here.'

I remember I'm still holding the whisky bottle, and quickly tuck it behind my back.

'Not that weird. You're right in front of my house and I'm heading out for my morning swim. Is your father with you?'

'Um,' I frown, pretending to look over both shoulders. 'Nope, nope. I don't think so. Not unless he's hiding.'

'I didn't realise you were so mobile, yet,' Linda says to me. 'Are you allowed to be out on your own?'

My hackles rise. 'Allowed?'

She corrects herself quickly. 'Is it safe, I mean, for you to be out and about on your own.'

'As safe as it is for you.'

My phone buzzes again, and I realise that if I don't answer soon, Dad will probably call the police to report me missing. I sigh. 'Fine. If you must know, I got a little lost last night, on the way home from my school reunion.'

'Might have something to do with all the whisky you drank,' Katie says helpfully.

'Yes, possibly,' I reply through gritted teeth.

Linda looks concerned. 'A taxi didn't leave you this far away from your house and expect you to make the rest of the journey on your own, did they? I know they complained about the state of some of these coastal roads at the last council meeting, but that's not on.'

'We have taxis in this town now?' Information I wish I'd known last night.

'Sure. It's not a big company,' she clarifies. 'Four drivers, two brothers and a couple of their friends. They only work on an on-call basis. It wouldn't be the first time I'd heard a complaint about them.'

'Well, unfortunately I had no idea they existed, so no. It wasn't them.'

Her concern deepens. 'Someone else abandoned you on the road, half a mile from your house? Who on earth would do that?'

'Look, it's a long and boring story, and I'm cold and tired.' I stifle a yawn. 'I've had a rough night. All I want to do is get home, shower and fall into my bed for a few weeks.'

She's clearly torn between wanting to respect my wishes and her desire to find out who treated me so badly, but in the end, she drops it. 'Fine. I guess we'd better get you home then.'

Realising I'm in no position to refuse her help, I give a tight, grateful smile. 'Thanks.'

Katie reaches out to take the whisky bottle. I hang on to it, flashing a guilty look at Linda.

'Don't worry,' she says. 'I'm not judging you. Made plenty of dumb choices myself, when I was younger. But you're going to have to let it go if you want to get back up this bank again. Katie can take the bottle up and put it in the trash for you.'

'Thanks,' I mutter to Katie, releasing the bottle.

'It's fine,' she shrugs. 'Nice to have a bit of excitement around here for a change.' She grins as she heads off along the beach. 'See you around.'

With Linda supporting my arm, we make our way back down the beach a small way to where the bank isn't anywhere near as steep and there's a small path carved into the dune by people using the reserve for beach access. She hovers behind me, her hands on my lower back supportively, as I awkwardly climb the path. When I stumble, she gently offers support. Once we're back up to the grassy reserve she guides me towards the road, then down her driveway to her cottage. By the time we get there, I'm sweating hard, sore and exhausted.

My phone buzzes again as we reach the side of her little white Suzuki Swift. This time I answer it, but don't give my father a chance to get a word in.

'Everything's fine,' I say curtly. 'I'll be home in a minute. Call off the dogs.' Then I disconnect.

'I'll get the keys from inside and then we'd better go,' says Linda. 'Knowing your father, he's probably worried.'

'Doubt it,' I say without thinking.

She pauses on the path, her back to me. 'I know you think he doesn't care, Zoe. But he does. Far more than you realise. You should cut him some slack. He's trying.' Then she continues walking and disappears inside her house, while I stand there feeling sheepish, like I've been told off. Which I have. She re-emerges without saying anything and pushes the button to unlock the car, then holds open the door while I climb inside.

214

'I'm sorry you missed out on your swim,' I say to break the silence, when we're on the road.

'Oh, I'll still go,' she smiles. 'A little bit later than normal, but that doesn't matter.'

'When I lived here before, I used to think you were so crazy, out there even on cold, rainy days.'

'A lot of people do,' she shrugs.

'I prefer being warm, myself. Not freezing my arse off on purpose.'

'It's cold, sure, but you soon get used to it. After that, well, it's addictive. Cold-water swimming is good for you, it provides pain relief and improves your general overall wellbeing.'

'Pain relief,' I snort. 'Yeah, right.'

'I heard you tell Katie that you're having phantom pains.'

'That was a private conversation.'

'I know, and I'm sorry for eavesdropping. Have you told your father?'

'No, and I'm not going to. I can handle it on my own.'

'Why? When you don't need to? I know what it's like living with chronic pain and if there is something that can help you, you should—'

'What would you know about pain,' I cut her off.

'I have rheumatoid arthritis. I know it's not the same as what you've been through, but I do have an inkling of what it's like.'

'I didn't know,' I grunt begrudgingly.

'There's a lot of things about me you don't know.' She flicks me a sideways smile that I don't return. 'But I'm hoping that will change. One day. No pressure from me.'

I swallow hard and look away from her, watching hedges and letterboxes flash past my window. Within a minute, she pulls

215

into Dad's driveway. The front door of the house opens, like he's been hovering at the window, and he walks out, concern and confusion etched on his face as he walks across the lawn to meet us.

Linda turns the car off and I reach to unclick my seat belt, jumping when she places a hand on mine. 'Zoe, I want you to know that I care about your father, a lot. He's not a bad guy, just someone who made some not-so-good choices once upon a time. But you have to remember, alcoholism is an addiction. He's told me how many times he tried to stop, to get help, how he knew he was failing you. It's the biggest regret of his life.'

'He's never mentioned any of that to me.'

'He doesn't know how to. You scare him.'

'I scare him?'

She shakes her head. 'Not scare. Intimidate. Frankly, he's in awe of you. How well you've done for yourself, despite ... everything. You're a success story, Zoe, and he's incredibly proud of you. All he wants to do now is try and make amends for the past, but he knows that he can't expect you to forgive him overnight.'

I shake off her hand and release the seat belt. 'Let me stop you right there. You have no idea what things were like for me after Mum died. You've heard one side of the story – his. Please stop trying to fix things between us. Even if it were possible, it's not your place.'

I pick up the crutches and exit the car as quickly as I can, which is not that quick. Dad comes down the steps and holds his hand out to help, but I refuse it.

'Where'd you get to all night?' The worry is heavy in his voice, and I'm taken aback by it. When I was a teenager, I could disappear to a friend's house for an entire weekend and he'd barely even notice, let alone worry.

'Out.'

Linda gets up, standing between her door and the car and looking at us over the roof.

His face falls, knowing he doesn't have the right to ask any more questions. 'Fair enough. Reunion OK?'

'It was fine,' I lie. 'Good to see some of the people again.'

'You want some breakfast? I've got bacon, eggs and hash browns in the warmer drawer. Might be a bit chewy now, but still edible.'

The thought of the food makes my stomach churn queasily. 'No thanks, I'm not hungry. I just want a shower and then some sleep.'

'Righto.' He steps to the side so I can have clear access up the path. 'I'll try and keep the noise down.'

I frown. 'What noise?'

'Oh . . . ' He looks flustered. 'I was kidding around.'

We both stare at each other, a little disconcerted. Joking is something other fathers and daughters do, not us, historically. It's weird, to see him act jovial like that, but I don't hate it and that surprises me.

'Bye, Zoe,' Linda calls out. 'I hope you feel better after some sleep.'

Dad instantly appears concerned again. 'Are you sick?'

I glare at Linda. There's no way I'm telling him about the whisky, or sleeping on the beach. 'No, I'm not sick. I'm tired. Thanks for the ride, Linda, but you can get going now.'

Dad turns to her. 'Unless you'd like some of that breakfast I mentioned. It'll only go to waste otherwise.'

'Thanks, but I'm going to head back and have my swim. You know how grumpy I get when I miss one.'

She winks at him. Actually winks. I want to throw up.

'OK, well then how about dinner? Tonight?' He looks at me. 'If that's OK with you, Zoe?'

'It's your house. You don't need my permission.'

'I know I don't need permission, but this is your home too. I don't want to do anything you're not comfortable with.'

'She can come if she wants,' I shrug. 'I don't care.'

Chapter forty-seven

After showering, which is a marathon effort in itself and uses up the little energy I have left, I bury myself in the billowy comforter on my bed, and re-read the email from Finn, over and over, tears streaming down my face because he's hurting so much and it's all my fault.

I'm grateful that he can't see me now. What would he think about me getting into the car with Brian? Even though I know that what happened wasn't my fault, I still feel guilty for putting myself in that position in the first place. I thought I had a better sense of judgement than that, but clearly my instincts were also affected by the accident. I don't know what to think anymore. Who to trust. It's like everything in my life is falling apart, and I'm powerless to stop it. Eventually I fall asleep, to dream troubled dreams of being chased while in a wheelchair. No matter how hard I turn the wheels, it's not fast enough, and the faceless/nameless entity behind me keeps gaining. I hear them getting closer and closer until a hand clamps down hard on my shoulder and I wake up with a start, my heart pounding.

'Zoe?' Dad asks, his voice muffled through the door. 'I heard you yell out, are you OK?'

'Bad dream,' I call, though I can still feel the weight of the hand on my shoulder as if it were really there, and I even touch it with my own hand, to make sure.

'Can I come in?'

'No, I'm fine.' I roll over, pulling the blankets up to my ears. 'I'm going to try and go back to sleep.'

The handle turns, hesitantly, then the door inches open a crack, wide enough for Dad to poke his head through. 'Please?'

Resentfully, I sit up against the pillows and pull my comforter up under my chin. 'Doesn't seem like I have a choice.'

He chooses to ignore this, entering the room and walking across to sit on the end of my bed. He stares out the window at the churning sea. The wind has picked up while I've been asleep, and out at sea, a storm is gathering.

'Looks like we're in for a wild night,' he observes.

'Did you come in here to talk about the weather?'

He sighs heavily. 'No. Linda mentioned that you've been having those phantom pains the doctors warned us about.'

My face flushes angrily. 'She only found out because she was being a nosy cow. I told her it was none of her business. Or yours. I can handle it myself.'

'Please don't be mad at her. She's worried about you. We both are.'

'She doesn't need to worry about me,' I say exasperatedly. 'I don't care what you two do, but we're not a family. I don't need some kind of . . . ' I pull my hands out of the covers and flail them around. 'Surrogate mother. I had a mother. A great one, the best. I'm sure Linda is OK, but I wish she'd mind her own business and stay out of mine.'

'I know she's still a stranger to you, Zoe, but she's been there for me. We have a lot of fun together. She makes me feel things that I haven't felt in a very long time.'

I pull a face. 'And there I was thinking this day couldn't get any worse.'

He looks at me sadly. 'When you left, did you really expect me to live here by myself and be lonely for the rest of my life?'

'Did you expect me to stay here and look after you?'

'No,' he shakes his head vehemently. 'Definitely not. That's the last thing I wanted. When you left, I was so happy that you were getting out there in the world. Making a life for yourself. All I ever wanted was for you to be happy. And I knew you weren't, not here with me.'

'Dad.'

'No.' He puts a hand up to stop me. 'Please. I have things I need to say to you but for years I've known you didn't want to listen. As hard as that was, I respected it because it was your choice. But now I think that, by staying silent, I've done more harm than good.'

I look down at my bed, bracing myself for whatever comes next.

'When your mother died, I couldn't see how I'd ever be happy again. She was my first love, my first everything. I'd known her since I was nine years old, for Christ's sake. She'd been a big part of my life, so when she was gone, and so suddenly, it was like a massive hole suddenly opened up and swallowed her. One minute she was here; warm, laughing, burning the potatoes . . . '

I smile at the painful memory. My mother was famous for getting distracted and letting the vegetables boil dry.

'...and then the next, she was gone.'

'I know,' I say carefully, feeling the pain as fresh as I did the day she died. 'I was here too, remember?'

He rubs his eyes, the network of wrinkles in the skin around them a testament to his grief. 'I knew you were suffering too,' he goes on. 'Of course, you were. You lost your mother. But at the time, I was so focused on what I had lost, I didn't know how to help you. I felt like it should have been me who died. Like you were robbed twice over, because not only did you lose a parent, you lost the one who would have known how to carry on in that situation. Your mother had always been the one with the words. The one who knew how to make it better when you fell off your bike or had a bad day at school. She knew when you needed to hear words of comfort, or when you needed a hug. I didn't. I wanted desperately to make it all better for you, but I couldn't fix it. All that you wanted was your mother back, and that was the one thing I couldn't give you. I felt like I'd failed you as well as her.'

'You stopped caring about me,' I say, my voice low in anger. Remembering the pain of feeling unwanted.

'No,' he says vehemently, shaking his head. 'I never stopped caring about you. I can't believe you even thought that, Zoe. I've loved you since the moment you were born. This tiny, red blotchy thing that cried and cried. My God, you pretty much cried for the first two years of your life.' He smiles through his tears. 'But you were still the most precious thing I'd ever seen. The best thing I've ever done with my life, was making you.'

I swallow the lump in my throat, feeling vulnerable all over again. I want to believe what he's saying more than anything.

'Things weren't always bad,' he says earnestly. 'Don't you remember? When you were little? Don't you have any happy memories of me? Please, Zoe, think.'

I close my eyes, let the past in. Memories, the ones I've blocked out because of the way they make me feel, drift to the surface. The way he was always there come rain or shine on the sidelines, cheering me on at school sporting days, and Saturday-morning netball. How he used to sit at the kitchen table with me every night after dinner and help me with my homework. I had trouble with some of my numbers and letters, used to muddle them up and write them around the wrong way. Most children grow out of it, but I didn't. The teacher turned a blind eye, she had thirty kids to worry about and I kept doing it no matter how many times she crossed my work out in red pen. But not him. He would patiently go over them with me, every night, until eventually it became natural for me to write them the correct way.

I remember how every Christmas, he'd make a big deal out of it. We always had a real tree, a huge one. He'd put it up at the start of December so that we had the whole month to get in the Christmas spirit. Even though it would be half dead come Christmas day, he'd still insist we had it for the whole month. It was all about making it magical for me. The buckets of water for the reindeer, the cookies and milk for Santa. And in the morning, there would be footprints in the sand we'd sprinkled around the bucket of water for the reindeer. Easter there would be an egg hunt. Fireworks every Guy Fawkes.

'I do,' I say, choking back a sob. 'Of course, I remember the good times. That's what made it so hard to understand. After she died, all you seemed to care about was the next drink. I made my own school lunches, every day. My own dinners, most of the time. Bought my own clothes, took myself to the hairdresser. I finished my schooling without any help from you. Sure, you provided money when I needed it, but I dealt with everything else by myself. Including making sure you didn't drink yourself to death. We were like . . . strangers, living in the same house.'

'No, you're wrong. I didn't care about drinking, I hated drinking. It might have looked like I wanted to do it, but I didn't. Maybe at first, when it helped to numb my emotions and get me to sleep. I couldn't bear thinking about her, but I couldn't stop thinking about her. She was everywhere around me, everything we owned brought back a memory of her.' He looks down at his hands. They still shake, I notice, though not as much. 'And you reminded me so much of her too. You look like her, you even sound like her sometimes. The way you smile. The things you say. It was too painful. Alcohol helped me forget. And then, I don't know when or how it happened, it became more than that, and I couldn't stop. I couldn't get through a night without it. I'd try, but I couldn't. I was too weak. And too pathetic to admit that I was addicted. I told myself that I was fine, because I still went to work, most days anyway. I still paid the bills, kept food in the house. An alcoholic couldn't do that, that's what I convinced myself.'

'It takes more than paying the bills to be a father.'

'I know. And I knew that then. But I didn't know how to stop, so I could be the father you needed. The father you deserved.' He takes a deep breath and looks me straight in the eyes. 'And I'll never forgive myself for that, Zoe. Never. It doesn't matter what I've learned during my recovery about self-forgiveness. I don't deserve it, and I don't expect you to forgive me either. I blew the one good thing I had going in my life: you. Sometimes, I thank my lucky stars that I can't remember a lot of that time, because if I could, I don't know how I could live with myself.'

He buries his head in his hands and sobs. Guttural, chest-heaving, shoulder-shaking sobs. From the heart.

'You weren't that bad,' I say, after some hesitation. 'I mean, you were, but you could have been worse. You were absent, but never violent. Not towards me, anyway. You smashed the front window once, because you'd lost your keys. And you almost burned the house down a few times, leaving something on the oven when you fell asleep. We're lucky the house never burned down.'

'Nothing but pure dumb luck,' he mutters into his hands. 'I'm more ashamed of myself than you'll ever know.'

I feel myself soften, seeing how much he hates himself. 'Most of the time, you used to drink and cry till you passed out, and then I'd put you to bed or chuck a blanket over you wherever you lay.'

'I should never have put you in that position.'

'No. You shouldn't. But,' I take a deep breath, 'you were sick. That's something I didn't understand at the time. I thought you were doing it on purpose, because you wanted to. I thought you chose drinking over me.' I look down at my hands, twisting my fingers, remembering how much it hurt. 'But a therapist helped me to realise that alcoholism is an illness.'

He lifts his head up and looks at me with surprise. 'You saw a therapist?'

I nod. 'A couple of years after I moved to the city. It was like all the buried anger hit me at once and I knew that I either had to see someone, or I'd find myself heading down the same sort of path that you did.'

I don't go into specifics. It was a brief phase of reckless behaviour. I drank a bit too much, trying to discover what was so enticing about it, why he preferred it over me. I also had a couple of one-night stands, regretted the next morning. Worse, I took a pill I was offered at a club once, not even knowing what it was. When I think about it now, it feels like it all happened to a different person. It only lasted a few months, but it was like the normal Zoe took a holiday. Thankfully, I retained enough sense to realise it was a cry for help. Bonnie took me to a therapist, and I saw them weekly at first, then monthly, for two years, until I'd worked through most of my issues. Or at least I thought I had, but being back here seems to have wiped everything I learned in those therapy sessions clean away.

'I'm sorry you had to do that because of me.'

I shrug. 'It is what it is. We can't change it.'

I watch his hand lift tentatively and slowly move towards mine before it stops, scared, his fingers falling back to the bed. Taking a deep breath, I meet it halfway, laying my hand gently on his and giving a little squeeze, before quickly pulling it away again. It's fleeting contact but seems momentous.

He looks at me, his eyes shining bright with tears. 'I love you, Zoe. I always have, and I always will. And if you can find a way to … not forgive or forget, I don't expect that. But if we can move on from it, I'd like the chance to prove to you that I've changed. That I can be here for you now. Obviously, I wish you didn't need me, not in these circumstances. But you do, and I won't let you down again. I love you.' He says it so fiercely that I'm left with no doubt at all that he means it.

'Just because I can't say it back,' I mumble, 'doesn't mean I don't feel it. I need more time, that's all.'

'I can wait,' he says, his voice wobbly with emotion. 'I'm not going anywhere.'

Chapter forty-eight

From: Finn_the_finster@gmail.com
To: ZoeCalloway@hotmail.com
Subject: have you ever been arrested?

Because I have, now. Well, cautioned. I guess I should have expected it. Loitering outside a ladies' gym all day and hassling everyone who entered is dodgy behaviour, however way you want to look at it.

It's winter. It's rained all week. People are wearing beanies, or hooded jumpers or big jackets with the hoods well over their heads to keep the rain off. It makes it hard to pick out faces, you know? I stood in the doorway of the gym you showed me, the one you said that you and Bonnie are members of, determined to check the face of every single woman who entered. But because of the hoods, this wasn't so easy. In hindsight, I can understand why some of the women thought I was 'crazy' and 'intimidating'. But I was desperate. I am desperate.

228

See, I don't have many clues left to find you. Like a trail of breadcrumbs that are being picked off one by one by a horrible black crow in a dark, demented fairy tale, the trail is getting smaller and narrower and colder, and my fear is getting worse and I can barely sleep or eat and I don't even know if my thoughts are rational or not anymore.

It's the not knowing that hurts.

Not knowing whether you're OK. Not knowing if I did something, or if you think I did something, but it's all a big misunderstanding and if I could only see you, talk to you, we'd figure it all out and everything would be OK again. See? It all keeps going around and around in my head like a big jumbled mess and I can't stop it, or understand it, or forget about you. That's what everyone keeps telling me to do. They reckon that anyone who could do this to someone they said they loved isn't worth it.

But you are worth it. I know you are. I know that we only knew each other physically for a few days, but in a way, I think that was a good thing. Because we had four months to get to know each other without that distraction. In our messages, our calls, I told you things I've never told anyone. I trusted you. I knew you felt the same.

Now I don't know anything anymore.

The apartment was a dead end. The bars were a dead end, although I'm not giving up, and I'll keep checking them, every Friday and Saturday night, searching for you.

They'll arrest me for trespassing if I go back to the gym. Not that there's much point – a couple of the women said they knew who you are, but not, crucially, where you are. They said they haven't seen you for a few months, or Bonnie. So, now I know that you've moved, you've stopped going to your gym. It's like I'm slowly being fed the pieces of a puzzle, but now I need to figure out how it all fits together, and then, maybe ... maybe, I'll figure out what happened to you.

It's all I have. All I can do.

I won't give up.

Chapter forty-nine

'Something smells delicious,' says Linda, sniffing the air with enthusiasm, arriving on the dot of six.

After the heart-to-heart with Dad, I pretty much alternated between crying, thinking and sleeping all afternoon. Hearing what he had to say had been cathartic for me, and I felt like I'd released some of the pain that I've been holding on to. Not all, not by a long shot. But some. Maybe that means the healing process has finally started. Only time will tell.

'Thanks for noticing,' my father says. 'I bought a new aftershave.'

Linda groans, while I look around the room as if I've been transported to an alternative universe. My father makes jokes? Twice in one day?

The house is bright and cheerful, the radio playing softly in the background and the air hazy with cooking smells. It's a stark contrast to the dark, cold and silent house I'm used to. It's weird but in a not entirely unpleasant way.

'Tough crowd.' He sighs theatrically. 'I hope you're both in the mood for sausages and chips.'

'Really push the boat out when you have company, don't you?' I say.

He waves his tongs at me. 'For your information, these happen to be the finest venison sausages that money can buy. And I made the chips myself. Hand cut. Seasoned with my own secret herb mix.'

'I made a chocolate cake for afterwards,' Linda says, placing a cling-film-wrapped plate on the bench. My father reaches for it and she slaps his hand lightly. 'Fingers off my icing, mister.'

He winks at her like it's some kind of euphemism, and I realise there are so many layers to their relationship that I'm not yet privy too. It clearly runs much deeper than what I thought. It's hard for me to face, even harder to accept. But I need to, for my own sake.

'Food's almost ready. Everyone take a seat at the table.'

I take my place at one end, where there's less chance of my leg being bumped, and also room for me to lie my crutches on the floor beside me. Linda sits on my left, leaving the other end of the table empty for Dad. He's put a lot of care into setting the table, I note. Even rustled up a pale blue tablecloth from somewhere. The cutlery is laid out, there is a glass of water in front of each setting and sauce bottles are ready in the middle.

'Grub's up.' Dad plonks the plates down in front of us proudly. He's done a pretty good job with the chips. Rough cut and still with the skin on, they look golden and crunchy, the way Mum used to do them. I wonder whether it's a fluke, or whether he remembered.

For a while, there's nothing but the sound of appreciative chewing, and then Dad clears his throat. 'How was your swim this morning?'

'Incredible, as always,' Linda replies. 'Nothing can beat the way you feel afterwards.'

'Why don't you tell Zoe a bit more about the benefits?' he says, in the world's worst acting voice.

'I can do better than that.' She puts down her cutlery and fishes around in the tote bag she'd brought with her, producing a load of papers and a magazine which she drops on the table and nudges in my direction.

Sensing a set-up, I put down my knife and fork. 'What's that.'

'Literature,' she says. 'If you won't believe me, you might believe science. These are some articles on cold-water swimming.'

'I'm not interested. And anyway,' I give Linda a pointed look. 'You shouldn't eavesdrop on private conversations. And you definitely shouldn't blab about anything you do hear.'

Linda puts down her own fork and gives me a level look. 'I told your dad that you're still in pain, yes. I thought that he had a right to know.'

'We want to help,' Dad says. 'That's all.'

'And I wouldn't suggest you come swimming with me if I didn't think it could help,' Linda adds.

'I told you, I don't do cold.'

'Some mornings, yes, it can be hard to get in. But you have to push through that. Because once you're in the water, you soon forget about the temperature and start to enjoy yourself and the benefits. And believe me, there are benefits. Proven ones. And not only for physical pain.' She points at her temple. 'Wild swimming can help up here too.'

I take offence at what she's implying. 'I'm not crazy.'

'Of course not. I meant with overall mental health. For

233

anyone, whatever their situation. It's obvious that you're struggling with a huge sense of loss . . .'

My heart starts pounding. Is she talking about Finn? If my
father has told her about him, it will be the ultimate betrayal.
Finn is my secret.

'. . . the loss of your life as you knew it,' she goes on, and I
feel intense relief flood through me. 'It's a traumatic change for
you. I think swimming might help, give you something else to
focus on. What have you got to lose?'

I scramble around in my head for an excuse, but can't find one
that I haven't already used, so I fall back on it. 'But it'll be cold.'

'Have you ever heard of Wim Hof's cold therapy?'

'No.'

'He was a Dutch athlete, also known as The Iceman. He was
renowned for his ability to withstand freezing temperatures.'

'Purely for the hell of it? Sounds like a fun guy to have
at parties.'

'Come on, Zoe. Like Linda says, you've got nothing to lose
by trying it at least once.'

'I don't have a bathing suit.'

'That's no problem.' Linda smiles the smile of someone who
senses victory. 'You can borrow one of mine.'

Chapter fifty

'This was a stupid idea,' I say petulantly, shivering. 'I want to go back to bed.'

'Come on,' Dad coaxes. 'You're here now, you may as well see it through.'

It's barely six, the sky is still quite dark, and I'm already in a foul mood, not helped by the fact that I hardly slept. After Linda left the night before, I'd checked my emails and found another message from Finn. It was heartbreaking, and he was clearly in a bad headspace. Half of what he said barely even made any sense. It didn't sound like the Finn I knew at all. He's obviously struggling, and I hate that I'm the one who's done this to him.

A cold wind blows in off the sea and I shiver again. I'm wearing a bathing suit that Linda brought with her. A sensible, unremarkable black number, with a big, slouchy jersey for warmth and shorts over the top. It's not shorts weather, but back in the warmth of the house, I figured they'd be easier to slip out of on the beach than a pair of track pants. Why risk falling flat on my face while hopping about on one leg trying to get pants off, if I can avoid it? I already feel conspicuous enough, and there's no one else around, because no one else is stupid enough to be preparing to swim in an icy cold ocean at dawn on a wintery morning.

'You ready?' Dad asks.

'Nope. Can we just get this over with?'

Dad takes his jersey off and then slides down a pair of track-suit pants. I'm surprised to see that he's wearing a pair of board shorts underneath.

'Are you coming in too?'

'Of course.' He stretches his arms above his head and to the sides a few times, like he's an Olympic swimmer limbering up beside a pool. 'As if I'd make you do this alone.'

When he's finished stretching, he helps me up, then lifts my left arm and places it around his neck, over his shoulders. Placing his right arm around my hip, he supports some of my weight as we hop/shuffle down the sand towards the water. I must admit that it feels nice to have something other than plastic or wooden floors underfoot again. Like I'm reconnecting with nature.

At the water's edge, I burrow my toes into the sand and enjoy the sensation. Taking a deep breath, I focus on the water. It's calm today, the surface unblemished. No surf breakers, just knee-high waves that swell and bob their way through the water then rush gently onto the beach where they are reabsorbed into the sand.

'I don't know if I can do this,' I say hesitantly, suddenly filled with fear. I have visions of sinking to the bottom, or being swept out to sea and being unable to swim myself back in. Going around in circles instead with my one foot.

'Yes, you can,' Linda says firmly, coming to stand beside me. 'And we'll be right here with you the whole time, so if you need help, ask.'

They're not going to give up, so I nod. 'OK.'

Dad and Linda scoop up my arms over their shoulders, and with my toes stepping on the sand, we take our first tentative steps into the water.

It's cold. Really, really cold.

'Fucking hell,' I squeal as the water bubbles around my ankle.

'Relax,' Linda coaches. 'Try and steady your breathing. It's better to immerse yourself slowly, acclimatise your body step by step.'

'We can stop here if you like,' Dad offers, as the water reaches our thighs. Linda frowns at him.

I can hardly talk, my teeth are chattering so much, but I shake my head. The water is painful, like thousands of needles poking into my body. The further we go in, the further the pain advances until we are in up to our chests and my whole body feels like it's on fire. And then it flips. No longer pain, but not quite pleasure either. Somewhere on the edge in between. It's the weirdest sensation I've ever felt.

I can't relax, worried that I'll be swept off my foot, so when the waves wash back out and the sand shifts I cling to Linda and my father harder, but the deeper we get, the more control over my body I begin to feel. It's the strangest thing, but if I focus hard, it feels as if my leg is still there. For the first time, I don't immediately feel my disability. It's no longer overriding everything else, instead it kind of recedes into the background and I feel like me again.

We stop when the water is at my shoulders, and I wait there

until my heart rate settles and my body adjusts to this new environment.

'OK, I'm ready. Let me go.'

Linda does so without question, lifting my arm off and gently moving away from me. She does a dolphin dive under a small wave and emerges, gasping briefly, then smiling at me encouragingly.

'You're doing amazing,' she says.

My father is more reluctant to let go. 'Are you sure?' he asks protectively. 'You don't want to get ahead of yourself. Maybe this first time I should stay with you, for support.'

'Dad. Please. You got me out here, now let me do this my way.'

'All right.' Reluctantly he releases me, ducking down and out from under my arm, disappearing into the dark water. He surfaces and shakes water from his hair, bobbing nearby, watching. Clearly nervous. I wait to feel unbalanced without his support, but surprisingly, I don't. My arms move in gentle circles through the water around me, keeping me steady. I slowly lift my foot from the ocean bottom and can't stop a smile forming when the embrace of the water keeps me from falling over. Since the accident, it's all been about balance, and when I haven't got that right, I've fallen. And the more I've fallen, the less I've been inclined to push myself or take chances. I've been playing it safe. In here, the water supports me. I feel buoyant, light and free.

I laugh, I properly, honestly, unashamedly laugh. It bubbles out of me, erupting joyfully as I swim around, using my leg to kick and my arms to pull me forward, the way I would have done before the accident. It doesn't feel anywhere near as weird or as scary as I'd feared. The opposite, in fact, and like Linda said, I forget about the cold and focus on how amazing it feels. Flipping over onto my back I float, rising up and down as the waves pass underneath me, watching the colours slowly seep into the dawn sky. I imagine I am out here alone, strong, capable and brave, like the Zoe I was before. Then I realise something. The pain in my stump has gone. For the first time, I can't feel anything.

On my back, I don't notice the wave coming. At the last second, I hear something and turn my head to the side – and there it is towering above me, its edge foaming as it curls and breaks and sends me plummeting underneath the water, spinning until I don't know which way is up and which way is down. Everything is dark and turbulently violent. In that moment, I honestly feel like death has come to finish off the job it failed to do the first time. That the universe is angry because I've been wasting the second chance at life I was given. I don't see my life flash before me, but I do see Finn. His smiling face fills my mind, giving me the strength I need.

My lungs are burning, they want air. Every instinct in my body is screaming at me to breathe, but I know that if I open my mouth and breathe in the water it will all be over. I don't want to die. Not today, not like this. I start kicking my foot and flailing, trying to find the bottom so I can push myself up. I feel hands on my arms, pulling me up until my head breaks out through the surface of the water and I take a huge, gasping breath of the sweetest air I've ever tasted in my life.

Coughing and spluttering, I hang on to my rescuer, Dad, as he holds me close and makes soothing noises.

'Are you OK?' Linda is beside me, her face creased with concern. 'I'm so sorry, Zoe, I should have warned you to watch out for rogue waves, we sometimes get them with a southerly wind.'

'You think?' I splutter. 'I ... told ... you ... this ... was ... a ... stupid ... idea.'

'Please don't let one silly wave put you off,' she says. 'It took you by surprise, I know. But don't give up now.'

'She can if she wants,' my father gently disagrees.

'No, she's right,' I say weakly. 'Before the accident, I was never one to give up at the first hurdle. I need to find that part of me again.'

He's not happy about it, but he understands. 'It's up to you, of course. As long as you're OK.'

I rest my head on his chest, his arms around me. A sense of déjà vu washes over me. Being held like this when I was a little girl. Feeling safe, the way I do now.

'Thank you, for saving me.'

He kisses the top of my head fervently, and it doesn't feel as weird as I would have thought. 'For the record, I think in another ten seconds you would have saved yourself. You were doing well there.'

'Maybe,' I say, feeling numb. 'But thanks all the same.'

He supports me on one side, Linda on the other, and we head for shore. 'I told you I'd never let you down,' he says. 'And I meant it.'

I hate to admit that Linda was right, but for the rest of the day I feel a weird kind of exhilaration. My skin is bright red and tingly, but I have no pain. I didn't hate the swim as much as I thought I was going to. So when that night Dad asks me if I want to keep doing it, I nod.

Chapter fifty-one

'I saw him.'

I don't need to ask Bonnie who she's talking about, I know straight away who she means. My stomach clenches, and my heart feels like it might palpitate out of my chest and right through my ribcage.

'Zoe? Did you hear me?'

'When? Where?'

'He showed up at work today. Luckily, I saw him coming through the window so I had time to duck into the storeroom. I told Dani to tell him that I no longer worked there.'

'And? Do you think he believed her?'

'I don't know. I think so. He seemed devastated. Kept asking if she knew where I'd gone, or if she knew you. Said he was trying to track you down and that I was his only chance. I swear to God, he looked so broken that she almost caved.'

I squeeze my eyes shut. 'How did he look?'

'I told you. Completely broken.'

'No, I mean physically.'

'Not great,' she admits. 'Sad. I don't think he's looking after himself very well. Zoe, I think you need to tell him about what happened. This is too cruel.'

'I can't, you know that.'

'I know you think you can't. But just because he said that one comment about his sister, doesn't mean he'll feel the same way when it's you.'

'I can't take that chance.'

'He deserves to know.'

'Of course, he does,' I snap angrily. 'It's not like I'm doing this on purpose to be cruel. I'm trying to protect him. Once he knows, he'll feel like he has to stay with me, even though he'll hate every second of it, because he's that kind of guy. I can't live the life he wants to live, or do the things he wants to do anymore, that's simply the way it is. I'm not going to hold him back.'

'Have you thought any more about having the operation?'

I don't answer straight away, because I don't want to get her hopes up. But truthfully, since the almost drowning at the beach (which, according to Linda, lasted less than ten seconds and wasn't as dramatic as it felt), I have been thinking about it. I've been thinking about it a lot. I realised that in that moment, I panicked. If I'd still had two legs, it probably wouldn't have been a problem at all, but with one leg, I felt completely helpless. But every time I think about having the operation, I can't get that voice out of my head . . . what if I die?

'Maybe,' I say. 'But I don't want to talk about it.'

She sighs. 'I miss you.'

'I miss you too.'

'How are things going with your dad?'

Bonnie is one of only three people in the world who knows

how bad things were after my mother died and how much it affected me. The second one is my therapist, and the third person is Finn, though he has a condensed, filtered version. It was somehow easier to pour it all out over the phone to his sympathetic ear than talking to anyone in real life had ever been.

'Things are … OK,' I confess. 'Better than I ever thought they could be. He's sober, has been for a few years apparently. He's trying hard to make up for everything.'

'That's wonderful. Do you think you'll ever be able to have a close relationship with him again?'

'Maybe? I kind of do. Sort of. I don't know. It's hard to trust him again. He's promised so much in the past and failed to follow through. But this time does seem different. And get this: he's found himself a girlfriend.'

'No way,' she gasps breathily. 'Go him.'

'Yes way.'

'Is it weird? It sounds weird. I think it would be weird.'

'It's weird,' I admit.

'What's her name? Is she nice?'

'Her name is Linda, and she's … OK.'

'You don't sound sure.'

'I wasn't. It was horrible at first, seeing her in my mother's house, with my father. I was a bit of a brat about it, to be honest.'

'I can imagine.'

'Shut up.'

'And now?'

'Now? She's kind of growing on me. She makes him happy, and I guess that's all that matters at the end of the day.'

'I suppose so. I mean, there's no age limit on happiness, is there,' she agrees sagely.

243

'Oh, how I've missed your clichés.'

She laughs. 'Hey, I was thinking Josh and I might come up and see you soon. His boss has told him to book in a couple of his annual leave weeks. Would that be OK? Is there room at your place for us to crash?'

'Yeah, of course,' I reply happily. 'I'd love that.'

But then I get off the phone after we chat for a while longer, and I realise it's not the best idea. What would we even do? They'd be bored stiff, coming here and spending a week sitting around the house with me. Sure, we could go into town, but it's not like there's heaps of things to look at or do there. Even the old cinema has closed down. They could go for walks along the (cold, forsaken) beach if they wanted, but I wouldn't be able to join them. How can I tell her no, though? I want to see her. She's the only link I have left to my old life. The only person with a physical connection to both Finn and me. It's not much, but it feels like all I have left.

Chapter fifty-two

A couple of days later, when I get out of the water, Olivia is sitting on the beach. Dad helps me up to my towel and I wrap it around myself hurriedly, sitting down to pull on my shorts.

'You're nuts,' she says quietly.

'Excuse me?'

'For swimming, I mean. Isn't the water cold?'

'Yeah,' I reply, a little sarcastically. 'It's cold. Usually is in winter.'

'I couldn't do it.' She picks up a shell and tosses it towards the water but it falls a few metres short.

'What are you doing here, Olivia?'

'I came to see if you were all right.'

'Why wouldn't I be?'

'Dr Ashton said you switched to home visits. I wondered if that was because you were avoiding me.'

I shrug my jersey on over my head and poke my arms through the holes. 'No, it's just easier.'

She stares at my leg. 'Is it sore?'

'Sometimes.'

'The reunion was a bit of a success, don't you think,' she says brightly, but it's an insincere brightness.

I give her a level look. 'That depends entirely on what your definition of success is.'

She deflates right in front of me. 'Yeah. You're right. It was a complete shit show.'

She looks so miserable, I take pity on her. 'It wasn't that bad. The drinks were cheap, food was pretty good, and it was nice to see some of those faces again.'

'It's crazy how much some people have changed,' she agrees. 'And yet others look like they've barely aged at all. Bastards.'

'Did you come all the way out here to make small talk?'

'No. I came to apologise.'

'For what?'

'The awards mess. We didn't even think about how you might not want to get up in front of everyone. Honestly, Kylie and I, we meant well.'

'I know you did. But yeah, I didn't appreciate the attention. Do you know, up until that point that was the first night since my accident when I'd felt almost like myself again?'

'And we ruined it.'

I tilt my head. 'Well, you and some other people. Yeah.'

She gives me a shrewd look. 'You mean Brian?'

I check to see if Dad is still within earshot, but he and Linda have retreated to a respectable distance, near the house. Talking to each other quietly while they wait. 'Yes, Brian. What was up with that, anyway? You were acting like you had a crush on him all night.'

She shudders, looking ashamed. 'I know. I wasn't half obvious, was I.'

'You're married.'

'It's . . . complicated. We haven't been happy for a long time. Got married too young. I feel like I missed out on life, and I guess sometimes, when I'm drinking usually, I try and make up for it.'

'There's probably ways to do that without cheating on your spouse.'

'Don't judge me, Zoe. You've got no idea what it's like to be so unhappy every day.'

My eyebrows shoot up. 'No. My life is a fucking pony ride.'

She screws up her nose. 'Right. Sorry. I know things are hard for you. But before that you must have had an awesome life in the city.'

'If you hate this town so much, why don't you leave?'

She looks genuinely surprised. 'I don't hate this town.'

'You don't?'

'It's not as bad as you act like it is, Zoe. Sure, it's suffering. But so are a lot of places around the country during these tough economic times. We'll bounce back, we always do. But behind the empty shops, there's a community of people all looking out for one another. Supporting each other. We're a small town with a big heart.'

'Three seconds ago, you told me you were miserable and considering cheating on your husband.'

'That's nothing to do with the town though, and it happens way more than you think. Wait until you're married – it isn't all surprise flowers and hot sex every night. That shit wears off, and it wears off pretty quick, especially when kids come along.'

'Olivia, you chose that life. I'm not going to feel sorry for you.

247

If you're not happy, do something to change it. But do it the honest way. At least give your kids a mum they can be proud of.'

She gets to her feet and brushes the sand off her trousers. 'A teacher never stops thinking about kids, eh?'

'No.' I feel a pang in my heart. I miss teaching. I miss the children in my class, and the class itself. I loved decorating the walls, making cosy corners for the kids to read and play. I wanted them to feel happy there, comfortable. I even miss the routine of it all.

'I have to get to work,' Olivia says, pulling her phone out of the pocket on her puffer jacket and checking the time. 'I only wanted to make sure you were OK.'

I give a little wave to Dad, who starts heading down the beach to help me up. 'Thanks, that's nice of you. I'm fine.'

She stands over me and lowers her voice. 'Zoe, I hate to ask, but ... did Brian ... did he try anything?'

'Why are you asking me that?'

'I ran into Nick at the supermarket, and he said that Brian's facing sexual harassment charges back in the UK. Apparently, he assaulted another player's wife when she was drunk. After that news got out, two other women also came forward to say he assaulted them too. The police have decided they have enough evidence to formally charge him, so he has to fly back next week to face the courts. Whatever the result, I'd say this is definitely the end of his sporting career.'

I remember his persistence that night.

'He's clearly not the hero we all thought he was,' she carries on.

'You thought he was,' I correct her.

'Come on, you fell for his nice guy act too.'

I remember how funny and kind he'd been at the start of the

evening, making me feel like I had an ally in the room. Like I wasn't so alone. 'You're right. I did.'

'So, did he . . . ?'

'No,' I shake my head. 'He didn't touch me. He tried, but I got out of the car.'

She sighs, relieved. 'Thank God. I felt like it was my fault that you left with him, because we put you under the spotlight with the trophies. I've been worried sick that he might have—'

'Well he didn't,' I say quickly and loudly, as Dad approaches within earshot. I shoot her a warning look. 'Honestly. I'm OK.'

She nods, her conscience clear. 'Good. Well, I'd better get going. Take care of yourself, OK?'

'I will. You too. Maybe I'll see you around, sometime.'

'I hope so.' She smiles. 'Remember what I said. You've clearly forgotten how horrible the winters are in this town, but the rest of the year' – she spreads her arms wide – 'it's as pretty as a picture.'

Chapter fifty-three

From: Finn_the_finster@gmail.com
To: ZoeCalloway@hotmail.com
Subject: It hurts

I never thought it would be possible to hurt this much. I don't see it ever stopping.

My friends and brothers staged an intervention. Apparently, it's 'unhealthy' how 'fixated' I am on you. Well, I told them, you'll have to fucking excuse me while I wallow in self-pity and grief, but the future I had planned with the woman I'd fallen in love with disappeared in a puff of smoke one day. No warning. Gone, without a trace.

You can see how that might mess someone up, right?

They can't. They kept banging on about how we only ever had a few days together, but they don't understand we had so much more than that. All the phone calls, the messages. The months of getting to know each other. Falling more in love. Anyway. It didn't end well. They don't think very highly of you, let's leave it at that. And they think that I should hate you too, that I should be angry with you for what you've done. I think I would be, if I wasn't so worried.

I didn't take very well to their opinions. Might have even told them all to fuck off if they can't be supportive. Which, ironically, is what they thought they were doing. They'll get over it. I'm sure their hearts are in the right place, but they've got no idea. They don't know you. They don't know us.

Eighteen. That's how many clothing shops there are in the vicinity of the – our – fountain. Putting aside how absolutely fucking ridiculous that is (eighteen!) I went into every single one yesterday. That night, New Years, I was too busy looking at you, to be honest, to pay much attention to the window display you showed me.

The other day I went into them all, asked for you, or your friend, Bonnie. At the door of every single one I got my hopes up. Walking in, I wondered if that was going to be the moment when I saw you again. I imagined someone saying, 'Zoe? Yeah sure, she works here. I'll get her for you.' I imagined it so many times I fully expected it to come true. But it didn't. No one had a clue who I was talking about.

I want you to remember how much you mean to me. I want you to remember how it was when we were together. I meant every single word I ever said to you. Every promise I ever made.

Don't do this, Zoe. Please. Whatever happened that made you doubt us, can be fixed. You said it wasn't me.

What does that leave? If you met someone else, it's going to crush me. But I'd still rather know. You owe me that at least. I'm not giving up on us yet, so if you want me to shut up and go away, you're going to have to front up and give me one good reason why.

Until then, I'm not going anywhere.

Chapter fifty-four

Getting into the water never gets any easier, and I have to psych myself up by remembering how good I will feel afterwards. It's addictive, as Linda warned, but it's an addiction I can live with. I sleep easier, my appetite increases, and my mood softens.

When the weather isn't so vile, I spend a lot of time on the front porch, watching the ocean and the horizon. Rugged up in layers of clothing with blankets wrapped around me and the wind whipping my hair across my face, I think about Finn. I relive every moment of our time together and I cry for how carefree and innocent I was; how easy life was then, how much I had to look forward to. I miss him with a physical ache that never goes away, but I don't want it to. I'll never stop loving him, I know that much.

About a week after that first swim, I start to notice something is up with my father. He keeps opening his mouth to say something, but then closing it and wandering away instead, looking worried. After a few days of this, it makes me start to worry. What is he finding so hard to tell me? I imagine worst-case scenarios, like maybe he's sick. It wouldn't be a surprise; his body has taken a hammering of abuse after all. But it would be terrifying.

As I watch him drift around the house with a worried expression on his face, I have a startling revelation.

I care.

I mean, I knew I loved him. Even when he was sick and I hated him, even when I told myself that I didn't, I did. I loved him because he was my father. But all those years I was away from him, in the city, I chose to distance myself from any feelings of concern or protectiveness about his health and wellbeing. It was the only way I could leave; to force myself to stop worrying about him. It wasn't easy, and it probably wasn't great for my own mental health either. But he was killing himself, and I sure as hell couldn't stop him from doing so, which made it even harder to stick around and watch. So I told myself that if he didn't care what happened to himself, then why the hell should I?

Now though, being back here with him, seeing how much he's changed through his own determination and effort, I feel like I have my dad back in my life. He's not the same man as he was before we lost Mum, but that's understandable. Death, grief, changes people.

However, there are sparks of the father I used to have. The smiles, the dad jokes, the fact that, so far, he's upheld every promise he's made since I woke up to see him beside my bed in the hospital. I can see that he wants to spend time with me. When the weather's bad, we spend hours playing board games that result in laughter and typically descend into cheating on my part, which he indulgently allows, claiming I've never been good at losing.

When it's not raining, we go for short, assisted walks on the beach or along the road, to try and build my strength up. Then there's the swimming. Since that first day, he stays protectively nearby, ready to react in a second should I need him. My guard is slowly coming down, my heart tentatively letting him back in.

But now this. The worried looks. The distracted pacing. The repeated attempts to say something before he stops abruptly, like he's changed his mind, or can't find the words. We go to Linda's for lunch one day and he is a bag of nerves. Fussing over his outfit, something he's never cared one jot about in the past. He laughs too quickly and too loudly, compliments the food more than it deserves. Even Linda looks taken aback.

'OK,' I say, when we're back in the car and heading home, a journey that takes all of a minute but during which he manages to drum his fingers a thousand times on the steering wheel. 'What's up?'

'Sorry?' He stops drumming and flicks me a distracted look.

'You're acting weird.'

He pulls into the driveway and gives me a surprised look. 'No I'm not. Am I?'

'Yes. You are.'

He takes the key out of the ignition and opens his door. 'No weirder than normal, I'm sure.' He closes the door and comes around to open my side, holding it open while I extricate myself.

'I disagree.' I wait for him to unlock the front door and then stomp down the hallway after him. 'You've been acting strange for a week or so now. I can tell you've got something on your mind, so come on and spit it out. It can't be any worse than anything I've imagined.'

He throws his keys on the bench and picks up the kettle, taking it to the sink to fill with water. 'Cup of tea?'

'Dad.'

'What? Nothing's wrong.'

I take a deep breath. 'You can tell me, if you're sick.'

'Sick?'

'Even if it's because of the . . . alcohol. I won't be mad.'

He gets two cups out of the cupboard and plonks them on the bench. Then he looks at me and frowns. 'You're serious? Oh Zoe, I'm sorry. I didn't realise you'd been worrying. That's my job. I promise you, I'm not sick. There's nothing wrong.'

I open my mouth to protest. 'But—'

He cuts me off. 'But if there was, I would tell you.'

I'm naturally relieved that he's not dying or anything scary like that, but I'm determined to find out what's up with him. I try a different approach.

'Maybe it's the teacher inside of me, but I know you're lying. There might not be something wrong, but there is something.'

He sighs. 'You're not going to let this go, are you?'

I back down onto the cream-coloured three-seater couch that's seen better days, lean my crutches against the small wooden side table, then cross my arms. 'Nope.'

He finishes brewing two cups of tea, discarding the bags into the sink – which he knows drives me nuts because he'll only have to fish them out later when he does the dishes. It's unnecessary double-handling. I keep my mouth shut this time though, not wanting to give him the opportunity to change the subject. He walks over and passes me my cup. 'Careful, it's hot.'

'Thanks. Now sit, and tell me what's up.'

He sinks down onto the other end of the couch and takes a

sip of his tea, wincing when it burns his bottom lip. Shuffling his bum forward, he prepares to stand again. 'I should have added more milk. Do you want me to get you some?'

'No,' I say, exasperated. 'I want you to talk to me.'

He settles back down. 'You should be an interrogator. You're just like your mother, she never let things go either.'

Normally, an impromptu mention of her would bring an awkward silence down between us. I hold my breath and wait for him to close off from me, but instead, I get a surprise when he smiles gently. 'She'd be so proud of you, you know.'

I look down at the surface of my tea and blow on it, watching the ripples fan out. 'I don't know about that.'

'I do.'

I wonder if she'd be as supportive of my decision not to have the operation, if she were still here. But then that's a moot point. Because if she were still here, that would mean she didn't die under the anaesthetic, and I wouldn't be terrified of doing the same thing.

'Do you ever feel like she's around you?' Dad asks, staring out the glass doors to where the sea is churning.

'I used to, but I think that was more wishful thinking on my part. I used to talk to her, at night when I was in bed. I'd pretend she was sitting on the armchair in the corner of my room, and I'd tell her about my day. Then, after you got ... sick, I used to beg her to come back. To help. I knew that she was the only thing, the only person, who could make you better again.'

'The only person who could have made me better,' he contradicts, 'was me. I wish it hadn't taken me so long to realise that. And I'll forever be sorry that you carried that burden. You were only a child.'

I reach out and put a hand on his arm, giving it a little squeeze. 'Stop. It's OK. You don't have to keep apologising.'

He grimaces. 'I'll never stop being sorry though.'

'Yeah, well. Enough of that. Back to what we were talking about.'

He takes another sip of tea and stares moodily out the window. 'I . . . ' he trails off, closing his mouth again, like he's been doing over and over.

'Oh my God, you're driving me nuts!' I shout, startling him.

'Steady on,' he says.

'Why can't you come out and say whatever it is you need to say?'

'It's . . . I think it might be too soon. That's all.'

'Too soon for what?'

'I mean, it's a massive, life-changing decision. Definitely not something that should be taken lightly. I know that. You know that. Everyone knows that.'

'What isn't?'

He carries on as if I hadn't spoken. 'Believe me, I've been thinking about it for a while now, weighing up the pros and cons. But that seems an awfully cynical way of looking at it. Unfair too, probably. I mean, look at the mess I made of everything. Plus, you and I are finally getting back to a good place, and that means everything to me. The world. So maybe I should be concentrating on that, you know? On you. Yes. I think that's the best thing all round.'

I blink, trying to keep up with his fast-changing train of thought.

'But then again,' he continues, 'why can't I have both? Is it possible? It could be possible. Other people manage, but I'm not other people. For the longest time, I didn't think I deserved to be happy, not after ... But, maybe I can. Do I deserve it? Probably not. I think it all depends on you, but then that's not fair, is it? Putting the decision in your hands. It's asking too much. It should be up to me and you. We're a family. We should make these decisions together.' He looks at me, his eyes confused. 'But how does one ever know for sure?'

'I kind of regret asking now,' I say, dazed. It's the most words I've heard him say in one hit, probably in forever. My head is reeling as it tries to keep up.

'I mean, the first time around it was easy,' he continues. 'I didn't even have to think about it, I just knew. But I'm older now. I know life isn't all rainbows and puppy dogs. Do I stick to what I know, or do I take a chance?'

'A chance on what?'

He finally stops talking and looks at me. 'A chance on love.'

'I don't understand.'

He takes a deep breath and then exhales it slowly. 'I've been thinking about asking Linda to marry me. But only with your blessing,' he adds hurriedly. 'I won't do it if you don't want me to.'

It's my turn to be speechless. In the space of five minutes, I've gone from being convinced that my father is dying, to finding out that, actually, he's thinking about proposing marriage to someone.

'You don't think it's a good idea,' he says.

'No, I don't.' He looks crestfallen, and I hurry to explain. 'I mean, I don't think that, that it's not a good idea.'

He looks understandably confused.

'Now I'm the one not making any sense,' I mutter. 'OK, I

don't think it's a bad idea,' I clarify. 'I'm surprised, that's all. I had no idea you guys were that serious.'

He looks guilty. 'That's because I asked her to give us some space, when you moved back home. Before that, we spent a lot of time together. Most nights, in fact.'

'Oh.'

'Don't worry, she understood completely,' he adds quickly. 'In fact, I didn't even need to ask, we sort of both reached the decision at the same time. She knows how much you mean to me, and how much I regret not being there for you. We both knew this was my chance to make up for it, and we were happy to take some time apart so that I could focus on you.'

For the first time, I understand the sacrifices Dad and Linda have made since I've been home. There they were, living a happy little life together, and I came along and ruined it for them. 'I'm sorry,' I say.

'For what?'

'I haven't exactly been very welcoming to her, have I.'

'That's not your fault. I should have told you about her before, instead of springing it on you.'

'Yes,' I agree. 'You should have. But still, I didn't need to behave like a spoiled brat. She's not such a bad person, now that I've given her half a chance.'

'She thinks the world of you.'

I shrug. 'I'm a pretty lovable person,' I say, then wait for him to contradict me. He doesn't. 'Well, normally anyway.' I add. 'I know I've been a bit of a nightmare lately.'

He gives me an understanding smile. 'You've had your reasons. Perfectly legitimate ones.'

'I think, in some sort of subconscious way, I was testing you.'

He frowns. 'What do you mean?'

'Last time when things got tough, when Mum died, you bailed. Emotionally, anyway. I was sure you'd end up doing the same this time, so I kept pushing you away. Waiting for the inevitable.'

'I told you in the hospital that I'd be there for you, and I meant it.'

'I know, but it's one thing hearing you say it, and another thing actually seeing it happen.'

He shakes his head ruefully. 'I guess I can't blame you. My track record isn't great.'

'You're still here though.'

'I am.'

'I mean, you live here, so it's not like you would have physically gone anywhere, but you haven't given up on me, no matter how horrible I've been.'

'And I won't.' He lifts his chin and looks at me proudly.

'I believe you.'

It's a huge moment between us, as far as moments go, but it's ruined when a particularly ferocious gust of wind bangs at the glass on the back doors. We both jump. I stare out at the darkening sky, and think about how Linda has been here for Dad these past few years. Supporting him. Helping him. Loving him. The fact he's doing so well in his recovery is mostly due to himself, of course. But I'm sure she played a part in it too.

'I think you should go for it. Ask Linda to marry you.'

'Seriously?'

'Seriously.' I nod. 'If she makes you happy, then you shouldn't let that go.'

'She does. I never thought that, after your mother, I'd find love again. But this is a different kind of love. We're older, wiser, more forgiving and accepting of each other's flaws. She's good company. I didn't realise how much I would miss her, until we started spending this time apart.'

'I'm sorry,' I repeat, feeling guilty.

'No,' he says. 'That came out wrong. Neither of us blame you, or would have things any other way. I guess what I'm saying is that the old cliché is true. Absence does make the heart grow fonder.'

I groan. 'You and Bonnie would get on great. She's a walking meme as well.'

'A what?'

'Never mind.'

'So you think I should do this?'

'You have my blessing, if that's what you're after. But only you can decide.'

'It's such a huge decision to make.'

'Well, if you ask me, I think you've already made your mind up and now you're letting nerves get to you, and that's giving you doubts. It's natural.'

'I am nervous,' he agrees. 'I'm far too old for this. I mean, I wouldn't even know how to ask. I figure I'll light a couple of candles and cook her dinner, but how do you drop something like that into conversation?'

I pull a face. 'I think we can come up with something a bit more romantic than that.'

He suppresses a smile. 'We? You mean, you'll help?'

'I'll help.'

'How did I get so lucky to have you, eh?'

I put my cup down and scoot across the couch until I'm

beside him. There's a moment of awkwardness, but then I look at his face and feel the awkwardness melt away. No matter what, he's my dad. I lift up his arm and snuggle in against his side. He breathes in sharply, surprised, then he drops his arm around my shoulder and pulls me in tight. I hear a catch in his throat, as he rests his head on top of mine.

'Dad?'

'Yeah?'

There's a weighted pause while I line the words up and make sure the timing's right. I don't want to say it just for the hell of it, or because I think I should.

It feels right.

'I love you too.'

Chapter fifty-five

'HAVE YOU SEEN ZOE?'

Underneath the glaring capital letters across the top of the page, there is a photo of me, and I cringe when I see it. I didn't even know he had it, must have taken it off my Facebook page before I deleted it. It's an old photo, from a picnic in the park Bonnie and I and a few of our mates had, about five years ago. He's cropped the people sitting on the blanket next to me out of the picture. Even though it's black and white and the quality isn't great because it's obviously been printed, photocopied and now scanned by Bonnie to me through email, I can't get over how young I look. But that's not what holds my attention.

In the front of the photo, stretched out on the blanket, is my leg. My right foot is tucked underneath my long, bohemian peacock-coloured skirt. But the other leg, my left leg, lays casually out in front. My sandals kicked off, my skin beautifully tanned and smooth. It's the weirdest feeling, looking at the slender toes, the rounded heel and the delicate ankle of a foot I no longer have. I've purposefully been avoiding photos of myself pre-accident, but this one I can't.

'Did you get it?' Bonnie asks in my ear, bringing me back to the present.

'Yeah, I got it.'

'I couldn't believe it when I saw it,' she says. 'Walked into the bakery and there it was, smack bang in the middle of the bulletin board.'

Bonnie and I used to love reading the notes and notices on the board while we drank our post-gym coffees and ate our sinful doughnuts, the ones with the custard centres and chocolate coating on top. We used to sympathise with the owners of the lost pets; the tabby cats, an occasional small fluffy dog and once, even, a colourful parrot. Sometimes, we'd scribble little messages on the bottom, something intended to be kind and uplifting, Good luck! Hope you find Ruffles! That sort of thing. There were adverts for flatmates and flats, people seeking employment – 'Anything considered!' – and all sorts of items for sale. Barely used expensive home exercise equipment; we used to snigger at those ones in particular, as we stuffed our faces with calorie-laden baked goods. Ironic, in hindsight.

I scan the rest of the flyer. It's pretty light on details. Basically says he's desperately searching for a very dear friend, and if anyone has any information that can help, to please contact him on any of the methods listed below. Then he lists his phone number, email address, and even his social media handles. I wonder whether he's had any prank messages because of it.

'I can't believe he did this,' I say, shocked at the lengths Finn is prepared to go to. 'Do you think this is the only one?'

Bonnie sucks air in sharply between her teeth, something she always does when she has bad news to impart. 'Bad news, I'm afraid. It's not.'

I sink back against my pillows, unable to take my eyes off my smiling, carefree face on the screen. 'Where else?'

'Well, I showed Josh, when I got home, and then he remembered seeing one, at the bookshop you used to always hang out at. The one on the corner of Queen Street. He noticed it in the window the other day when he was walking past, but at the time he thought nothing of it, only that the photo kind of looked like you. He figured it was like, your doppelganger or something.'

'You mean my name across the top wasn't a bit of a giveaway?' I shouldn't be surprised. Josh isn't known for paying attention to anything that doesn't directly affect him, but only because he runs his own plumbing business and he's distracted by that most of the time.

'Apparently not, but you know what he's like. It's a miracle he noticed it at all. Anyway, after I showed him the one from the bakery, he realised it must have been you in the other flyer, so we went to check, and sure enough. Don't worry, I ripped it out of the window when they weren't looking.' Her tone drops. 'It's kind of spooky though, don't you think? I mean, how does Finn even know all the places you used to hang out? You said you showed him the shop, but all these other places?'

'It's no mystery. Do you remember I told you how we walked around the city that night, for hours, before we ended up on his brother's roof?'

'Yeah?'

'I showed him then. The gym, the bakery. The library, the bookshops.'

'So, wait, what you're saying is that there's probably more of these flyers around the city?'

I groan. 'Probably.'

I hear her exhale heavily. 'Don't you think enough is enough? He's not giving up; these flyers clearly indicate that. What if someone who knows you gets in touch with him?'

'Like who?'

'Someone from the school, one of your old colleagues ... Isn't it better he finds out about the accident from you, not someone else?'

'You know how I feel about that.'

'Yes, I do. But for the record – and you know I love you, so don't take this the wrong way – I think you're wrong. I think you owe him an explanation. What you're doing is cruel, Zoe.'

Her words sting. 'That's the opposite of what I'm trying to do. Anyway, what's that saying? Sometimes you have to be cruel to be kind.'

'Now who's spouting clichés.'

'I'm doing this for him. And yes, selfishly, for me too.' Tears well up in my eyes as I look out of the window at a grey world. 'I'd rather he remembers me how I was. Full of life, active. Brave.'

'You're still all those things.'

'He won't see it that way.'

'You don't know that.'

'Bonnie, please,' I say resignedly. 'This is my decision. You don't have to like it, but I'd be grateful if you could at least respect me enough to drop it.'

'Fine,' she says stiffly.

'Don't be mad at me,' I beg. 'I couldn't bear it. You're my best friend, my only friend.'

'As if I'd ever be mad at you,' she scolds affectionately. 'All I want is for you to be happy, and I know that Finn made you that way.'

I squeeze my eyes shut tightly. 'He did.'

I hear a rustle. 'What do you want me to do about these flyers?'

'Pull them down,' I suggest. 'Any that you see. He'll have targeted the places I showed him that night.' Bonnie's words catch up to me. An old colleague. The school. He knew where I worked, has he been there?

The school secretary, Sarah, answers the phone when I ring.

'Miss Calloway,' she exclaims. 'How are you? I heard about the accident. I can't believe they had to cut your leg off. I mean, how ridiculous. Were there no other options?'

The last thing I want to do is make small talk with her and act like we're friends, because we're not. Never were. In fact, out of a staff of nearly sixty, there were probably two teachers who liked Sarah, at least when I was there. The rest of us tiptoed around her, for fear of triggering one of her outbursts. From her swivel chair in the office she believed – and behaved – like she ruled the school. I dreaded ever having to interact with her, because she could deflate a good mood in two seconds flat. It was like her special talent. Seek out joy and destroy it.

'Hi, Sarah, uh, no. No other options, I'm afraid, or I'm fairly sure they would have explored them. Hey, is Kendra there by any chance?'

Kendra is the office manager, and a much nicer human being all round.

'No, she's out to lunch. Should have been back ten minutes ago, but you know what she's like.' She gives a long-suffering sigh. 'Leaving me to carry the weight. I do the job of three people. But is it appreciated by the staff around here? No.'

I resist the urge to remind her that she works five hours a day, five days a week, and has almost twelve weeks of holidays a year, yet she carries on as if it's the teachers who have the easy life. She's also notorious for being rude to both the children and their parents, and has had more complaints made against her than I've attended assemblies. The rumour was that the only reason she still had a job at all was because she'd once had an affair with the principal.

'OK, well could you please ask her to call me when she gets back?'

'Is it not something I could help you with?'

As the person who answers the phones, she might have been able to, but anything to do with staff and human resources is Kendra's domain, so I'm hoping that she would have been the one to speak to Finn. Plus, I remember how much Sarah thrives on gossip, so I don't want to get into it with her. It would be all over the school within minutes.

'No, it's Kendra I need to speak to,' I lie. 'It's ah . . . pay-related.'

'You're not thinking about coming back to work, are you?' she asks sharply.

Her tone clearly indicates that she thinks that wouldn't be a good idea, and it pisses me off. I lost a leg, yes. But I didn't forget how to be a teacher, and a damn good one at that. It's bad enough I'm down on myself, I don't need her making me feel any worse.

'I'm sorry, but that's confidential,' I say firmly, in a tone

269

that I hope conveys it's above her pay grade. Petty, but satisfying. 'You'll need to give Kendra my new number. Have you got a pen?'

When she sullenly confirms that she does, I rattle off the digits.

'Great, thank you, enjoy the rest of your day,' I say chirpily, disconnecting the call before she has the chance to probe any further. It's funny how much pleasure I derive from standing up to her, something I'd have been too afraid to do back when I worked at the school. I know it'll be driving her nuts now, trying to figure out what's going on and why she doesn't already know about it.

Kendra calls half an hour later, and unlike Sandra, the sound of her voice makes me happy. She fills me in on the goings on of the last few months, and my stomach feels all funny when I realise how much I miss being part of a community. Not every day was easy, and there were definitely times I'd roll out of bed and dread going into work, but for the most part, I loved it. I knew that what I did made a difference in the world. I was helping to shape the next generation.

She asks about me, in a way that is genuinely caring, not nosy, like Sarah. I give her a brief rundown of life since the accident, though I try to keep it from sounding as grim and lonely as it truthfully is. I also lie, and tell her I'm on the path to getting a prosthesis, but have hit a few speed bumps along way. It's almost true.

'I guess the one blessing to come from it, if you can look at it that way, is that you get to spend some time with your father again,' she says. 'It's so hard to maintain a close relationship with your parents when you live so far away, and yet such an important thing to do.'

I hear the wistfulness in her voice and recall that she has a son who's somewhere overseas. I'm guessing he hasn't been home in a while.

'Mm,' I agree vaguely. 'Hey, um, this is kind of a weird question, but I was wondering if you'd had anyone calling the school about me? Trying to get information maybe, that sort of thing?'

'Yes, as a matter of fact,' she says, sounding surprised. 'Last week. I'd forgotten about that.'

'Did you happen to get a name?' My heart beats faster as I wait for her to respond, even though I know full well who it was.

'No, he refused to give one. I think he was drunk. He was quite belligerent at the end, when I refused to tell him anything. He stopped short of insisting it was life and death, but he was pretty adamant that he needed to get in touch with you. I told him firmly that there are privacy laws at stake, and that I was not prepared to break them. Not that I had anything to tell. We don't have a forwarding address for you, and clearly your number has changed.'

I swing my leg off the bed and push up, hopping towards my bedroom window, holding on to the frame for support. Hopping without crutches is strictly frowned upon by my occupational therapist, but sometimes I feel the burning need to move without assistance, even if it is dangerous and awkward.

'I'm sorry if he was rude,' I apologise to her, resting my forehead against the cool glass. 'He's not normally like that, he's a nice guy. But he's been ... well, he's still going through a rough time.'

'He wasn't rude, as such,' she answers. 'But it was obvious he was upset. Frustrated. Zoe, I don't like to pry, but ... is everything OK?'

271

'Everything's fine.'

'Is he someone that you need to be worried about?'

'Oh no, not at all,' I reassure her. 'It's nothing like that.'

'Good.' She sounds relieved. 'I'm glad. You've been through enough.'

I hear a phone ringing persistently in the background, and she sighs. 'I'm sorry, I'd better get that. Sarah has disappeared from her desk.'

'Nice to know that some things never change. Or should I say, people.'

'You're not wrong there,' she chortles. 'Hey, when you get back on your feet and ready to get into teaching again, give us a shout. We'd love to have you back here.'

I feel choked up, unable to answer. She says it so casually, but it's probably the nicest thing anyone could say to me right now. Someone wants me. Someone considers me functional; that I still have something to offer. I clear my throat and mumble, 'Sounds great, I'll definitely keep it in mind.'

After I hang up, I watch the ocean for a while, hoping it will calm me. It doesn't. Finn wasn't lying when he said he won't give up. The flyers, contacting the school. What's next? A full-page advertisement in a national newspaper? TV advert? I'm lost as to what to do to make this easier for him. I don't like admitting it, but there's also a small part of me that's glad he's not giving up, as selfish as that is. Because I don't know what I'd do if he did.

Chapter fifty-six

'What do you think? Is it too much?'

I study the pergola that Dad and I have spent most of Saturday afternoon constructing on the back lawn. Well, I say Dad and I, but for obvious reasons he's done all the grunt work while I've sat in the hospital wheelchair with a blanket wrapped around me, calling out instructions from the brochure in my hands. It's a kit set, bought from the hardware store in town. They had one option and one option only: a light-coloured pine affair that looks unfinished, like it's missing a coat of paint. Frankly, it wouldn't have been my first choice, but it'll do. Anyway, by the time I've finished with it, it'll look like something from a Nicholas Sparks movie.

After it's erected, and we're satisfied it'll stand up to anything the unpredictable weather might throw at it, we move on to the final touches. The weather is supposed to stay calm for the next four days, no rain or gales, but they're often wrong, so I keep one nervous eye on the sky. I've been planning this since Dad asked me to help, and I have no plan B.

Sitting in the chair, I use a knife to open the boxes that have been arriving almost daily since I started ordering everything at the end of last week. Most of it has turned up, though I'm a bit devastated that the black iron brazier hasn't. I had visions of an open fire beside the pergola – can you get any more romantic than that? – but instead the old outdoor heater Dad has in the garage will have to do. It won't have quite the same effect, but beggars can't be choosers. He drags it out and sets it up, plugging it into the lounge power with an extension cord. It still works, and we high-five each other.

At my direction, Dad then moves the round outside table – after a good scrub first –underneath the pergola, arranging it nicely in the middle. I hand him swathes of white material and he wraps them around the four outer poles and along the top beams. Then he goes over the same areas with outdoor fairy lights, hundreds of them. Small ones tightly wrapped around the wood, and then bigger, globe-shaped ones dangling from the centre of the roof part, out to the four corners.

While he's doing that, I lay a plain white tablecloth on the table, then set to making a flower arrangement in a big white vase. Being the end of winter, pickings are slim, but I sent Dad out with a pair of scissors earlier and he managed to rustle up some winter roses, pansies, calendula and polyanthus from the garden. It might not win any flower arrangement awards, but I think it looks rustic and pretty in the centre of the table. When that's finished, I stuff small strings of star-shaped fairy lights into little jars, which I then place around the base of the vase. Dad brings all the cutlery and glassware out on a tray for me to arrange while he lays out solar lights in two lines, a metre apart, making a pathway from the bottom of the porch steps to the pergola. We've had them charging on the deck all day, and a couple of them flicker on as he presses the on button. The sun is starting to go down.

'Are you sure she's going to like this?' Dad asks, pausing from his hard work to wipe his brow and stand back, appraising his handiwork.

'What's not to like? It's romantic. Chicks dig romance.'

He looks at me. 'Chicks? I'm not sure a woman of Linda's age qualifies.'

'I was being silly. Relax, she's going to love it. How are the nerves?'

'Getting worse,' he admits. 'Do you really think I'm ready for this?' He looks at me imploringly. 'I mean, am I making a big mistake here? What if she laughs in my face?' He starts pacing the makeshift path and I eye the grass nervously. Wouldn't take much to turn it into mud after all the winter rain. 'I mean, look at us. Maybe we're too old for this sort of carry on. Things are fine as they are. I don't know what I was thinking.'

'Calm down,' I say firmly. 'You're talking yourself out of it.'

He buries his face in his hands. 'What am I doing?'

'Dad.'

He looks up.

'Do you love her?' I ask.

He nods.

'And she loves you too, right?'

He nods again. 'I think so. She says she does.'

'Then stop stressing. Everything's going to be fine.'

He checks his watch. 'Oh God, there's only an hour to go.'

'Still time for you to change your mind then.'

'What?' He looks at me panicked. 'But you said—'

275

'Sorry.' I hold up my hands. 'Sorry. Bad time for jokes. OK, an hour. Enough time for you to shower and put on a nice shirt.'

He looks down at himself. 'I have to shower?'

'Yes, Dad, you have to shower. You're about to propose marriage to someone, after an afternoon spent digging post holes and hammering bits of wood together. The least you could do is make yourself smell nice and dress like you've made an effort.'

'Good point,' he concedes. 'I'm glad you're here. I'm no good at this sort of stuff.'

'Bonnie always told me I'd make a good party planner,' I say wistfully. 'I have an eye for detail, that's what she said.'

'I'd have to agree. The place looks great. Shall we turn the fairy lights on now?'

I shake my head. 'Not yet. We don't want her to see it before we're ready. Go and take a shower. I'll make sure everything is tidied up.'

'Be careful, I don't want you falling over if I'm not out here to help.'

'I'm not completely useless.'

'I didn't mean that you were. I'm only worried because the ground out here is uneven.'

My anger deflates in a heartbeat. 'I know. Sorry.'

'Are you OK?'

I smile brightly. 'Of course. I'll have a new ... family soon, and a big fat Nugget Bay wedding to plan.'

'Um, I think we'd probably both prefer something simple. A casual backyard affair. But that's up to Linda. She might not even say yes.'

'If she doesn't, then she's a fool.' I smile. 'And I was kidding

276

about the wedding. You're not used to my sense of humour. We'll get there.'

He nods in agreement. 'We will. I'm grateful, to you ... for being OK about all this. You know, Linda and everything else. And for your help. It means a lot.'

'Dad.'

'Yeah?'

'Shower.'

'Right.'

Chapter fifty-seven

To say Linda is surprised would be an understatement. She's speechless, standing on the deck and surveying the backyard scene for a good minute or two, without saying even a single word. The solar-light path is all lit up, and the pergola is even better than I imagined it. Nicholas Sparks eat your heart out.

'Did you guys do this?' she finally asks when she finds her voice again.

'Yep,' I answer proudly. 'Well, mostly Dad.'

'Don't be modest,' he says, from Linda's other side. 'You did all the planning and design. I'd have never come up with something like this on my own, not in a million years. Romance isn't exactly my forte.'

Another understatement.

'You guys,' she gushes. 'This is beautiful.'

I've never seen my dad beam before, but he's sure as hell beaming right now.

'Thanks,' he says. 'I'm glad you like it.'

'Like it? I love it.' They walk down the steps and Dad leads her to the table, one of her arms linked through his. He pulls back her chair for her, then after she's settled he comes back up on the deck to where I'm standing in the open door.

'Come on,' he says, jerking his head and crooking his arm towards me, waiting for me to link mine through.

'What?' I say, frowning. 'Not me. I'm going to grab something out of the pantry and hide out in my room. This is for you guys.'

'Zoe,' he says firmly. 'You and I are a package deal. I'm not doing this without you.' He steps closer and lowers his voice. 'Please? I'm terrified. What if I screw up and say something stupid?'

'Don't know how I could fix it if you did.'

'Please, Zoe?'

I can tell by his eyes that he's serious, and not doing this because he feels sorry for me. He wants me to be there. To be honest, I'd rather skip it. Although I've given him my blessing to propose to Linda, and in theory I am OK with it, I don't know how I'll feel . . . or react . . . when the actual moment comes.

'I only set two places on the table,' I tell him.

'Already sorted. I added another one while you were getting ready. Come on.' He wriggles his elbow.

'This is ridiculous,' I mutter as I let him help me down the ramp. 'You're a grown man. You don't need me to hold your hand.'

He ignores me, helping me across the lawn to a seat under the pergola. Full credit to Linda. If she's surprised or annoyed that I'm joining them for their romantic dinner for two, she doesn't show it.

279

Dad flicks the switch to ignite the outdoor heater and instantly it helps ward off the chill of the night. 'There's a blanket on the back of your chair if either of you get cold,' he points out. 'I'll go and get dinner.'

'You two have thought of everything,' Linda says, turning slightly in her seat to run a hand over the wool surface of the blanket neatly folded over the back. 'I feel underdressed for such a beautiful setting though. If I'd known you were going to go to this much effort, I'd have worn something nicer.'

'It was a surprise,' I reply, lifting up my water to take a sip. 'We couldn't exactly issue you with a dress code.'

My father brings out a huge lasagne, still in the pan, and warm dinner rolls, then dishes it onto everyone's plates at the table, heaping generous portions. We eat under the soft light of the fairy lights. For once, the weather forecasters were right and the sky stays clear. No clouds, and no rain. It's not the warmest, but with blankets over our knees and the outdoor heater, it's not as bad as I'd have expected. We're too busy enjoying ourselves to notice the cold, anyway. The food is delicious, the company fun.

After we've finished dessert – a chocolate cheesecake – Dad clears the table, making several trips inside. On the last trip, he turns the radio up loud and invites Linda to a dance. Some old love song from the seventies. The kind of thing that would normally make me cringe, but tonight, I have a lump in my throat and I'm feeling all sorts of emotions. It's good to see him so happy. She gets to her feet and accepts his hand, and they twirl slowly around the lawn, their heads close together, arms around each other. It's a personal moment, and I feel horribly like I'm intruding, but I'd have to interrupt them to ask Dad for help getting back into the house, so I stay silent.

When the song finishes, Dad gently pushes Linda away, awkwardly sinking down onto one knee and reaching up to take her left hand in his. She looks momentarily confused but as I watch, her features change as she realises what is happening. She covers her mouth with her free hand.

'Linda,' Dad says, his voice croaky. He clears his throat. 'I'm no good with fancy words, or poetry, or things like that. I did think about trying to learn something for the occasion, but then I realised, that's not me. This is. And you'll either take me for that, or leave it.'

She opens her mouth to speak but he cuts her off.

'Wait, I'm not finished. The simple fact of the matter is,' he continues, 'I love you. And you make me happy, which is more than I ever thought I'd deserve.'

I feel sadness when I hear him say that, but it's tinged with relief. Sadness that for all these years he's been hating himself, believing himself unworthy of love or happiness. But also, relief that we've finally started to mend our relationship, even if we've still got a long way to go. If there's anything I've learned this past year it's that trauma, and grief, affects everyone differently. When you're in the thick of it, it's like being on a raft in the wildest white-water rapids in the world. All you can do is hang on for dear life as you get thrown about at the mercy of your emotions. You can't control water any more than you can control feelings. I know that now.

With a start, I realise I've missed the rest of Dad's speech, but I tune back in just in time to hear the important bit.

'... if you'll have me, that is.'

He looks up at her with such a mixture of hope and fear that it makes my heart physically ache.

She nods, one hand still covering her mouth.

It's not enough. Dad seeks clarification. 'Is that a yes?'

Finally, she removes the hand, revealing a quivering lip that can't hide a genuine smile of happiness 'Yes,' she says. 'Definitely yes. Nothing would make me happier.'

Dad's forehead irons out with relief and he starts to smile.

'But,' she holds up a finger. 'Only on one condition.'

He immediately looks worried again and my heart starts racing as I feel a protectiveness towards him that I've never felt before. How dare she? If she hurts him . . . my hands involuntarily curl into fists.

She turns to look straight at me. 'You have to be OK with this.'

My fists unclench as my shoulders sag with relief. I don't think I'd have actually hit her if it came to it, but wow, the ferocity of my feelings is a complete surprise. 'I am.'

'I don't want to do anything that might upset you, Zoe. So if this is too much, or too soon, I'm quite happy and willing to wait until you're sure.'

'I'm sure.' I nod. 'I am. Dad and I have already talked about this and I gave him, as I give you, my blessing. I want him to be happy, and you clearly do that for him.'

'Thank you. That means a lot.' She turns back to Dad. 'I guess we're getting married.'

'I guess we are.'

They embrace, she squeals, and he lets out a bellowing laugh that makes me wince. They're kind of cute, but there's a limit to how much of their cutesy, loved-up joy that I'm prepared to bear witness to.

'Dad,' I call out. 'You forgot something.'

He pulls back to look at me. 'I did?'

I hold up my left hand and tap my fingers.

'Of course!' He taps all his pockets until he finds the one he's looking for, then pulls out a simple gold band with a pretty ruby stone set amongst a circle of small diamonds. I helped him pick it out of a catalogue earlier in the week. He lifts her hand and slides it onto her ring finger, giving it a little tug when it gets stuck on her knuckle.

'Damn arthritis,' she sighs, helping him. Then she holds her hand at arm's length to get a better look. 'Look at that. What a beautiful ring, I love it. Though if I'd have known you were going to do this, I would have at least slapped on some moisturiser, or painted my nails,' she says dolefully. 'You can tell these hands have spent the week in the garden.'

My father kisses the back of her hand. 'You don't need to put on a show for me. I love you just the way you are.'

'Hey, you can talk,' she exclaims, gesturing around the garden. 'Look at all the effort you went to.'

'I wanted it to be special. Show you how much you mean to me.'

She smiles. 'It's the most romantic thing that anyone's ever done for me. But all I really need,' she wraps her arms around his waist and snuggles in tightly against him, 'is you.'

They start dancing again slowly to the music, sharing the occasional kiss, murmuring to each other.

I watch them, and I can't help feeling nostalgic for Finn. A picture of us together, that night on the roof, springs to mind. Lying next to him on that rickety old lounger chair, butterflies in my stomach as we kissed. And then our time at the lake.

283

The feel of his body touching mine in the water. The way he looked at me so intensely right before he picked me up and we made love for the first time. It felt so perfect. He was so perfect. I was so happy.

Chapter fifty-eight

It's gone eleven when I leave Linda and Dad to celebrate in private and slip off to bed, but I can't sleep. I'm genuinely happy for my father, but seeing their love, so honest and unconditional, only serves to drive home how much I've lost. Lying there, in the dark, listening to the sound of the ocean outside, and muffled conversation through the wall, I feel like my heart could burst right out of my chest. The longing for Finn hasn't abated with time. If anything, it's getting worse. I miss him. I miss him, I need him, I want him. I close my eyes and imagine him lying beside me, his arms around me, his lips on mine, his breath on my skin. I want it so much I can almost feel it. But then I open my eyes, and he's not there, and the loneliness and the heartbreak flood in and I start crying so much I honestly think I'll never stop.

I do, eventually. The tears trickle to a halt, the sobs that catch in my throat and make my chest heave gradually subside. The feelings remain, my whole body aching with the bruise of sadness. I hear the noises that signal Dad and Linda going to bed.

Toilet flushing, running water as teeth are brushed. The click of the front door being locked. The lights under the bottom of my door flicks off, but still, I wait ten, twenty minutes to be sure they're out of the way before I throw off the covers and shuffle out of bed, reaching for the head torch Dad bought me for when I need to use the bathroom in the night, to keep my hands free, and then my crutches. The metal is cold, and I resent it. I resent those crutches and everything they stand for. If I didn't need them, I'd burn them.

In the kitchen, I flick the range hood light on and boil the kettle, carefully making myself a hot chocolate when it switches itself off again, the way my occupational therapist has taught me. Instead of feeling a sense of accomplishment, like I did the first time, I feel a stab of anger at how something that I could once do without thought, now requires such concentration and effort. If I don't concentrate, there are consequences. Potentially serious ones. I could fall, or spill the boiling water all over myself. The last thing I need is burns on top of everything else.

The lights are all still on outside. Being solar-powered, they'll keep going until they run out of charge. I drink my hot chocolate at the bench because I can't hold it and walk with the crutches. When it's finished, I leave the cup in the sink and make my way around to the glass doors, flicking the lock and opening the door as quietly as I can.

The shock of the cold night air causes me to suck in my next breath sharply. When I release it, it takes the form of a plume of steam that drifts away into the night. I'm wearing long pyjamas, flannelette ones, but I may as well be naked for how quickly the cold seeps through the layers. I can see the blankets down on the chairs still, and debate trying to get one, but I know better

286

than to attempt the steps at night, by myself. A dew is already settling, the wood is treacherously slippery, I picture myself sprawled at the bottom and quickly dismiss the idea. Instead, I sit carefully down on the old, faded outdoor chaise and bring my knees up against my chest, hugging them, feeling spectacularly sorry for myself, as a fresh batch of tears threatens. I don't realise the door has opened behind me until Linda speaks.

'Are you OK?'

I jump, clutching my chest. 'Jesus, Linda. You gave me a fright.'

'Sorry. Can't sleep either, huh?'

I shake my head.

'Mind if I sit with you?'

'No. I don't know why you want to though, it's not exactly pleasant out here.'

'You're right. Hang on a tick.' She disappears back into the house, emerging a few minutes later with the large knitted blue throw blanket that's usually draped across the back of the couch. It was my mother's, but I'm so grateful to see it that I don't fall into petulant old habits. She sits beside me and spreads it over both of us.

'How's that?'

'Better,' I admit. 'Dad asleep?'

She nods. 'Within minutes, as usual. Drives me nuts.'

I frown. 'You still want to marry him though, right?'

She looks surprised. 'Of course. You know what it's like, being a couple. There's always little quirks and habits in the other person you find annoying.'

I try and think of something, anything that Finn might have done that annoyed me. Nothing springs to mind, but

287

then we've never lived together. For all I know he might be a toilet-seat-leaver-upper, or a clips-toe-nails-in-the-lounge-while-watching-television kind of guy. I wish I'd had the chance to find out.

'Your dad tells me you were seeing a guy, before the accident,' Linda says carefully, sensing she's bringing up something that's not only painful, but also not really any of her business. A few weeks ago, I'd have been angry, fuming, that Dad had told her. But the new, calmer, determined-to-act-like-an-adult again me takes a deep breath before responding. She is my father's fiancé. It is only natural they talk about things, even things to do with me.

'Yes,' I say shortly.

'Do you miss him?'

I look down at the lights on the lawn, remembering the lights of the city spread out beneath us. 'More than I miss my leg,' I reply. It comes out of somewhere deep inside of me, my core, the place where truth and feelings collide, and it takes us both by surprise.

'That's ... a lot then,' she says slowly. 'He must have been pretty special.'

'He was. He is.'

'Do you mind me asking what went wrong?'

'Everything ... changed, after the accident.'

'Maybe he needed a bit of time to adjust. Have you talked to him lately?'

'No. And I don't want to talk about it.' The new me still has limits. Some subjects remain out of bounds.

'OK.' She nods, respecting my wishes, which I'm grateful for. Then she carries on talking. 'But I do want to talk to you about something, and you might not like it.'

My walls go up immediately. 'If you know I'm not going to like it, then maybe you shouldn't say it.'

'I have to. Believe me, I don't want to upset you, or risk alienating you again. And I'm not bringing this up now because I'm marrying your dad and that kind of makes us family. I'm saying this as someone who'd like to be your friend, one day, if you'll let me. It hasn't been easy, this last month or so, watching you struggle, both physically and emotionally.'

'It hasn't exactly been a walk in the park for me either.'

'I know. And that's why I wanted to talk to you about having the second operation.'

'Oh, here we go. Did Dad put you up to this?'

'No, he has no idea I'm talking to you.'

'Oh, I see.' I face her off. 'Let me guess, you want me out of here, now that you and Dad are getting married. I'm an inconvenience, cluttering up the place, and you figure the operation is the best way to get me out of here so you can enjoy your merry little retirement with my father without the responsibility of his useless, pathetic daughter getting in the way.' I spit the words out bitterly – and regret it instantly.

She stares at me, in a way that doesn't make me feel good. Then she exhales heavily.

'Whoa. Zoe, do you honestly think that badly of me?'

I chew my lower lip angrily, staring out at an ocean I can't see, but I can hear.

'Maybe this engagement was a bad idea,' she says. 'You're clearly not ready, and the last thing I ever wanted to do was upset you. I'll talk to Greg in the morning, explain that—'

'No!' I shout, cutting her off. 'Don't do that, you'll break his heart. He'll blame me.'

'He won't blame you. He loves you. All he wants is to help you to feel good about life again.'

'Bit hard when life is so fucking unfair.'

'But that's that thing. No one knows why bad things happen to good people, they do. No, what happened to you wasn't fair, but it happened, and no amount of wishing otherwise will change that. You can't drive yourself crazy trying to find a reason, because there isn't one. And if you focus too much on the unfairness of it all and what you can't do, you won't ever realise all the things that you can do.'

'I can't do anything.'

'It's natural to feel like that. It's still early days, you're still recuperating from the accident. But Zoe, you're wrong, and you'll see that one day. Your life isn't over. There are millions of amputees in this world, all living all sorts of extraordinary and perfectly normal lives. You can let this defeat you, or you can choose not to let it define you. You're still you, Zoe. And I might not have known you before the accident, but I know what I see in your heart, and you're not the kind of person to roll over and let life defeat them.'

'You make it sound so easy.'

'It's not easy. But you've already proved that you're not afraid to work hard for what you want. We don't choose everything that happens to us, and we can't change the past, but we can choose how we adapt and move forward. We can choose to accept, and we can decide to live life the best way we possibly can.'

'Wow, you're like a motivational speaker. Tony Robbins and Rhonda Byrne all rolled into one.'

She smiles. 'I've listened to a lot of those kinds of podcasts and read a lot of books, yes.'

'Because?'

She hesitates.

'Come on,' I prod. 'You're the life coach here. It's only fair you share your own motivation, isn't that how this works?'

'I was married once before. A nice guy, Paul. Met in our early twenties, married, bought a house. Followed the usual trajectory. We were happy, rubbed along well, never really argued.'

'And? What happened?'

'I was twenty-eight when I was diagnosed with rheumatoid arthritis. It came on suddenly. One minute I was fit and active, enjoying life with my husband. We liked to spend our weekends hiking, or riding our bikes around the country until we'd find a B&B to stay in. Then I began waking up stiff, swollen and in pain. Knees, feet, hips, wrists – you name a joint, it hurt. I thought I was dying, so the diagnosis was both a relief and a shock. I wasn't dying, but I had RA, an autoimmune disease. The medication they gave me back then was hard-core stuff. It came with a lot of side effects. I gained weight, lost my confidence and my libido. Irrational mood swings. Paul tried to be supportive, but I pushed him away. I insisted we try for a family, to prove I was still OK. He was worried about how I would cope, how it would affect my body. Wanted to wait. I took his hesitation as rejection, and not long after that, we separated.'

'He left you?'

'Only because I made it unbearable for him to stay. When I was having a flare-up, I could barely walk to the mailbox, let alone throw my leg over a bike. I would encourage him to go without me but he wouldn't, and his being so noble about it only made me feel worse. I could see I was holding him back from doing the things he enjoyed.'

I shift uncomfortably in my seat. It's like she can read my mind. Her words, the way she felt? It unnervingly mirrors my own feelings towards Finn. That I'd be holding him back.

'It took me years to accept my illness,' she says. 'I was angry, like you, for a long time. Fixated on the unfairness of it.'

'What changed?'

'Honestly? It wasn't one thing in particular. I didn't wake up one day feeling better.'

'Great, so no quick fix.'

'No. Sorry. No quick fix. It took some soul searching, as well as reading some books and talking to people in a support group with the same or a similar diagnosis. I did some research, took ownership of my diet and lifestyle. Kept records of what helped, what didn't, that sort of stuff. That's how I started wild swimming. A daily dip has been the best pain relief I've found. I learned how to manage my health – along with the medication, when needed. It gave me back some of the feeling of control over myself that I felt I'd lost.'

'I don't think diet and exercise is going to fix this,' I say, rubbing my thigh under the blanket.

'No. Nothing can fix it. But, if you have the operation, you can take back some of that control for yourself. Imagine, Zoe. Imagine yourself walking again. Driving. Teaching.'

I swallow the hard lump in my throat. 'Do you think I haven't? I'd do anything . . .'

'Anything? Including the operation?'

'I can't.'

'What's stopping you?'

'I'm scared.'

'I understand.'

'No, you don't. With all due respect, your illness isn't going to kill you. If I have that operation, there's no guarantees I'll survive another anaesthetic.'

'The chance of—'

'The chance of it happening is slim, sure. But there's still a chance.'

She leans her head on the back of the seat and exhales noisily out of her nose, staring up at the sky, only there's nothing to be seen. A vast empty blackness, like there's nothing out there at all. Her fingers fiddle with the new ring on her finger.

'I don't all have the answers,' she says finally. 'I wish I did. All I know is that I'd hate for you to waste as many years as I did, feeling bitter and hard done by.'

'It's only been a few months,' I point out. 'I think I'm entitled to wallow a bit.'

She lifts the blanket off her knees and, on the third attempt, gets to her feet. 'I'm going to hit the hay. Do you need me to help you to your room?'

I shake my head. 'I'm going to hang out here for a bit longer.'

'OK. Goodnight.' She takes a few steps, then pauses with her hand on the door handle. 'I'll say one last thing and then I promise I'll drop it. If there's even a chance that you could fix things with this man, shouldn't you take it? Stop thinking about all the things that could go wrong if you have the operation, Zoe, and dream about all the things that could go right. The life you could reclaim. Be brave and take the first step. The rest will follow.'

Chapter fifty-nine

Linda's words keep echoing in my head. Even though it was unsolicited, her advice made sense in a way that has my heart racing. She made it sound so simple. Can I get my life – and Finn – back? It's easy for her to tell me to be brave though, she's not the one needing surgery, potentially life-threatening surgery.

Dream about all the things that could go right, the life you could reclaim.

I push the blanket off my legs, to one side, and take a deep breath. My left pyjama pant leg has been cut off at mid shin to stop it getting tangled around the stump when I roll around in bed. I gently pull it up even further, to my knee, and for the first time, I take a proper look at my leg. I mean really look at it. I've washed my leg in the shower. I've even shaved part of it, though not near any of the scars. But I haven't looked at it. Now, with the light of the range hood in the kitchen beaming out over me, I do.

It's not easy. I still can't reconcile what I see with how I feel. My sense of identity doesn't match what I'm seeing. Every single fibre inside me still feels able-bodied. Two-legged. The way I have been all my life. If I'm to accept my new reality, I have to first face it.

I examine the long scars, still red and lumpy, and the misshapen abrupt end of my leg where the bone was cut off. Sometimes, in the night when I can't sleep, I've looked up other amputees on the internet, so I'm well aware that no two stumps look the same. I also know that it will change even more as it heals. It is still, even after all these weeks, swollen.

Closing my eyes, I take one deep breath in, then deliberately exhale as I reach for my leg, sliding my hands down my thigh, over my knee, until I reach the stump. Softly, my fingers light and cautious. I explore how it feels, the scars, the shape, cupping the end of it in my palm. I try to imagine it even shorter. Neater, less . . . abrasive and ugly. I visualise myself pushing the stump into a prosthetic leg. Attaching it. Standing up, walking. Somewhere, anywhere, without the aid of crutches or a wheelchair. I picture getting dressed without planning an outfit that hides my leg. Maybe even, one day, being proud to show off my prosthetic. (See how far I've come!) I imagine teaching again, the faces of the children looking up at me without fear, only curiosity.

I feel my heart rate quicken as I imagine living a life like the one I lived before.

I want it, I really do.

I want it so much.

'What do you think, Mum?' I ask, looking up at the black sky. 'Do you think I can do this?'

She doesn't answer, of course. There are no shooting stars or streaking meteor showers. I've never had a sign from her. No feathers or pennies in my path, no butterflies around me, that sort of thing. The lights have never switched on and off, and her favourite song has never come on the radio when I've been thinking about her. But somehow, I know she's still listening. I feel it. When my gut instincts tell me to trust something, it's like she's still guiding me in some way. Those instincts told me I could trust Finn, and they were right.

Right now, tonight, my gut is telling me that I can do this. I have to do this.

I'm going to have the operation.

Chapter sixty

I'm going to have the operation.

I'm going to have the operation!

Even though it's almost one in the morning, I clump down the hallway like a kid on Christmas morning, throwing open Dad's bedroom door with such force it bangs hard against the wall behind.

'Oops,' I say, as Dad kind of half leaps, half falls out of bed, swearing his head off. Linda lifts a head off the pillow, reaching for the bedside lamp switch.

'Who's there? I'm armed!' Dad babbles, then blinks a few times as the light comes on, his face flooding with relief when he realises it's only me.

'Bloody hell, Zoe, you gave me a heart attack!'

'Sorry,' I apologise. 'But I couldn't wait.'

'Wait for what? What's wrong?' He hurries across the room to stand in front of me, looking me up and down as if in search of a clue.

I take a deep breath, knowing that saying it out loud will

make it real. Determination sets in. No going back. 'I'm going to have the operation.'

Dad is speechless for a few seconds as it sinks in. 'Oh,' he says. 'OK. If that's what you want, you know I'll support you.'

I nod. 'It is.'

'This isn't because I proposed to Linda, is it? Because you know that changes nothing for you, right? You'll always have a place here. This will always be your home.'

'I know. This has nothing to do with that. I'm doing this for me. I want to get my life back. I appreciate everything that you've done, but I want to teach again, travel, live independently. I want to be me again.'

Behind Dad, Linda gives a satisfied smile. He nods slowly as he absorbs what I'm saying.

'Well, I guess we'll call the doctors tomorrow, get the ball rolling. If you're still sure in the morning.'

'I will be, and we'll call first thing,' I reply. Now that the decision is made, I'm impatient. I have seen, felt and imagined the life I had, the life I can have again. I don't want to wait any longer.

There's something I haven't dared to think about yet though, and that's Finn. I don't know if Linda's right and there's any chance for us still, not after how I've treated him. I don't want to even allow myself to hope. I need to focus on one thing at a time. Getting through the operation first. Like Linda said. Be brave, and hope that the rest will follow.

Chapter sixty-one

Three weeks pass. Three of the longest, yet somehow also the quickest, weeks of my life. In a few days' time I am booked in to have the second amputation, and I am petrified.

Not always. Sometimes I'm excited, my stomach on fire with nerves as I think about what will come after the operation, not so much the operation itself.

I wake up in the early hours of the day before the day we have to leave to go the city, two days before the operation, screaming, a horrible feeling of dread settled over me like a cloying blanket, suffocating.

A light flicks on in the hallway and then my door opens.

'What's wrong?' Dad asks, hurrying over to my bed, where I'm sitting up, breathing shallowly.

'I . . . can't . . . breathe.'

'Where's your inhaler?' He fumbles to open my bedside drawer, knocking a glass of water to the floor. 'Shit.'

'No, not . . . asthma . . .' I reassure him.

'Are you sure?'

I nod.

He sits on the edge of the bed and rubs my back until my breathing slows down, the air getting deeper into my lungs, oxygenating my blood. The heavy feeling of dread remains.

'I don't think I can do it, Dad,' I say tearfully. 'I'm sorry. I don't want to disappoint you.'

'Shush,' he soothes, pulling me in against his side. 'It's OK. You could never disappoint me. It was a nightmare, that's all.'

'No, it was more than that. I saw someone, lying on a table. You were crying. I don't know if it was me, or Mum. I couldn't see a face.' I look at him earnestly. 'Maybe it was a vision? Like, a premonition.'

'You're not psychic,' he says gently, tactfully. 'It was just a bad dream. Don't let it get to you.'

'It felt so real.'

'Lay down,' he encourages me, standing up and lifting the blankets so I can snuggle down under. He drags the armchair over from the corner. 'You need to get some sleep. I'll sit here awhile.'

'Like you used to do when I was little and had a nightmare,' I say, as the memory comes to me. He smiles.

'You remember.'

'I do now.'

'Everything's going to be OK, Zoe. Close your eyes, go back to sleep.'

I roll over onto my side and pull the covers over my chin, but every time I close my eyes I see the same thing.

Chapter sixty-two

From: Finn_the_finster@gmail.com
To: ZoeCalloway@hotmail.com
Subject: What I want for you

My sweet, wonderful Zoe,

OK. So, you're not going to change your mind, that much is finally, blindingly, obvious. I guess I've been a little slow on the uptake to have held on to my hope this long. But now, enough is enough. I need to claw back some dignity, for my own mental health if nothing else. I've thrown myself at your feet, begged you for a second chance, to no avail.

Here's what I do know. You're not a bad person. Despite what any of my friends and family might say to the contrary, I know you have a good heart. Because of that, I must assume that whatever reason there was behind you making the decision to cut me out of your life, it has to have been a bloody good one. You wouldn't have done it otherwise.

So here is what I want for you, Zoe.

I want you to find peace with your decision. I know it can't have been easy. But I forgive you. I hope you've forgiven yourself.

I want you to find someone who loves you as much as I do. Who'll never stop remembering how damn lucky he is that you love him back. Don't settle, promise me that. I would have given you the world without hesitation, so if he offers you anything less, don't accept. Find happiness. Find love.

I want you to find the guy who can give you whatever it was that I couldn't. Someone who will spend all night on a chat call with you if you're feeling low, not even talking, just listening to you breathe. Someone who every single time he kisses you hears fireworks go off in his head. Who kisses you the way you should be kissed, like he'll never get enough.

I knew from the moment I first looked into your eyes that something huge was about to happen. That my life was about to change. I don't know whether it was the universe or what it was that brought us together that night, but I'll never stop being grateful. I can't remember what my life was like before you were in it, and I don't know how I'm supposed to live without you now. It hurts so much to even consider it. I thought I was going to grow old with you. I was even prepared to have the five children you want, if that's not love, what is? We could have had a good life, you and me. An amazing life. A life.

My brother, Connor, thinks that love is everywhere. That

when you fall out of love with someone, you soon chance upon it again with someone else. I don't know what that is, but it's not love. What I feel for you? That's love. It will never stop, and I will never forget you, Zoe.

Chapter sixty-three

In the morning, Dad is gone, but the chair is still beside the bed, confirmation that the nightmare wasn't a bad dream in itself. The water has been mopped up, the empty glass back on the drawer beside my phone. I pick it up to check the time and there is an email from Finn. As I read it, I weep. There is an air of finality to the email. He is saying goodbye. My heart, already in bad shape, hardens a little more. I have lost him forever.

Later, when I have no tears left, I clomp out to the kitchen in search of coffee. Linda is there. She takes one look at my face and can tell immediately that something is wrong.

'You look awful,' she says, chewing on a corner of a piece of toast.

'Gee, thanks.'

'No sleep?'

Outside the window, it's raining steadily. The sky and the sea are their usual winter shade of pale grey. I push the button to boil the kettle and open the drawer to search for a teaspoon. 'Not much. Where's Dad?'

'He called me in the middle of the night, some problem at work. A machine malfunctioned. Asked me to come over and sleep here while he was gone. Said you'd had a bad night and he didn't want to leave you alone.'

The dream, or whatever it was, is still unnerving me. Teaspoon found, I add two heaped spoons of coffee into the mug, then on deliberation, add a third.

'That bad, huh?' Linda quips, observing.

I exhale heavily. 'I don't think I can do it.'

'What?'

'The operation.'

She puts the piece of toast back down on her plate, and wipes her hands together. 'I've been expecting this.'

'Expecting what?'

'It's only natural for you to have second thoughts, now that the operation day is so close. It's nerves, that's all.'

'I'm not nervous, I'm fucking terrified. I had a dream last night that I died on the operating table.'

'Perfectly natural. Your fears are manifesting in your subconscious.'

'Oh cut the psychobabble bullshit. I think we should postpone.'

She weighs up her next words carefully. 'Until when?'

'Until I'm feeling more prepared.'

'You'll only feel the same way then too. Like I said, it's natural to have nerves this close to the day. I'd be more worried if you didn't.'

'Yeah, well, I'll ask Dad to call. Tell them I've come down with a cold. That'll push the date out.'

'Lie, you mean.'

I glare at her and fake a cough. 'Not completely. I am feeling a bit like I'm coming down with something.'

'Mm-mm.'

'It's true,' I protest.

'Mm.' She picks up the toast again and takes another bite, her expression neutral.

'Fine,' I say in exasperation. 'I'm not sick. It's . . . the thought of something going wrong.'

'Everyone worries before surgery.'

'Yes, but not everyone has a genetic condition that means they could die during surgery though, do they.'

'No,' she admits.

'Right, so stop judging me.'

'I'm not judging you.'

'It kind of feels like you are.'

She shrugs. 'I can't control how you feel.'

'Sounds as though I should've waited for Dad.'

'I only want what's best for you, same as he does.'

The whistle on the kettle fades away and I pour the boiling water into the mug, stirring it until all the brown granules dissolve.

'Are you sure there's nothing else going on?' she asks.

I take a mouthful of coffee and close my eyes. 'I had an email from Finn.'

'Oh?'

'He's had enough.'

'He said that?'

'Read it yourself.' I pull my phone out of my dressing gown pocket and find the email, slapping it on the bench in front of her, then turn my back so I don't have to watch her read it.

'Easy,' she says, picking it up. There's silence for a few minutes, during which I listen to the rain drumming on the roof, and watch it pockmark the surface of the ocean.

'What a beautiful email,' she says finally, her voice emotional. 'But I don't understand.'

'He's given up on me.'

'But your father said he broke up with you weeks ago, when you told him about the accident. He's under the impression that Finn couldn't handle what happened to you. Your father is still very angry about it.'

I turn to face her, leaning my back against the bench to support myself while I drink my coffee. 'Dad assumed that's what happened,' I admit. 'And I didn't correct him.'

'So . . . ?'

'It was me who broke things off. Only I didn't have the guts to do it, so I stopped replying to his messages. And deleted all my social media profiles so he couldn't find me.'

Her eyebrows shoot up. 'You ghosted him?'

'You know what that means?' I ask, equally surprised.

'I read a lot, remember. Including psychology and behavioural magazines. Why on earth would you do that? That's a horrible thing to do to someone, especially someone you profess to care about.'

'I know,' I wail, feeling awful. 'But every time I tried to tell him what had happened, I froze up. It's not exactly the easiest thing to say in a message, so I thought I would wait until he was home again. I didn't want him to cut his trip short because of me. But as time went on it got harder. He was talking about all the things we were going to do together, and I couldn't tell him that I was no longer physically able to do some of those things, because that meant I'd have to tell him about the second operation, and that I was too much of a coward to face it. I didn't want to disappoint him. He's brave, fearless, he wouldn't understand.'

'You don't know that.'

I drain the last of my coffee and turn to put my cup in the sink, running the tap to keep it from staining. 'It's too late now, anyway.'

'It's never too late.'

'I think in this instance, it is.'

She sighs, exasperated. 'There's only one way to find out though, isn't there. But back to the operation for a second: is this why you want to postpone it? Because of him?'

'No. I don't think so. I mean, sure, a part of me was secretly hoping that I'd get my leg fixed and then maybe, somewhere down the track I could try and explain, sort things out with him. But that's not why I decided to do it. I meant it when I said I want to teach again, and live on my own. I want my life back.'

'And you can have it. You just need to push through these nerves.'

'I don't know if I can.'

'I do. You're stronger than you think you are.'

Her phone emits a merry tune and she picks it up. 'Your father, checking up on you. I'll tell him you're awake.'

'Please don't tell him about Finn,' I say quickly. 'Or that I'm thinking about postponing the op. I'll tell him when he's home.'

'I wasn't going to do it in a text, but I don't like lying to him.'

'I'm not asking you to lie, I'm asking you to ... hold off. Please? I need to think about it some more.'

She regards me thoughtfully. 'On one condition.'

'Which is?'

'Come for a swim with me this morning.'

'It's raining.'

'You're going to get wet in the water anyway,' she points out. 'You haven't been in a while, I think it would do you good. I always find I think clearer after a swim.'

I look back out the window. She's right, I haven't been for a week or so, and I do miss it. I don't miss the cold, but maybe it will shock me into thinking straight. Worth a try.

'Fine,' I sigh. 'But let me eat some toast first.'

She fires back a reply to my father. 'You going to be OK for a while if I shoot home to grab my suit and sort out a few things?'

'I don't need a babysitter.'

'Have the operation and we'll stop worrying about you so much,' she says, as she gets to her feet. Her phone beeps again. 'Your father says he'll be home in an hour or so. Perfect. Enough time for us to have a good dip. OK, you eat and then get ready. I'll be back soon.'

Chapter sixty-four

The water is warmer than expected, which I'm guessing is thanks to the rain. I frustrate Linda by complaining repeatedly as we make our way down the beach, and again by inching into the water slower than she would like, but bugger her. She made me come out here; she can wait while my body adjusts.

As soon as we're deep enough for the water to take over the supporting role, she releases me, never straying more than five metres away, in case I should need her. She needn't worry; since that first swim, I've learned to keep a wary eye out for rogue waves, and haven't been caught unawares again. I flip over onto my back, and sweep my arms leisurely through the water, drifting. My favoured position. With my ears under the water and my eyes on the sky, everything else disappears and I feel alone, but in a way that I appreciate. The rain falls gently on my face so I close my eyes and open my mouth, catching droplets that I let run down my throat.

It's like being part of another world out here, but between swims, I forget. I forget the buzz you feel afterwards, when your skin is a jangle of thawing nerve endings. I forget how utterly exhilarating it is. Out here, it's like I'm one with the natural world. There is no ending or beginning, we merge, blending together seamlessly. I am accepted, embraced, part of the landscape, rather than merely an observer.

Out here, all my worries are washed clean away. When you're so focused on the here and now, floating, staying warm, monitoring your breathing and your core temp, there's little room to fret about much else. Including the operation, and the decision I have to make. Linda was right again, damn it. I needed this.

We haven't been out long, ten minutes maybe, when I catch sight of Linda waving at someone in the distance. Flipping over onto my stomach and paddling in place, I see a figure standing at the top of the dunes below our house, a hundred metres or so from where we are. The rain has turned into a steady drizzle, and the air is murky but I can still see that it's Dad, home again. I smile, lifting my own arm to wave. He waves back, starts walking down the beach towards us.

'Well?' Linda says. 'Has the water helped?'

'Yeah. You were right, as usual.'

'What are you going to tell him?'

'I'm going to tell him he needs to get my bag down from the top of the wardrobe. I have an operation I need to pack for.'

Chapter sixty-five

'Dad, stop pacing.'

He stops to blink at me. 'I'm not pacing.' He looks at Linda. 'Am I?'

'You are,' Linda answers him affectionately. 'It's a little distracting.'

'Sorry,' Dad says sheepishly. 'I can't seem to stand still.'

'Don't worry,' I tell him. 'If I wasn't attached to this thing' – I wave my hand, the one with the cannula poked inside – 'I'd already be halfway out the front doors.'

He crosses the room to hover beside the bed. 'Don't say that. You're here now. You may as well go through with it.'

'Thanks for the inspiring pep talk.'

'You're welcome. So you're feeling OK about the operation, then?'

'I wouldn't say that. How I'm feeling, on a scale of one to ten ... one being this is all a walk in the park, and ten being completely, utterly, out of my mind terrified ... is about a thirty-six.'

Dad nods. 'That sounds normal.'

There's a knock on the door and my nurse, Melissa, pops her head in. 'The orderly has arrived to take you down to theatre, Zoe.'

'Can we go with her?' Dad asks quickly.

'Of course. I'll be coming, to do a pre-op handover to the nurses down there. I can show you where to wait, if you like.'

'That'd be great, thanks.'

This is it, I think, as Dad and Melissa open both doors wide and lock them into place so my bed can pass through. This is actually happening.

'You're going to be fine,' Linda smiles, holding her handbag tight against her chest as they wheel my bed through the narrow gap past her. 'And we'll be right here waiting for you when you wake up, ready for your new life to begin.'

I exhale heavily, nodding. She's right. I have to remind myself of the end goal, the reason why I'm doing this. That's the only way I'll be strong enough to go through with it.

I look up at the lights flashing by on the corridor roof, drawing on an inner strength I honestly didn't know I had. I can do this.

'I love you,' Dad says, when we reach the doors they're not allowed through. He hovers over me, his face a puddle of emotions. Fear, pride, anxiety all battle to the surface.

'I love you too.' I can do this.

In theatre, the anaesthetist smiles down at me as I try not to look at the implements of torture laid out on trolleys nearby. Is that a saw? Fuck.

'Take some deep breaths into the mask,' he says. 'It'll all be over before you know it.'

I want to tell him that's exactly what I'm worried about, that something will go wrong and it'll all be over as in over, dead, and I'll never get the chance to see Finn again, to tell him how much I love him, that I never stopped loving him. That I'll love him always.

Instead I do as I'm told and breathe in the horrible-tasting chemicals, my eyes darting between the blue-suited and masked figures in the room. There are so many of them. Is that normal?

I can do this, I think, my blinks lasting longer as my eyelids grow heavy. I picture my dad, and Finn.

I can do this.

Chapter sixty-six

Beep

'Where is she? Where is she? In here? Oh God, Zoe.'

'I'm so sorry, Mr Calloway.'

'Sorry? Sorry isn't going to fix anything.'

'Greg, I'm sure they're doing everything they can.'

'No, Linda, they're not doing anything. She looks so vulnerable, lying here. Why aren't you doing something?'

'Believe me, we're doing everything that we can.'

'What the hell happened?'

'Zoe had a laryngospasm under anaesthetic, which brought on a hypoxemic episode. During this time, her brain and other organs were deprived of oxygen.'

'Oh my God.'

'As you know, there was a risk of something like this going in to the operation, because of her condition. We were prepared for it, and started treating Zoe very quickly.'

'So she's OK? I don't understand, why is she still asleep?'

'I'm afraid it was more difficult than expected to get oxygen to Zoe. We've had to place her in an induced coma, to give her brain time to recover.'

'Then she'll be OK?'

'Unfortunately, we won't know for sure until she wakes up but, as the episode lasted less than two minutes, we're hopeful that any damage will be short-term, and minimal.'

'You're hopeful?'

'There's no way of knowing, not until we're able to bring Zoe out of the coma.'

'And when will that be?'

'A few days.'

'Few? Few isn't a very precise form of measurement, Doctor.'

'Greg ...'

'No. This is my daughter, Linda. I don't need vague estimates, I need facts. I need to know that she's going to be OK. I need to know that they're doing everything that they should be doing.'

'We are. I assure you. I'm sorry, that I can't be more specific, but it depends entirely on Zoe, and how well she responds. Some patients don't cope well with anaesthetic and its effects. Some take their time waking up, and we don't always know the reason why. The best thing we can do right now is be patient.'

'I can't believe this is happening.'

'I'll let you have some time alone with her. Here in ICU she's continuously being monitored, and if you need something, press this button. Someone is always nearby.'

'What I need is to go back in time and stop Zoe from having the operation.'

'I understand.'

'Do you?'

'I'll be back to check on Zoe later.'

'Wait!'

'Yes?'

'Her leg?'

'From that regard, the operation was a success. We were close to finishing up when Zoe stopped breathing, but the amputation went exactly as planned.'

'That won't mean anything if she doesn't survive.'

'I'm sorry, I have somewhere else I need to be, but I'll be back later.'

'This is all my fault.'

'No, Greg. You can't blame yourself.'

'Can't I? I knew the risks, Linda. I've been here before! I should have protected Zoe, instead, I encouraged her. What the hell have I done?'

'Zoe knew the risks too. We all did. And this was her decision, not yours. You couldn't have stopped her. It wouldn't have been right for you to try.'

'Look at her, Linda. Look at her. Hooked up to a bloody machine. She can't even breathe for herself.'

'No, not yet. But she will. You know Zoe. She won't give up.'

'What if she doesn't wake up?'

'Don't think like that. She will.'

'Why? Why Zoe? After everything else she's been through this year. The accident, losing her leg. That asshole, dumping her.'

'Who?'

'Finn! That coward. She loved him – I think she still does, not that he deserves it. Why are you looking at me like that?'

'I think you should sit down.'

'Why?'

'I promised Zoe I wouldn't tell you this, but you need to know the truth.'

Chapter sixty-seven

It smells like Christmas. Pine trees, shedding their needles, everywhere. They crunch underfoot as I step on them, releasing even more of the delicious scent that makes me think of Christmas lights and Santa, candy canes and Christmas carols. 'Fairytale of New York', my mother's favourite. I've never understood half the words.

It's not Christmas though, and it's not carols I can hear as I walk through the woods, but birdsong. Above me in the trees. All manner of pitches and tunes. It's beautiful and I wish I could see them, but when I look up all I can see is sunlight streaming down towards me through the natural green canopy.

I feel incredibly relaxed, surrounded by nature. This place is familiar, but I can't put a name to it. I just know I've been here before.

The trees and the carpet that smells like Christmas give way to grassy ground. A lake is in front of me, the water as still as bathwater, the surface dazzling in the midday sun. There's a jetty, twenty, thirty metres away from me, and I walk towards it, marvelling at how beautiful everything is here. How pristine and untouched the land and the water are, like I'm the first person to ever come here.

The wood on the jetty is faded, lichen sprouts between some of the cracks. The eighth board has a crack in the middle and the wood dips down towards the water, I step over that one.

'Hello,' I call when I am standing on the edge of the jetty, looking out over the lake and at the Christmas tree laden hills all around. My voice skims the surface of the water and echoes back to me.

'Zoe.'

I close my eyes and smile to myself. Happiness floods through me at the familiar sound of his voice. Then I open my eyes and turn to face him.

'Finn.'

Chapter sixty-eight

I feel him pick up my hand, the one without the needle in. He is painfully gentle, as if afraid he'll hurt me. I want so badly to see him, but despite summoning every ounce of will I have, I cannot open my eyes, or even move. I don't know why, and it's terrifying, but I can't physically react. All I know is that he is here, finally.

'I don't know where to start,' he says, and his voice is hoarse, anguished.

Then I will. I'm sorry, Finn. For everything.

'Why didn't you tell me?'

I had so many reasons, so many valid reasons. None of which make any sense right now.

'I have about a billion questions for you,' he says. 'But don't let that keep you from waking up. In fact, wake up, for me and I promise I'll forget all the questions, except one. Do you still love me?'

I never stopped.

'You have to do this for me, OK? You have to wake up.

Please, Zoe, I've only just found you again, I can't lose you. I need to see your eyes, hear your voice. I need to hear you say my name.'

Finn. I'm trying. I am.

Chapter sixty-nine

'Morning, Finn.'

'Morning, Mr Calloway.'

'Jesus it's hot in here.'

'Yeah, the radiators have been stuck on full all night, the dial doesn't work. Where's Linda?'

'She's gone home, sort out a few things, get some clean clothes for us both. An elderly neighbour has been feeding her cat while we've been away, but they've run out of food and don't drive.'

'Right.'

'I told her to go, she could do with a break from all this . . . sitting around, and waiting. The last three nights in the motel she hasn't slept much. I think the constant city noise is a little unnerving for her.'

'Yeah, it can be if you're not used to it.'

'How was Zoe during the night?'

'No change. Same as the last three nights.'

'I'm glad they finally caved and let you sleep in here on a chair beside her, at least.'

'Yeah, guess they got sick of me on the floor outside the ICU doors every night. Tripping everybody up.'

'You don't have to stay here all the time, Finn. There must be other places you need to be?'

'No, sir, nowhere. Even if there was, I'm not leaving her.'

'Call me Greg.'

'O . . . k.'

'Don't sound so nervous. I like you more now that I know you didn't break my daughter's heart.'

'I could never do that. I love your daughter, I want to spend the rest of my life with her. These last few months, not knowing where she was, or why she'd cut off all contact, I felt like I was going insane.'

'The thing you have to understand about Zoe is that she can be stubborn once she makes her mind up about something, and pride won't let her admit when she's in the wrong. Her mother was the same. She shouldn't have treated you the way she did, but I'm sure you can understand that she was in a pretty bad headspace. Losing her leg like that . . . '

'I do understand. Well, I'm trying. I just, I wish I could have been there for her. It frustrates me that she didn't think I would want to. I could have helped her through it.'

'Maybe, or maybe she would have driven you away. Truthfully, I'm kind of glad you weren't around. It gave Zoe and me the chance to reconnect.'

'I'm glad to hear it.'

'I don't know how much Zoe's told you, about her and me, and how things were when she was growing up.'

'I know you were an alcoholic, and that she felt you weren't there for her.'

'OK, right, so ah, I guess that's all out in the open then. Wow, you don't beat around the bush, do you?'

'No. Sorry.'

'Don't be. I own my past, it's part of my recovery. These past few months, I've had the chance to prove to Zoe that I wasn't going anywhere this time, that I'm here for her, whatever she needs. And I always will be.'

'I want the chance to prove the same.'

'You'll get one.'

'She has to wake up. I don't ... I can't ... '

'She will.'

Chapter seventy

I run from the lake, laughing, wringing the water out of my hair. There's no towel, but I don't need one. Instead I lay on my back on the tickly grass and let the warm sun overhead evaporate the droplets on my body, deliciously warming my skin as it does. A shadow covers the sun and I look up. Finn grins down at me, his teeth white against his tanned skin, his hair dark and curled from our swim.

'Would you mind moving?' I ask. 'You're blocking my sun.'

He grins wider and shakes his head furiously, like a retriever. Water flies in all directions, most of it down on to my sun-warmed skin. I squeal at the shock of it, and he laughs, dropping down to the grass beside me, also on his back. He lifts one arm and I snuggle in against his side, my head on his shoulder.

'Tell me again, where we'll go.'

He kisses my hair. 'I think the easiest answer would be where won't we go.'

'OK, where won't we go?'

He thinks about it. 'Nowhere.'

'Do we have enough time? To go everywhere?'

'We'll make time.' He kisses me again. 'It doesn't matter if we don't manage it, anyway. As long as we're together.'

I open one eye and look up at his chin, hidden under a layer of stubble. 'You haven't shaved.'

'You don't like it?'

I reach up and rub one hand along his jawline. 'It feels funny, kind of softer than it looks.'

'When we travel, I might not shave it for months. Will you still love me with a little beard?'

'I would love you even if it came down to your knees.'

He props himself up on one elbow, rolling me onto my back, looks down at me seriously. 'Promise me one thing, Zoe.'

'What's that?'

'You won't stay here.'

Chapter seventy-one

'Are you sure she's breathing?'

'Yes.'

'How can you tell?'

'The machines tell us, Mr Calloway. Her oxygen saturation level is good. Believe me, we're monitoring Zoe closely. If the levels start to drop, alarms will go off. But you can tell by looking at her anyway. See how her chest rises and falls?'

'I can't tell. Finn, can you see?'

'No. Maybe, I'm not sure.'

'No? Doctor, maybe you should check her again.'

'Please don't worry, like I said, we are monitoring Zoe very closely. We wouldn't have taken her off ventilation if we didn't think she was ready.'

'And you're sure she's breathing?'

'Yes.'

'On her own?'

'Yes.'

'What if she stops?'

'Then we'll deal with it. But she's doing well, she's been breathing on her own now for . . . almost an hour.'

'You're absolutely sure?'

'Yes.'

'When will she wake up?'

'That I can't answer. Soon, hopefully. But prepare yourselves, it won't be like waking from sleep. She has been in an induced coma, heavily medicated. It will take some time for those drugs to work their way out of her system before she'll become fully conscious. It's a marathon, not a sprint.'

'So . . . today? She might wake up today?'

'You might begin to see something today, Mr Young, yes. Twelve to seventy-two hours is when we usually expect to see a patient begin to respond.'

'Respond how?'

'You'll see Zoe start to open her eyes, but don't be alarmed if she doesn't seem to see you, or she can't focus. It's perfectly normal. After that, uh, she'll begin to respond to simple commands from the nurses or myself, she'll show recognition of her name. Things like that.'

'And if she doesn't?'

'We try not to worry about things that haven't happened, Mr Calloway. Let's give Zoe some time first, OK? See how she gets on.'

'The other doctor, the one after the operation, he said there could be . . . brain damage.'

'Any time that the brain is deprived of oxygen yes, there is the potential for long-term debilitating effects. But we won't know if that's happened in Zoe's case, or to what extent, until she wakes up.'

329

'Seems like no one can give us a damn straight answer around here.'

'Finn, I know you're frustrated, I am too. But we can't take it out on the doctors. They're trying to help Zoe.'

'I'm sorry.'

'It's OK, Mr Young. I understand. The best thing for Zoe right now, is—'

'Rest, yeah, we know.'

'I know it's hard, but try to be patient.'

'Thanks.'

'I'll see you later.'

'Doctor?'

'Yes?'

'Are you sure she's breathing?'

Chapter seventy-two

'Linda says hi. She's on her way back, should get here before dark tonight. I told her to head straight to the hotel though, she'll be tired and, well. There's nothing she can do here, not until you . . .'

Wake up. I know.

'She'll come see you in the morning. Says everyone back home is thinking of you. Olivia's started a web page, or something. People can donate money, in case you need rehab when you wake up, or to help with any prosthetic costs. It's a nice thought.'

Yeah, I suppose she's not all bad. I was too quick to judge, and it's not like I'm perfect. I should give her a chance.

'Maybe you can take a holiday with it. You and that fella of yours. God knows you deserve it.'

My fella. I like the sound of that.

'He's devoted, I'll give you that. Well, devoted doesn't cover the half of it. He's fallen hard for you, Zoe. I've made him go for a walk. He looks like hell, but that's because he's barely left your side since I called him here. I wish you'd told me it was you who cut him out of your life, but I know we've still got a way to go until we can talk about anything. I'm just glad you told Linda.'

Who obviously blabbed straight to you.

'I know when you wake up you're probably going to be grumpy with her for telling me, and even grumpier with me for going through your emails, but if I hadn't, Finn wouldn't be here. So just remember that, OK?'

I'm not angry.

'Come on, Zoe. It's been two days since they took you off the machines. You're supposed to be waking up by now. Give me a sign, here, squeeze my hand. Go on, as tight as you can. Don't be worried about hurting me.'

I am, I'm squeezing. I'm squeezing, Dad. Why do you sound upset? Can't you feel it?

'I'm trying not to freak out, but I'm scared. And I know I probably shouldn't be saying that to you, because if you can hear me, I'm sure you're scared too. But you can do this. You're strong, Zoe. You're the strongest person I know. And I need you. Who else is going to plan my wedding for me? I can't even orchestrate a bloody proposal, remember? I was going to ask you this after the operation, but now I realise that these things shouldn't wait. I'd be grateful if you'd consider being my best man. There's no one else I want standing by my side, but you.'

I'd be honoured.

Chapter seventy-three

'Your dad's gone back to the motel for a sleep. He doesn't like leaving you, but I think it's easier for him, knowing that I'm here with you.'

It's easier for me too. I'm scared, but hearing your voice is like a lifeline. As long as you're with me, I'm still here, still tethered.

'The doctors reckon you should be awake by now. It's been four days, Zoe, and the longer this goes on, the more worried they are. I can tell. They're not exactly good poker players. I need you to show them that they've got nothing to worry about. I need you to wake up so they'll stop with the worried looks and consultations in the corridor. Show them, Zoe, wake up.'

I don't know how.

'I couldn't take my eyes off you, that night we first met, and I can't now. You're so beautiful, Zoe. Sometimes, at night, I pretend you're only sleeping. I sit here beside the bed, holding your hand, wondering if you even know I'm here.'

I know.

'Open your eyes. I want to see you smile at me again, the

way you used to. I want to see that moment in your eyes, right before I kiss you. I'm here, waiting for you. Wake up. Wake up, wake up, wake up.'

I'm sorry. I'm so sorry. I hate that you're upset, and I'm the reason.

'Your leg is fixed. You can get the prosthesis now. You can walk and teach and do all those things you said you want to do. Travel. We can do it all together. Well, obviously not the teaching part. I don't have a lot of experience with kids. I've always thought that raising kids is a lot of pressure. I mean, what if I stuff it up? Remember that night on the roof?'

How could I forget.

'You said you wanted a whole bunch. Well guess what? Wake up now, and you can have six kids, if you want. Hell, you can have a whole football team. I don't care, as long as you're OK and we're together. Wake up. Please! I can't imagine living without you. It was hard enough the first time, but at least then I had hope of seeing you again. There's so much I need to say to you. Please, Zoe. Please. Wake up.'

Chapter seventy-four

The water is so warm, like bathwater. I float gently, languidly waving my arms like I'm making a snow angel. Clouds drift overhead.

'You can't avoid me forever.'

'I'm not.'

Finn has paddled out to join me.

'It's so warm,' I tell him.

'It is,' he agrees.

'I don't think I've ever felt so warm. It's comforting.'

'You have a decision to make, Zoe.'

'I don't have to make it now, though, do I?'

'Soon, yes.'

'But not now. Swim with me. Tell me again when you fell in love with me.'

He floats along beside me. We float for miles, past the Christmas trees, under the brilliant sun.

'I'm not sure. I could say it was when you asked me to kiss you and I looked into your face for the very first time, but I don't know if that was love or curiosity, to be honest. Maybe it was infatuation.'

'I remember the way you looked at me. I knew my life was about to change.'

'Do you regret anything?'

'No. Do you?'

'Never.'

'Tell me what we'll do.'

'Like what?'

'I don't know. Will our lives be ordinary or extraordinary?'

'Both. Everything will be extraordinary when we're together. We'll get married, do some travel. You'll teach, until it's time to have our own children, and then whenever you want to again afterwards. I'll run our own bar. Maybe we'll live above it, at least at the start, when it's just us. The children will need somewhere to play when they come along. A lawn to run on, trees to climb. We'll work hard. In summer, once the kids are in bed, you and I will drink beer on the back porch to escape the heat inside. Watch the sun set and the stars wake up. In winter, I'll show our kids how to crack the ice on a puddle without slipping over. We'll have a dog, help out at the jumble sale on school gala day. Dress the kids up for Halloween, bake cakes for their birthdays, whatever they request. We'll stand on the side of the court, or the field every Saturday morning in winter and cheer our children on, and in summer, we'll take them swimming at the lake house, and fishing in the river. Everything will be extraordinary, as long as we're together.'

I roll over in the water to face him. 'You make it sound wonderful.'

'It will be wonderful.'

'Don't you like it here?'

'I do,' he says carefully. 'But I can't stay here. And I don't want you to either.'

I look at the trees, the gentle blue sky, the softly wafting clouds. 'It's so . . . warm here. I don't remember ever being cold.'

'No, Zoe. Please don't get comfortable. This isn't where you belong.'

'Where do I belong?'

'With me.'

Chapter seventy-five

'Hey, Finn.'

'Bonnie.'

'How is she?'

'The same as she was last time you came.'

'So ... nothing? No, flickering eyes, no, moving fingers? Nothing?'

'Nothing.'

'Fuck. They must have some idea why she hasn't woken up yet, surely?'

'If they do, they're not telling us.'

'This is insane. This is absolutely fucking insane. This sort of stuff shouldn't happen in this day and age.'

'And yet ...'

'Where's Greg?'

'He and Linda went for a walk.'

'If you want to go outside yourself, for a coffee or something, stretch your legs, fresh air, whatever, I'll sit with her a bit.'

'I don't know.'

'Come on, Finn, I'm sure you're sick of the sight of these four walls.'

'I don't look at the walls, I look at her.'

'You know what I mean.'

'Fine. I'll go grab a shower down the hallway, on the ward. I won't be far away, and I won't be long. If anything changes . . . '

'I'll call you.'

'You have my number?'

'You put it in my phone last time.'

'OK.'

'Go. I'll stay with her.'

'OK. I'll be back soon.'

'Hey, Zoe. I'm sorry I didn't come yesterday. Truth be told I was pretty upset the night before, after I visited. I hate seeing you like this. And I know that sounds as selfish as hell, and I feel bad, believe me, and if you want to give me shit about it, go for it, but you got to wake up first. Come on. I know Finn's all tortured by love, so I'm sure he's not giving you the hard word, and your dad, well . . . your dad's a mess. So I will. Wake the fuck up. This isn't how you're supposed to go. You survived the accident, losing your leg, and then what, you slip off quietly like this, for no real reason? Nah-uh, no way. That's bullshit. You can't do that to your dad, or Finn, or me. If you die, I'll never forgive you. I need you in my life, you're my best friend, and . . . God, this is so not how I wanted to tell you this, but you don't really leave me any choice. I'm pregnant. Eight weeks. I was going to tell you once I passed that magical twelve-week safety point that everyone says you have to wait for, but forget that, forget the rules. I need to tell you now, because what if I don't get another chance? I'm scared, Zoe, absolutely shitting myself.

Josh and I didn't plan this, and I'm sure as hell not ready, but . . . we're doing it. We're having a baby. And I need you to be there for me. I want you right by my side when I push this baby out, and I want you to be the godmother, and I want you to answer your phone in the middle of the night when the baby won't stop crying and tell me that everything is going to be OK. OK? I love you, Zoe. I need you – my baby needs you – WAKE UP.'

Chapter seventy-six

'What are you saying? She might never wake up?'

'We have to start considering all possibilities, Mr Calloway.'

'But . . . you said that she would.'

'Zoe has been withdrawn from all sedative medication for a week now. She should be awake. Frankly, we're baffled.'

'OK, well find someone who's not. There must be another doctor, if not in this city then in this country, who has more of an idea than you clearly fucking do.'

'Finn.'

'Sorry. I just . . . this can't be happening.'

'People handle trauma differently. Zoe's been through a lot this year. Her brain possibly thinks it's protecting her from further trauma by keeping her in this unconscious state.'

'That can happen?'

'Obviously, we're theorising at this point. Her EEG shows brain activity. We know she's not in a vegetative state, she's just . . . not waking up.'

'This isn't a fairy tale. She's not sleeping beauty. There must be something you can do.'

'We've tried everything that usually works, and we're speaking to experts all over the world, in case there's anything we've missed. But I'm afraid, at this stage, it's all up to Zoe.'

Chapter seventy-seven

'I'm sorry, Zoe. I'm sorry that I wasn't here for you when you needed me the most. I should have tried harder to find you. I should have known that you wouldn't have pushed me away like you did for no good reason. I should have known that you were suffering. When I think about everything you've been through, it breaks my heart, and I hate that it happened to you. If I could change it I would, but I can't. I'm so grateful that you're still here. You could have died when that van hit you, but you didn't. You survived for a reason, and this might sound corny or clichéd, but . . . I think that reason was us. I know everyone thinks their love is special, but I really believe that ours is one of the rare ones. I'm under no illusions that everything will always be perfect and easy. Your dad has told me some stories. I know that you can be moody when you haven't had enough sleep, and that when you think you're right you're too stubborn to back down, even when proven wrong. Hey, I'm sure as hell no angel either. But I love you. And I know that you love me too. Together we can be happy.

I'll protect you, Zoe. If you're too scared to wake up, don't be. I'm here now, and I'm never leaving you again. We can have a good life, you and I. A wonderful life. All you have to do is come back to me.'

Chapter seventy-eight

'Tell me how much you love me.'

Finn smiles patiently. 'I've already told you.'

'Tell me again.'

'I love you more today than I did yesterday.'

'Good.'

'And tomorrow I will love you even more. And the next day, and the next day, and every day until I die.'

'Is there enough love in the world?'

'There is enough love in my heart.'

'What do you think happens when we die? Where does all that love go?'

'I think it stays with you. Why are you asking?'

'I'm not sure.'

'You're not dying.'

'I'm not living either.'

'Yes, you are. Your heart is beating. Your lungs are breathing in oxygen. Your skin is warm. You are alive.'

'I'm scared, Finn.'

'I know. So am I. But we can be brave together.'

'I don't know if I'm strong enough.'

'You don't have to be. You just have to want to try.'

'If only it were that easy.'

'It is.'

'It's so warm here, and quiet. I like it. There's no pain, no danger, no loneliness or heartbreak.'

'That's not living, Zoe. Don't you want to live? With me?'

'I love you.'

'Enough?'

'I'm scared.'

'Life is messy, and loud and real, and sometimes, yes, it hurts. It hurts so much you don't understand how your heart can keep beating. But life is also wonderful. We only get one, and it's over in the flash of a shooting star in a galaxy a million miles away. Remember, Zoe. Remember how it felt to be alive. Remember.'

Chapter seventy-nine

I remember

I remember a kiss in a crowded room, my life course altered . . .

a rooftop, falling in love in front of a sea of lights. A beautiful man, his beautiful soul exposed

a lake, dancing in the rain, his laughter, his arms carrying me, our bodies joined together

I remember . . .

I remember pain, heartbreak, despair. Everything changed, my life over

I remember . . .

pain, anger, fear

No

I remember

love

love

love

Chapter eighty

It's so bright, the light. Pure white, blinding. It gets brighter as it gets closer, then there is a brilliant flash, like the universe has imploded. Noise rushes into the space left behind.

I blink, until my eyes adjust.

the clouds? the trees? the lake? tranquillity?

a dream

it's all gone

Replaced by plain walls, a cupboard, chaos . . . life.

I see his head. His beautiful, dark curly head. He is face down, buried in the blankets over my right leg. His shoulders shudder. I hear him sob.

I wriggle my fingers experimentally. They move, stiffly at first, slowly loosening up. I reach them out, it takes every bit of effort I can muster. Every ounce of energy I have, I direct towards him. When I touch his head, it's as if I've hit him with an electrical current. His head jerks off the bed and turns to me, his face streaked with tears, his eyes disbelieving.

'Zoe? Zoe! You're awake, oh thank God.'

He stands and moves so swiftly it's a blur. His eyes bore into mine, as if he can't believe what he sees. 'I knew you'd come back to me.'

'Finn.'

He reaches over my head, I hear an alarm sound. Then he fumbles in his pocket and pulls out his phone, his eyes never leaving my face. I drink in the sight of him. He is here, with me.

'Greg? She's awake. Just now, she just opened her eyes. Yes, I've pushed the button. You guys need to get back here. *Now.*' He disconnects and lowers his head, pressing his forehead against mine. His tears drip onto my cheeks, their warmth reminding me I am alive.

'Oh God, oh Zoe. Promise you'll never leave me again,' he sobs.

'I promise.'

'I thought I'd lost you forever . . .'

'You didn't.' I lift my hand and place it against his cheek. 'You won't.'

'I love you, Zoe Calloway.'

'I love you too, Finlay . . . Archibald . . . Bradford . . . Young.'

He laughs through his tears. 'At least we know your memory's OK.'

Chapter eighty-one

'Kiss me,' I say, in the sultriest voice I can muster. The night is hot, the air thick with the humidity of summer. I move my shoulders in time to the music, not even realising that I'm doing it. There is the hum of conversation and laughter all around, but I only have eyes for the man sitting at the table beside me.

Clearly amused, he considers my request. Eventually, regretfully, he shakes his head. 'I'm sorry, but I'm not sure my wife would appreciate it.'

My eyebrows shoot up. 'You're married?'

'I am.' He holds up his left hand, waggling the ring finger at me. I peer closer, admiring the thick gold band.

'Pretty. Are you sure I can't tempt you?'

'I'm sure.'

I pout. 'Your wife must be quite special.'

'Oh, she is. She's perfect in every way.'

I smile smugly.

'Well,' he goes on. 'Almost perfect. She does have some flaws, of course.'

'I'm sorry, did you just say flaws?'

He nods. 'I did.'

'Really. Such as?'

'Well, communication, for one.'

'*Communi* . . . what's wrong with the way I communicate?' I demand, temporarily slipping out of character in my outrage.

'You completely ghosted me, remember?'

I roll my eyes. 'Pfft, that was ages ago.'

'It was seven months ago. Seven months.'

'Like I said, ages. And frankly, if I knew you were going to bring it up every two seconds, I might not have been so quick to agree to this.' I hold my own left hand up, admiring the diamond and plain bands that now adorn my own ring finger.

'Regrets? So soon? That's got to be some kind of record. I mean we've only been married all of' – he checks his watch – 'five hours.'

I push out of my seat and climb onto his lap, wrapping my arms around his neck. 'No regrets. Not now, not ever, Mr Young.'

'I'm awfully glad to hear that, Mrs Zoe Archibald Bradford Young.'

'Oh no you don't.'

He looks wounded. 'You're not going to take my name?'

'Oh, I am, I'm just not going to take all of your names.'

He sighs. 'Fair enough.' Then he pulls my head in close and kisses me, softly at first, then with more urgency. We break apart only when a throat is cleared pointedly close by.

'Hey, Dad,' I grin, after pulling back to see who it is.

'Zoe,' he says stiffly. 'Finn.'

'Sir.' Finn picks up his drink and takes a sip.

'Christ, Finn, we're family now, and you still can't call me Greg?'

'Habit, sir. I mean Greg. I'll get there.'

Finn proposed when I was still in hospital, a few days after the operation. He'd even gone and bought a ring, with Bonnie's helpful assistance. When he asked me, I cried. Not ashamed to admit it. I couldn't believe how quickly my life had changed in the space of a few weeks. I'd had the operation, survived my biggest fear, and been reunited with the love of my life.

If someone had told me ten years ago – actually, at any point during my life – that I'd one day have a double wedding with my father, I'd never have believed it. And yet here I am, on my wedding day, and five hours previously I'd stood under the arch of the pergola and declared my love for Finn, with my father and Linda standing nearby doing the exact same thing. We tweaked our vows, personalised them. Made them our own. I didn't mind sharing my big day at all. Dad and I had come so far, it felt right to share such a special occasion with him, and Linda. It was her idea to combine the ceremonies. Neither Finn nor I wanted or needed a big, fancy wedding. Here, by the beach as the sun set, was perfect. Olivia was right. I had forgotten how beautiful Nugget Bay is in summer, when the sea and the sky are blue and the surrounding land a lush green. There's a warm breeze blowing in off the ocean, and the perfume of blooming roses in the air.

'Almost time for the first dances,' Linda smiles.

Finn gives me a questioning look. 'You don't have to, if you don't want to. If you're not ready.'

'Oh I'm ready,' I tell him confidently, sliding off his lap and standing up. It still thrills me every single time I stand on my own two feet. So what if one of them is mechanical? It's mine, and it's as much a part of me now as the other one is.

'City lights or starry skies,' Finn asks, as he steers me gently around a dance floor constructed of polished paving stones that Harry Taylor has set into the lawn.

I look up at the vast Milky Way overhead. Its beauty never fails to astound me, but I do sometimes miss the city. You don't see stars like this back there, but it has its own beauty, its own display of lights. I've realised though, that I don't care where in the world I am, as long as I'm with Finn. 'I love both, for different reasons.'

'Are you going to miss it here, if we move back to the city?'

I fail to notice the if, not when. 'Don't tell anyone I said this, because I'll only deny it,' I answer in a hushed voice. 'But yeah, I will. Mostly I'll miss Dad though. I lost a lot of years with him, and we're in such a good place now. We'll have to make sure we come back and visit often.'

'Funny you should say that,' Finn clears his throat. 'I noticed that Charlie's, the bar, is up for sale. I called the agent, made some enquiries.'

'Oh?' I get the goose-bump feeling you get when something in your universe aligns. I had it the night I met Finn, and I have it now.

'Zoe, I've got some savings, not much, but some, and I reckon the bank will lend us the rest.'

I stop dancing and look up at him, unable to believe that I'm even entertaining the idea, and that I'm feeling excited at the thought, instead of panicked. 'You want to stay here?'

'Well, you've got the teaching gig. I know it's only a couple of days relief teaching at the moment, but they said you could have a more permanent role if you wanted one, right?'

I nod.

'Like you said, I think it would be good for you to stay close to your dad for a while. I think we could build a life here.'

'You'd do that for me?'

'I'd do anything for you, Zoe.'

I throw my arms around his neck and we kiss, as I marvel yet again at how I got so damn lucky.

'Speaking of doing anything,' I break away to murmur. 'Was I dreaming in the hospital? Or did I hear you say something about having a whole soccer team?'

I laugh as his face turns ashen.

'Er,' he says. 'You were under a lot of medication . . .'

Fireworks explode into the sky above us, offering him a temporary respite.

'Happy New Year, Wife,' he says.

'Happy New Year,' I reply. 'The first of many to come.'

He leans his face down and nuzzles my lips with his own. 'You better believe it.'

Acknowledgements

A massive thank you for reading this book, and to *anyone* who has ever read or recommended ANY of my books. The book community is such a special one, and readers are my favourite kind of people. I love connecting with you, so feel free to look me up on Instagram or Facebook and flick me a message.

Thank you to all the wonderful booksellers and librarians across this country and the world, for both supporting my books and for helping to get books into people's hands.

Huge gratitude to everyone in the Piatkus office, particularly Emma Beswetherick, Eleanor Russell and Anna Boatman. My thanks to you and all of the people there who have worked to make this a much better book.

To everyone in the New Zealand and Australian Hachette offices, you all do such an incredible job, especially with championing local authors. Thank you for everything you do, it is so appreciated.

My agent Vicki. What can I say? This book would never have made it into the hands of readers without you and your guidance, encouragement, belief, and tough-love. You've always believed in my writing, and that means the world. I know you work tirelessly every day to help me become as successful as I can be, and for that I can't say thank you enough. I consider you a friend as well as my agent, and I think you're simply marvellous.

Big thanks to my friends all over the world who support my writing by buying my books, attending my events and listening to me moan on the bad days when the words are not flowing as easily as I'd like them too. You know who you are.

Lorraine & Kevin Tipene, for everything you've done for us over the years, with both my writing and in general. You're both beautiful people who brighten up the world.

Marika Pollard. Thanks for being such a big-hearted, generous, kind, funny, non-judgemental all-round wonder woman. Wine and Thai soon?

Love and thanks to my family, especially Tony Ryan, Rob Ryan, Kerrie Ryan, Angeline Ryan, Jack Morrissey, Jacqui Morrissey, Catelyn Morrissey and my late mother, Patrice Ryan. You guys are the very best family a girl could hope for.

And last, but certainly not least, all my love and gratitude to my husband, Karl, and our beautiful, precious children, Holly, Willow and Leo. I am beyond grateful every single day that I have you in my life. You guys are my everything, and I will always keep striving to make life as wonderful for you as I possibly can.